# THE YARDS

ALSO BY A. F. CARTER:

*All of Us*

# THE YARDS

*A Novel of Suspense*

# A. F. CARTER

THE MYSTERIOUS PRESS
NEW YORK

THE YARDS

Mysterious Press
An Imprint of Penzler Publishers
58 Warren Street
New York, N.Y. 10007

First Mysterious Press edition

Interior design by Maria Fernandez

Library of Congress Control Number: 2021912474

ISBN: 978-1-61316-235-4
eBook ISBN: 978-1-61316-236-1

10 9 8 7 6 5 4 3 2 1

Printed in the United States of America
Distributed by W. W. Norton & Company

# CHAPTER ONE

## GIT

Even without makeup, I'm not bad looking. True, my face is a little too thin, my nose too short, my chin a bit too firm. But if my likeness won't be appearing on the cover of a fashion magazine anytime soon, it isn't a face that men reject. No, attracting men has never been my problem. It's the choosing part that escapes me.

The way I figure now, the first link was in place long before my outing. Two years and three months before, give or take a few days. That's when I gave up on having a man in my life. Twenty-five years old, and enough was more than enough. I wasn't a man-hater. I have girlfriends who married decent men, not perfect, but decent. You could imagine putting your arms around them twenty years down the road. Not me, though. My first love punched me in the face when I wouldn't go down on him—I was twelve—and my last love, Franky Belleau, emptied my bank account before he headed off to fame and fortune in Las Vegas. Franky's in prison now, though he did have his moment of fame. A two-inch story on page eighteen of the *Las Vegas Review* after he shot a grocer.

Maybe choosing badly just comes natural to girls who grow up on the trashy side of the tracks in a broke-down city like Baxter. Between an alcoholic mother who changed lovers monthly and a missing father who showed up occasionally with his hand out, my life illustrated every cliché in the book. There are times when I think that's all women like me are good for. I think maybe God created us to be living examples of how not to raise children.

But I'm not a whiner, and I don't have my hand out, either. By waitressing part-time, I managed to finish a year of nursing school after I graduated from Dunning High, and that makes me a licensed practical nurse.

My original goals were much higher. At the least, I wanted another year's schooling and the title of registered nurse. RNs make a lot more than LPNs. But it wasn't happening, not even close. The country fell into recession, my Pell Grant went the way of the economy, I couldn't qualify for another student loan, and Franky ran off with my cash reserves.

If the men in my life were consoling types, I would have cried on somebody's shoulder.

With little choice, I took a job working three twelve-hour shifts at Resurrection Nursing Home. This was two years before the virus hit. The thirty-six-hour schedule allowed the Baptists who run the dump to classify me as part-time and not entitled to benefits like health insurance or paid vacations. And what they paid me for those thirty-six hours wasn't enough to cover the bills, not with Charlotte to care for. Which is why I found a second job.

Now I work three nights at Resurrection and three nights as a home care nurse for an old man who claims he was a gangster. Zack's full of advice but too old to grab my ass, though he checks me out every time I cross the room. Just as well, because I'm not willing to have my ass grabbed, no matter how bad I need the job.

The saddest part is that I'm mostly proud of my achievements. I rent a small house in Dunning, a neighborhood where people turn down their sound systems at ten o'clock. Respectable's probably the right word—respectable, but still poor. I can see the railroad tracks from the top of the rise behind the house. I can hear the trains go by at night. Should I get sick or hurt, maybe lose a couple of months' pay, I'll be recrossing those tracks. Me and Charlie both.

If I hadn't gotten married, I would have started nursing school two years earlier. I still don't understand why Sean picked me, because there were plenty of girls in the neighborhood who would've jumped at the chance to wear his ring. But pick me he did, always charming, always considerate.

My girlfriends warned me. Sean's playing you, Git. When you're not around, he calls you his redneck. It's supposed to be a joke, but it doesn't sound like a joke. If you marry him, he'll own you.

Par for the course, I didn't listen to a word. I married Sean at age nineteen and had my reception in the back room of a roadside bar.

So, yeah, I was young and soft. A little girl looking for a daddy, any daddy. But give me credit, I hardened in a hurry. Sean used his fists to enforce his ownership rights, fists and threats. That ended on the afternoon I shot him with the Glock he kept in a night-table drawer. The bullet grazed his ribs, but I'd been aiming at his head and Sean knew it. He turned and fled, through the door, up the street, and out of my life. Leaving the Glock and his unborn child behind.

My daughter—Charlotte on her birth certificate, but Charlie everywhere else—was born eight weeks later, a few days after my twentieth birthday. And not in prison. Sean never went to the hospital or the cops. We don't, people like us.

Charlie became the focus of my life when the delivery nurse laid her in my arms and said, "Say hello to your daughter." I felt nearly destroyed at the time. I'd been in labor for hours, my head was throbbing, and the stink rising from my armpits was thick enough to light with a match. Charlie cut through all that bullshit. I knew exactly what I had to do, knew that my own life was down the tubes if I fucked this up. My job was to love Charlie, to care for her, to protect her, to raise her until she didn't need any more raising. My job was to give my daughter more than I ever had, to give her a chance.

I want Charlotte to move up. I want her to live in a neighborhood too far away from the tracks to hear the trains pass, but that takes money.

Sean contributes a few bucks every month, enough to prevent his arrest, not enough to make a difference in Charlie's life. So it's on me, my daughter's fate, and I'm holding my own, now that I've sworn off men. These days, I generally make do with a vibrator and my imagination, but there are still times, no lie, when I really need an outing.

The word libido didn't enter my vocabulary until I was twenty. That's because the only word used on my end of the food chain is horny. Truth to tell, I'm horny most of the time, and like I said, I usually take care of it by myself. It's only every couple of months when I reach the point where I have to have a man. That's where this story begins, the last link in a chain that marks the days since I swore to go it on my own.

# CHAPTER TWO

## GIT

**M**om sits on the edge of the bed, an unlit cigarette propped between her fingers. She'll have to go outside to smoke it. I'm sitting in an office chair with a wicker seat and back, staring into a mirror propped on my vanity. There's no reason to hurry. It's not seven o'clock yet, and prime outing hours don't begin until after ten on Saturday. I chose Saturday because it's my only night off.

"I think the green dress," Mom tells me.

"Not the black?"

"The black makes your ass look flat."

My rented home is a three-bedroom house on Booth Lane, with a kitchen, a living room, and a too-small bathroom we have to share. There's me—Bridget O'Rourke—and Charlie, who's eight, and also my mother, Celia Graham.

Charlie's in her own room now, watching a television I can hear through the drywall. Mom and I are alone.

I'm not exaggerating when I say that my mother put the trash in trailer trash. Cross-addicted to whatever somebody else paid for, she was absent more than she was home when I was a kid. That was a blessing because my mother's conversation, drunk or sober, tends to include all the rage she's accumulated over a hard and bitter lifetime. As a kid, I took it. What choice did I have? Still, I was happiest when she was gone, even though I sometimes had to beg my Granny Jo for something to eat.

Mom was as surprised as everyone else in the family when I completed that first year of nursing school and moved out. At the time, I hoped to leave her in that rearview mirror, so long, sayonara, and goodbye. But then I became a single mother, and there was no way I could work and afford day care. Even in depressed, post-Covid Baxter, professional day care runs a thousand a month. So I cut a deal with my mother: I put a roof over her head and food in her belly, and she became . . . maybe not a real grandmother, but at least a nanny. By then, Mom's liver had reached the point of no return, and she was in bad shape. The bones of her shoulders and hips were sharp enough to pass for offensive weapons. Her face was a mass of deep creases. Her mouth had caved in so far that it looked as though she was trying to swallow her lips.

Sorry if I'm not mincing words. My relationship with my mother is strictly one of convenience, and my grievances run deep. As far as I'm concerned, I owe her nothing. All debts run in the other direction. But at least she's sober these days, and for good reason. She knows I'll kick her out on her ass if she starts drinking again. She also knows that she's likely to need a piece of my liver somewhere down the road.

"Okay, the green." I get up, put the black dress in the closet, and lay the green on the bed. The pale fabric is laced with small sequins. They look cheap and brassy under the harsh bedroom light, but I'm seeing the dress in a dim barroom, reflecting whatever light's available.

I know where I'm going in a few hours, know where I'll sit, know that a bloodred neon sign announcing the name of the bar, Randy's, will explode in the sequins on the left side of my dress and the silver bangles on my wrist.

"'Bout time you got out somewheres, Git." Mom's on her knees, rummaging through a pile of shoes for the pumps that match my dress. They're more silver than green, but close enough to work. "Got 'em." Mom displays the shoes with their six-inch heels. My feet hurt just looking at them, but I do like the dressing-up part one night every couple of months when I can pretend to be what I can never be. Not with a child to raise.

Mom puts down her unlit smoke and takes the small case that holds her cosmetics, brushes, and sponges out of the vanity's middle drawer. At one time she made a half-assed living as a beautician, but she was always too unreliable to succeed. She has talent, though, along with a small but noticeable tremor that disappears when she's at work.

"You comin' home tonight? Tomorrow?" Without looking up, she plucks an eyebrow pencil from the case. "What am I supposed to tell Charlie if you're not here when she wakes up?"

This from a woman who disappeared for weeks at a time.

"If I'm not home by sunrise, call the cops."

"And tell 'em what?"

When I don't answer, Mom goes to work. She sharpens the angle of my eyebrows and extends the outer edges by a quarter of an inch. The lids come next. She applies three coats of base, the color gradually darkening until both eyelids are a pale green that echoes the green of my dress. A spatter of silver glitter on the inner half of both lids and a curving black line that extends about an inch from the corners of each blue eye complete the package.

"Whatta ya think?" she asks.

Mom slips off to one side, leaving me face-to-face with the mirror. I find what I hoped for in my reflection. Party girl, not street whore, the main difference being that while you have to pay a whore, I'll do it for nothing. That gives me the right to be more selective, but not by all that much.

The mirror holds my attention for another moment. There's still a lot of work to be done on the too-pale skin and the ruler-straight blond hair that advertise my hill-billy roots. My grandparents—the only ones I knew, my mother's parents—came out of West Virginia in search of a better life. Which, according to Grandma Jo, they found.

Not long before she died, Granny Jo announced that she was proud of me. I was moving up, just as she'd moved up.

"It don't matter how hard we lived once we come to Baxter, life was a bunch meaner back in the hollers. You didn't have a job in the mines, you was likely to find your sorry self eatin' grass."

"Did you decide where you're goin' tonight, Git?" Mom returns to work, applying concealer to a small scar above my right eye, then foundation to the broad planes of my face and brow.

"I'm thinkin' Randy's."

The name fits the joint. Randy's Tavern is a bar where randy men and women congregate. You don't patronize Randy's unless you're looking for sex. It might be a couple in search of another couple or a married woman with an out-of-town hubby or me in search of a one-night stand.

The tavern's located at the edge of Mount Jackson, Baxter's only affluent neighborhood. The mount part's a joke to those of us who grew up on the southern end of the city. Mount Jackson could only be called Mount Anything in a city surrounded by hundreds of miles of flatland. The affluent part is just as misleading. True, the Baxter mansion, sixty-five rooms, dominates the top of the hill. But the family hasn't visited the place in years, and rumor has it they're preparing to close their plant. There are smaller mansions as well, most of them abandoned, and still smaller homes occupied by professional types—doctors, lawyers, small business owners.

At one time, our city had six major processing plants, each family owned. The Gauss Plant was the first to close, in 1994, and the fifth one, Dunning Pork Products, locked its gates six years ago. There's only the one left now, the one constructed by George Baxter in the early part of the last century.

And when that plant closes?

They don't locate tech companies in midwestern states dominated by corn, cattle, and hogs. Barring a miracle, it'll be run for your life when Baxter Packing shuts its doors.

"You can't maybe stay with your own kind?" Mom, as usual, drags me back to earth.

"And where would that be?"

Satisfied with my face, she pulls a curling iron from her bag of tricks and begins to curl the slightly thinning hair I intend to cover with a hat. Almost done now, I'm eager to get moving. With any luck, I'll stagger home tomorrow at sunrise with the itch thoroughly scratched. The earlier I start, the better.

"Lawton's would do."

Mom's probably right, on one level. If I went to Lawton's, I wouldn't need to buy a drink. I could stand in the doorway, beckon with a finger, and have a dozen unemployed rednecks named Austin, Clint, or Boyd competing for my favors. Maybe we'd ride to the motel in a pickup truck. Or maybe, if the guy was broke, we could screw in the truck bed.

An hour later, I'm staring into the vanity mirror, fascinated with my appearance. I'm almost beautiful, the effect so exotic I'm not sure what to do with my face. And though I know I'm playing above my weight, that's the basic idea. My panties and bra cost a hundred dollars. They're pale blue, trimmed with lavender lace and almost transparent.

Charlie walks into the room as I slide eight silver bangles onto my wrist. They'll also catch that red light.

"Mommy," Charlie says, head cocked to one side, "you look beautiful."

I take my daughter into my arms and give her a quick peck that doesn't smear my lipstick. Then I go into the vanity's drawer, take out my wedding ring, and slip it on my finger.

Good to go.

# CHAPTER THREE

## GIT

People in real cities like New York and Chicago would laugh at Randy's. I mean the upscale part. But I have to admit that Randy's owner, Mason Cheat, made a sincere effort. From the stone floor to the metal ceiling, the joint's sleek. A curved bar is wrapped in quilted leather, the lacquered crimson tables are glass-topped and square, and a white-metal sculpture that reminds me vaguely of a bird in flight dominates the main wall.

It's all nice, the effort I mean, but to my way of thinking, the bar's main claim to upscale status lies in what it doesn't have. A pool table in the back.

The lighting at Randy's is mostly provided by wall sconces and is very dim, which you'd expect and which I appreciate as I come through the door. We're far enough west in Baxter for me to get away with a broad-brimmed hat made by a local artisan, which conceals me still further. Hats aren't really in fashion, even in Baxter, but this close to cattle country, the Stetsons come out at the county fair to celebrate a time when cattlemen drove their herds through town. And on Wild West nights at the local clubs, where the Texas Two-Step prevails, they're more or less required.

Satisfied that I'm still anonymous, I cross the room. I can feel the eyes following me. You might call it self-arousal—to be desired, that's the first step—and I put a little extra into my gait. Not too blatant I'm hoping. Just a bit more bounce to the part of my body currently drawing the most attention.

The bartender approaches. I've seen him before, a middle-aged guy with a beard and sad eyes, like he's been at this way too long. His name is Shiloh and he's got an easy smile. But if he recognizes me, he's not giving it away.

"What can I get ya?"

"A martini."

"Comin' up."

The last half of my adolescence was spent downing shooters in one or another of the many bars in the Yards, the low-rent neighborhood surrounding Baxter's last processing plant. Lesson learned, I don't plan to get drunk tonight. I don't need that, and my drink is just part of the show.

My dress stops north of mid-thigh when I'm standing, and its neckline reaches my throat. The armholes are cut deep. They're open almost to my waist, and only the built-in bra keeps me on the right side of Baxter's indecent exposure laws. I don't know about the hem, which naturally moves up when I set one foot on the stool's polished rung and cross my legs.

Settled in, I take a closer look at the available talent, finding professional types mostly, along with a few overdressed rednecks, the usual stew, with a single exception. I don't stare at the man sitting at a table within ten feet of the bar. He's older than I am, though not by much, wearing a black jacket over a silk T-shirt that models his chest without being obviously tight. The T-shirt's indigo blue, a contrast to the faded blue of his jeans.

Bad boy? Boy toy? Something in a tiny smile that appears as we make eye contact tells me that he's nobody's toy.

But he's not moving. Instead, he lifts his drink, sips, and again makes brief eye contact before looking away. I'm not fooled. I know he's seen my wedding ring. It's on the hand raising my drink. There's only one reason a married woman would be in Randy's on a Saturday night, sitting by herself, no husband in view. Another man would already be standing next to me.

My first suitor—I love that word, though it has nothing to do with the situation—approaches a few minutes after I sit down. He's got recently divorced written all over him, from the frightened smile to the carefully tailored comb-over.

"Buy you a drink?"

"I'm good for now."

A little more experienced, and he'd understand the signal and head off to greener pastures. But he's not, and he pours out the bio he decided to reveal on the way to the bar. Recently divorced, as I predicted, his name is Owen and he's originally from Baxter. He teaches American history at the University of Wisconsin in Madison, and he's come home to visit his folks.

Encouragement is off the table, but I can't make myself tell him to get lost either. I look past Owen's left ear at the man in the silk T-shirt. He's smiling that same narrow smile, watching the show, in no hurry. What would he do if I took off with the college professor? If I had long-term plans, I just might do that—Owen's a mate-for-life kinda guy—but I'm not in search of a life sentence, and I take advantage of a pause in his monologue to spin back to the bar.

"Another, Shiloh. On *my* tab."

I can feel Owen's crest as it falls. Rejected, again. Can't help it, though, and I watch him drift away. He's replaced within a minute, this time by a paunchy middle-aged man wearing a gold chain thick enough to anchor a cruise ship.

"Buy you a drink?"

Shiloh chooses that moment to lay my drink on the bar.

"Thanks," I say, "but your timing's off."

"Franklyn Wallace here." He offers his hand, which I barely touch. No matter, Franklyn's quick to lay his credentials on the table, what he has to offer. He owns houses in Prairie Meadows, a gated community outside the city line, and in Boca Raton, Florida. He can afford these properties because he also owns the largest car dealership in the county, Toyotas, Chevys, Hondas, Audis, hundreds of cars. I should come by if I'm in the market, ask for Franklyn.

Franklyn's wearing a diamond ring, the diamonds arranged to form a horseshoe, and I instantly make him for the guy who never got the girl in high school. He's a winner now, right? Maybe?

I don't wanna hurt the guy, any more than I wanted to hurt Owen. I hold up my left hand. "Married."

"Me, too. I left my ring in the car."

"So what? Is that the question?"

"Yeah, like so what? We both know what we came for."

"You're right. I do know what I came for, and it isn't you." I look into his eyes for a moment. "Nothing personal, but my fantasies for the night run in another direction."

That gets me a shrug and a little speech I'm thinking he's made before. "All right, I could live with that, and thanks for not wastin' my time." He tosses a business card on the table. "Call me if you're in the market for a car, new or used. I'll beat any deal on the table."

Franklyn walks away, and I'm wondering if I made a mistake. Franklyn's not much to look at, but I know he'd be a by-the-books lover trying to make up for lost time. That we'd never meet again wouldn't matter. He'd go at me stubbornly, trying this, trying that, until he finally pushed the right button.

He's gone, though, and my attention returns to my boy toy. He looks at me for a moment, then stands, a leather gym bag I hadn't noticed before in his left hand. If the bag's snakeskin, which is what it looks like, it has to be worth a few hundred dollars. At the least.

Time to make his move? I'm expecting him to approach me, but he takes a step toward the door before looking over, a question in his dark eyes: Yes or no? He's taller than he looked sitting down, his shoulders broader, but something nags at me, some measure of doubt. I get up anyway, pausing long enough to leave a twenty on the bar top. Shiloh nods to me, then looks at the man, now standing halfway between the bar and the door.

"He okay?" I ask.

"Seen him before, honey. Name's Bradley Grieg and he comes in pretty regular."

Feeling safer now, and a lot more confident, I follow Bradley out of the bar and into the parking lot. I think he means to have me trail two steps behind, but the sex-slave thing doesn't get me off.

"That's far enough, Bradley."

He turns to me, smiling at the sound of his name. I come straight up to him. "We gonna play tonight, Bradley? Because if the answer's yes, then I gotta tell ya, I'm not into handcuffs or ropes or calling you master. You need that, better we should part friends."

He looks at me for a minute, looks directly into my eyes, like he's checking me out. But then he smiles and says, "I aim to please."

My internal alarms are ringing. He hasn't even asked my name, though I've said his aloud. Those fears vanish, replaced by a quick flush that reminds me of why I'm here, when he takes me in his arms for a gentle, lingering kiss that only gradually becomes more probing. I feel him stiffen as we press into each other.

"We good?" he asks.

"Yeah," I tell him, "we're good."

Bradley already has a room at the Skyview Motor Court on Baxter Boulevard. The Skyview may not be the Hilton, but they don't rent their mini cabins by the hour, either. I follow Bradley's Audi along Baxter Boulevard, the only surface street that crosses the entire city. Traffic lights on every block slow us down, raising expectations, my impatience somehow erotic. I open a window, then close it when I hear thunder roll in the distance. We're close now, and I imagine, in a few seconds, a joining that takes hours, everything and anything. It's my outing, and I plan to work it hard.

Bradley turns into the Skyview's parking lot and I follow, not quite riding his bumper. It must be a slow night because only a few cars front the cabins, none close to ours. Bradley's standing in front of our cabin, holding the door open when I get out of my little Ford. As I slip by, he slaps me on the ass. And then . . .

Less than ten minutes later, he's on his way, naked, to the bathroom. I'm still bent over a small dresser, half paralyzed. Bradley hasn't spoken a word, hasn't kissed or caressed me, and I have to think he bothered with me only because I was better than a sock. I hear the shower running, hear it shut down a minute later, then nothing.

My brain's a supercharged roulette wheel, spinning, spinning, spinning. I need to get out of here while some little piece of my dignity remains intact, but I can't seem to move. And my panties are nowhere in sight. I vaguely remember throwing them toward the bed, but I can't see them, and I can't leave without them. They're too fucking expensive.

Instead of crying, which is what I want to do, I drop to my knees and search for the damned panties. They're behind the headboard, and I'm holding them, standing in the middle of the room, when the bathroom door opens. Still naked, Bradley staggers into the room, stoned out of his mind, his eyelids at half-mast. His voice, when he speaks after a long moment, is slurred.

"You still here?" He flops onto the bed, then sits up. "Wait a minute."

Bradley's jeans are next to him on the bed. He reaches into a pocket, withdraws a roll of bills, peels off three twenties, and tosses them in my direction.

"Fuck off."

I watch the bills flutter and separate as they fall to the carpet. Bradley snorts once, then falls onto his stomach and begins to snore.

It takes a few minutes, but I recover. Furious, I look around for some heavy object, something I can smash into his helpless skull, maybe a lamp. But the lights are attached to the walls or in the ceiling. There's only the chair I'm sitting on.

My brain still roiling, I head for the bathroom. I'm thinking I should clean up before I go home, but the cigarette lighter, the burnt spoon, and the syringe on the edge of the tub stop me in my tracks. I turn around, catching sight of the leather gym bag on the room's small table, then quickly check on Bradley. He's halfway to an overdose and won't be conscious anytime soon.

Where I grew up, honesty was rarely considered the best policy. My mother lied so often I lost count. She lied to me, to social workers, to Granny Jo, to my teachers, to the boyfriends she cheated on.

The first thing I see when I open the bag is a large handgun, a semiautomatic. I don't flinch. They call my part of the country the Bible Belt, but they could easily call it the Gun Belt. Pistols don't frighten me, rifles or shotguns either, just ask my ex-husband. Anyway, I'm a lot more interested in the banded stacks of twenties and fifties beneath the gun. There's enough here to alter the course of my life, and much for the better.

Charlie's, too.

My day-to-day schedule wouldn't change all that much, not at first. Quitting my job would attract too much attention. But I could probably take enough part-time classes to earn my RN. As a registered nurse, I'd earn enough to get out of Baxter before it falls apart. I could set up a new life in a new city where nobody knows where I came from or how I grew up. I could free myself and Charlie from the chains that bind us.

At one time, herds of cattle were driven through Baxter's streets. Nowadays they come by truck and rail. Either way, on quiet mornings you can hear the animals wailing as they're led to slaughter, the bellow of the steers, the screams of the hogs.

I could free myself from that, too.

# CHAPTER FOUR

## DELIA

When Chief Black phones, I'm not busy in the squad room, although I'm the chief of Baxter's detectives and always on duty if an emergency warrants my presence. No, I'm sitting in the pastor's office at Trinity Lutheran Church, answering for my son's unacceptable behavior. Trinity's one of Baxter's more prosperous churches. Upper galleries run the length of the church on both sides, and chandeliers hang from a coffered ceiling. The altar is flanked by stained-glass windows, the maple pews are highly polished. Trinity's congregation reflects the church's sedate prosperity. Baxter's mostly a city of poor and poorer, but what middle class we have attends Trinity or the local Catholic churches.

Religion holds no great attraction for me, but a number of my twelve-year-old son's buddies attend Trinity Lutheran,

so I dutifully drive Danny to morning services every
Sunday. I don't want to know what they're teaching him,
but I'm pretty sure it hasn't affected his behavior. This
morning he punched a kid in the mouth for still unex-
plained reasons.

"Your son is quite intelligent, Lieutenant Mariola,"
Pastor Grange tells me. "But his attitude is . . . how shall
I put it? Not quite belligerent, I won't go that far, but certainly on the edge." He smiles, revealing yellow, uneven
teeth. "Yes, that's perfect. Daniel is an edgy child with
little respect for authority."

Grange's smarmy tone pushes me to my own edge, and I
have to fight an urge to say something obscene that I'll later
regret. I am, after all, a respected public servant, the first
female detective on the Baxter Police Department. Now,
I'm the head detective no less. True, the city's population
is only a bit over a hundred thousand. True, the Detective
Division's limited to six investigators. True, the department emphasizes moneymakers like traffic and parking
violations. But I'm still the officer Chief Black chose when
Tommy Harrigan retired.

"A wop for a mick, Delia," was the folksy way he
explained it. "And a girl wop at that."

Pastor Grange isn't too happy when my cell runs off the
first few notes of "Fast Car," a Tracy Chapman tune. He's
unhappier still when I answer. Too bad. It's my boss and
I can't ignore the call.

"Where are you, Delia?"

"Trinity Lutheran. My son—"

"Forget the kid. We got a body out at the Skyview, a homicide. I need you on it. Like yesterday."

It should be a joke, but it's not. In the last year, little Baxter's seen ten overdose deaths and five drug-related suicides. No big deal. No rush. Now we have our second murder, and the chief's sweating. That it's Sunday and my scheduled day off matters not at all.

"I gotta go," I tell Pastor Grange. "Duty calls."

On the way to my car, I stop in the room outside Grange's office to confront my son. Dan's wearing a resigned expression. He knows he's in for a lecture, and he doesn't like it.

"You wanna tell me what happened?"

"Barry called you a dyke."

"He did, huh? Well, I hope you at least broke his legs."

Danny finally grins. "Nah, I just ripped off his ears."

Tall for his age and blond, Danny's a natural athlete. He plays Pop Warner football and Little League baseball. A perfect life . . . except for his mom's inconvenient sexual preferences. Not that I bring women home or hang out in Baxter's one gay and lesbian bar. No, I'm discreet, an absolute necessity in a Bible Belt city. Still, my preferences are no secret, and Danny's adolescent world is honor bound. He had to respond to Barry's taunt, true or not. Either that or be marked a coward, a punk, a target for bullies. That's not a fate either one of us is prepared to accept. You back away from a confrontation once, you'll back away forever, a chiseled-in-stone truth familiar to every cop. Character counts.

"Let me tell you a story," I say, ignoring his resigned expression. He's been here before. "You know how I used to play junior varsity baseball in high school?"

"Yeah, second base."

"Right. So, there was this one boy who stayed on my case every second." I have to think for a minute before his name comes back to me. "Jimmy Leland. He never let up, kept calling me Butch Mariola when the coaches weren't around. So one day we're playin' an inter-squad game and he's on first base with nobody out. I'm shaded toward the middle when the batter—I don't remember his name—slaps a ground ball past the pitcher. The ball takes a big hop right into my glove, and I step on second, then turn to complete the double play. At that point, Jimmy Leland's supposed to get out of my way. He's already been called out. But he's blocking a throw to first, and he's got this big smirk on his face, and he's screaming, `Yah, yah, yah, yah.' Well, I threw the ball anyway, and it hit him square in the forehead. Trust me, the jerk dropped like a stone."

"So what happened?"

"That's what I'm getting to. Jimmy was okay, but the coach sent him to the emergency room to be checked out. And it didn't matter that he was supposed to give me room to throw to first, that he was wrong. I got tossed off the team, and that was the end of my baseball career. You understand, Danny? It felt good takin' the jerk out, but what did it really get me?"

Give Danny credit. He doesn't go with the first thing that comes into his head. He thinks it over for a minute. "Mom, I couldn't let it go."

"True enough, but you could have waited until you got him alone. Reverend Grange, he's got the power, like my coach. If he kicks you out, you're out." I give it a couple of beats, then change the subject. "I just got a call from the boss. A murder, okay, at the Skyview Motor Court. Tonight, when I get home, I'll tell you all about it."

Dan's face brightens at the prospect. This is something he can brag about to his friends. A real murder. He kisses me on the cheek—too old, apparently, for the mouth—and I'm out of there.

The sad truth is that Danny's the product of an acquaintance rape. Or so I've come to believe. In fact, I found out I was pregnant only after weeks of morning sickness. Shock doesn't begin to describe my reaction when the doctor delivered the news. I was nineteen, a freshman studying criminal justice at Southern Illinois Community College. I was also a committed (if still closeted to all but my parents) lesbian. This commitment followed my only experience with a male, a true disaster that resulted in the loss of my virginity and a determination never to repeat the experience.

So . . . pregnant?

Two months earlier, I'd been to a party. At the time, I was drinking pretty hard and doing the occasional line of coke, just like most kids my age. When I woke at dawn on a made bed, I simply assumed that I'd passed out. I was drinking gin that night, mixed drinks poured by a man I'd known for years. A mentor, almost.

I'd like to claim that I sought and got revenge, but the reality was that I could do exactly nothing. I couldn't be sure I was drugged, or that Kyle Spyros was the father. I couldn't accuse him, either, not without proof. No, I had only one question to answer: whether or not to abort.

My parents were devout Catholics, yet they'd accepted my gay orientation. That's how much they loved me. But abortion was a step too far. Way too far. This was back in Centralia, Illinois, a town of twelve thousand in the very conservative, southern part of the state. Unwed mothers were too common to reject altogether, but abortion was unforgivable. If I didn't feel that I could raise the child, my parents would take on the responsibility.

Maybe they feared that I'd resent having motherhood forced on me, that I'd reject my baby. In fact, I loved Danny without reservation from the first day, though I didn't make an especially good mom. Too selfish, really, and too committed to a job that forced me to work odd hours. That first year, while I finished my education, I relied on my parents for childcare. It was only after I took the only job offered to me in faraway Virginia that I learned how hard it is to be a single mom. There's the never-ending guilt about leaving your child in someone else's care and the unending financial burden. You learn to muddle through, juggling bills at the end of every month, always looking for the next opportunity. My move to Baxter was all about money.

The city of Baxter was built in pieces, neighborhood by neighborhood, as the packing plants went up, leaving Baxter Boulevard the only through street. The boulevard runs ten miles from the southeast corner of the city to the northwest. Except for a cluster of municipal offices downtown, it's bordered by strip malls, car lots, gas stations, and fast-food joints. Empty stores and weathered For Rent signs confirm an economy on the permanent downside. We'd been well on our way before the virus hit Baxter Packing, but Covid-19 was the last nail in the city's collective coffin. Baxter Packing closed and opened, then closed and opened again. This was before testing determined that more than eighteen hundred of its three thousand employees had been infected. They carried the virus to every corner of the community, and I ceased to be a detective. Instead, I spent my days, like every other member of the force, responding to the 911 calls of the desperately ill, so many that our volunteer ambulance corps was overwhelmed and we often transported the sick in the backs of our patrol cars. We transported them to our one small hospital, Baxter Medical Center. Each trip had the feel of an execution. Gurneys filled the parking lot, the coughing of the men and women who lay on them sounding to me like the babble of geese on the Southern Illinois lakes where I grew up. Sure of one thing only, that my time would come, I worked day after day until my knees buckled.

These days, except for Baxter Packing, most people work outside the city. Truckers going over the road, a Walmart box store one county to the east, an Amazon warehouse two counties to the south. The luckiest endure an eighty-mile round-trip commute to a unionized GE plant or find government jobs at Ackley Air Force Base even farther away.

Unsynchronized traffic lights slow me down as I make my way along Baxter Boulevard. I'm forced to observe the remnants of Baxter's glory days. The pitted sandstone blocks of the courthouse and the jail, City Hall Park with its untended shrubs and lawn. Baxter's population numbered 103,412 at the last census. If it should fall below a hundred thousand at the next census, a near certainty, Baxter will cease to be a city and become a town.

Mayor Venn and the city council are obsessed with keeping our city a city, despite the cratering economy. They want to attract new business, using our low homicide rate to bolster a claim that we're family friendly. That's bullshit. The opiate crisis didn't just roll through town, here and gone, it set up permanent residence. Burglaries are as common in Baxter as they are in third-world cities.

Irrational or not, the mayor will lean on Chief Black, who will lean on me. But that's Baxter's story. Nepotism, cronyism, pay-to-play. The politicians are tearing the last bits of flesh from the city's bones. I'm not going to wait until those bones are bare, and I work my cases hard while I apply to police departments in viable cities like Minneapolis or Chicago. These are cities that all patriotic

Baxterites pretend to despise, even as their college-bound children seek them out.

The streets are still wet from last night's rain, and little ponds surround plugged drains at the curb. Most of our businesses are closed this early on a Sunday morning, but the churches I pass are doing good business. We're big on Christianity in Baxter. Big on every brand from St. Paul's Roman Catholic Church to the Tabernacle Church of God, where the pastor handles rattlesnakes. Religion doesn't appeal to me, but most of these churches have a second mission that does. By midafternoon they'll be transformed into food pantries, feeding hundreds of destitute families. That's how far down we've come.

The atrocity at the Skyview doesn't surprise me. But atrocity it is. First, it rained last night. Second, the Skyview's parking lot is in need of maintenance, and there are muddy potholes. Third, mud records and pre- serves the tire treads of any vehicle passing through it. Fourth, this end of the parking lot contains six cruisers, an ambulance, a fire engine, the coroner's van, and an Audi that I'm guessing belongs to the victim. All have passed through the same potholes that might have cap- tured the perpetrator's treads. All have deposited their own tire impressions in the mud.

Did I mention that our cops are paid, on average, twenty- five percent less than cops assigned to similar duty in other parts of the state? Factor in rampant nepotism, and you have the makings of a truly incompetent force.

The Dink's standing in front of the last in a line of cabins maybe twenty feet apart. That would be Detective John Meacham, brother of Gloria Meacham, city council president. You can give the Dink a direct order and assume that he'll make at least a half-hearted attempt to follow it. But that's all you're likely to get. And don't expect him to report back when he finishes the job. Look for him in the nearest coffee shop.

"Who was first on the scene?" I ask.

"Harvey and Morello."

"And when did you get here?"

"A few minutes later. I was right around the corner."

"And you didn't think to seal off the parking lot? *Never* crossed your mind?"

One thing about the Dink, he knows he's protected. "Nope," he tells me. "It never did."

"Seal it off now, Detective. Except for the Audi, I want every vehicle moved."

The Skyview Motor Court's seen better days, much better. The twelve little buildings are supposed to resemble log cabins, but the logs were never logs, only siding that weathered badly over the years. Now the phony bark is peeling, reminding me of a long-haired dog shedding its winter coat.

I step onto the small porch that fronts Cabin 909's open doorway just as our coroner emerges. Most communities of any size employ full-time medical examiners. Baxter has a coroner-cardiologist, Arshan Rishnavata, who gets paid by the body.

Arshan likes talking tough. "Somebody jammed a pillow against the back of his head and put a bullet through it. His forehead and most of his brain are all over the sheets."

I lay a hand on his chest. "Forget the brains, Arshan. It's the *mayor* who's all over this. Do the autopsy right. Give me a full tox screen, scrape his fingernails, check him for cancer, heart disease, and STDs. No shortcuts."

# CHAPTER FIVE

## DELIA

Two of my detectives, Vernon Taney and Laura Udell, stand by the body of a man. The man's naked and stretched out on the room's only bed. He's lying on his stomach, his face buried in a pillow that's soaked in blood. Brain matter and stuffing from a blackened pillow blot the entry wound. The head injury is the only visible wound on the body.

Vern Taney's not only my partner of choice on investigations, but along with his wife and son, he pretty much defines my social life. Vern's a local, with family ties reaching back a hundred years. Unlike the Dink and most of the other locals on the force, he's as dedicated to Baxter and the craft of policing as he is to his family. Laura Udell, by contrast, is the chief's sister-in-law. Or maybe cousin or niece. It's reached the point where it's hard to keep track.

"The staties on the way, Vern?"

"Less than an hour out, Lieutenant," Vern tells me.

Baxter doesn't have a crime scene unit. Instead, we have a few cops who can fingerprint a burglarized house or a stolen car. But systematically identifying and collecting well-documented blood and DNA evidence? Sorry, can't afford the training. We use the state's crime scene unit. Their lab, too.

"Detective," I tell Laura, "I want you to supervise a search of the parking lot and the area around the cabin. Photograph anything you find before you collect it."

"Got it, Lou."

Laura out of the way, I turn back to Vern. A football hero back in his high school days, Vern is amiable and folksy with his colleagues. Just another local, a guy you can talk sports with at the corner bar. But don't disrespect him or the department, or resist arrest. Vern's hands are almost as big as my head.

"You find his cell phone?" I ask.

"Nope, but the coroner's done, so we can turn him over. We know the asshole, by the way."

"That right?"

"Name's Bradley Grieg, according to his driver's license."

It takes a moment, but then it comes back to me. A woman beat to shit, cheeks the color of an eggplant, eyes swollen shut, jaw fractured. I move closer to the bed as I examine Grieg's hands. I'm looking for bruises, but they're both clean.

"What was her name again, Vern? The victim?"

"Cindy Sherman."

"Right."

Cindy was only nineteen. Way too young to be married to an asshole like Bradley Grieg. But she'd named him as her attacker, and we had him in a cage when she decided not to testify. Instead, she hired an attorney who told us that the matter had been "addressed" and Bradley would no longer be part of Cindy's life. By then we knew that Bradley was buddy-buddy with Connor Schmidt, son of Carl Schmidt.

Carl Schmidt's the head of what passes for a mob crew in Baxter. Unlike the city, he's prospered, what with the permanently unemployed consoling themselves with dope, coke, meth, and alcohol. But that's been the pattern from the beginning. As the packing plants closed one by one, the number of addicts grew, as did the robbery and burglary rates, as did incidents of domestic violence and the number of families headed by women.

"Word out there," Vern explains, "is that Connor stepped in. Told Cindy if she didn't testify, he would guarantee that she'd never hear from Bradley again. Cindy took the deal."

Vern rolls Grieg over in my direction. Grieg's mouth is open far enough to reveal a gold tooth far back in a shattered jaw. Most of the rest of his face is gone.

"You speak to the motel manager, Vern?"

"Owner-manager. That would be Felice Gaitskill, who I knew back in high school. She was a few years ahead of me. Felice told me Grieg checked in yesterday afternoon. No idea where he went from there, if he went out at all."

"What about video?"

"Three cameras mounted over the door to the office, facing left, right, and forward."

"That's it?" Two stories high, the office is closer to a house than a cabin. It's also a hundred yards away.

"Fraid so, Delia. And I understand why Grieg chose a cabin on the edge of the motel. His home is only a mile from here, and the boy wasn't married, so he musta been up to some kinda bullshit. But check out this here." Vern lifts Grieg's left arm to reveal the healed tracks of a reformed junkie, along with enough fresh punctures to transform his arm into a pincushion.

"Now check out the bathroom," Vern tells me. "The man's works are spread out on the edge of the tub."

"Yeah, I will. But what about the video? We gonna see it today?"

"The Gaitskills were reluctant. That would be Felice and her son, Richard. So I explained how we'd have to seal off the motel until we got a warrant. Said it nice and all, like I didn't have any choice in the matter. That's when they decided to cooperate."

I dispatch Vern to make sure the video's not accidentally deleted. Motel owners believe that, to many of their customers, privacy is more important than clean sheets. I also want a few minutes to let my thoughts run where they will. Vern was right about one thing. With Grieg's home only a short distance away, he hadn't come to the Skyview for a night's sleep.

A drug deal gone bad? That's my first thought. Connor Schmidt and his father are known dealers, and I've been after them for a long time. So far, they've been too quick. By the time we learn of a deal, it's already gone down. I'll probably nail them sometime in the future, but I'm not holding my breath. When the stars line up, they line up.

I check the bathroom first. On the edge of the tub I find a syringe, a teaspoon, a ball of cotton, and a tiny plastic vial holding a bit of brown powder. A pair of towels on the floor and the bottom of the shower stall are still damp.

Back in the main room, I take another slow inventory, listing each item as I proceed. A three-drawer bureau, a desk and hard-backed chair, an upholstered chair in the corner, a queen-size bed, its sheets and blankets, though bloodstained, almost undisturbed. The room's flat-screen TV is mounted above the desk. A print above the bed depicts a woodsman bent over a mountain stream.

The pants Grieg had been wearing lie in a heap on the upholstered chair. A T-shirt, silk from the look of it, and a thin black jacket have been tossed onto the carpet.

In a hurry when he came through the door? That's what it looks like. But there's another item in the room, this one definitely out of place. An expensive snakeskin bag lies open and empty on the bureau.

The earliest stage of an investigation, at least for this cop, is packed with questions. Was the snakeskin bag full before Grieg carried it from the car into the room? Why is it open? Were its contents stolen? Or were its contents exchanged before Grieg checked in? After? If so, exchanged for what? Cash? The only cash in the room is still in Grieg's pocket. The only drugs, a vial of what's probably heroin or fentanyl, rests on the edge of the tub.

The empty bag indicates robbery. But that doesn't jibe with Grieg's lying naked on the bed after a shower. Drug dealers rarely conduct business in the nude. And I'm almost certain that Grieg hasn't been moved. Lividity is pronounced, with Grieg's blood pooled on his chest and the front of his legs. No, he died where he is right now. Lying naked on that bed.

Always begin with the most likely explanation. Only move on when you've proved that explanation false. The strewn clothes? The damp towels? Naked on the bed? Bradley Grieg brought the wrong woman to Cabin 909.

# CHAPTER SIX

## CONNOR

"**D**o me a favor and try to organize your fuckin' thoughts. For once in your life, tell me what happened, exactly. This, then this, then that. Okay? One, then two, then three."

That's Carl Schmidt talking. My dad. Dad's pissed off, but then he's always pissed off. At me, at Mom, at the asshole thugs who work for us, at the dry cleaner for leavin' a stain on his jacket. My best guess? Dad's anger began as an act designed to keep his workers (and his customers) in line. But then it grew into a habit he couldn't break. I say this because Mom claims that once upon a time her husband was even tempered. Like her son.

In other words, Dad's a bully and a jerk. True, he's made a very good living by scaring everyone around him. Except me. I stopped being afraid of him a couple of years ago. That's when I realized that I might have to kill him someday. That's when I realized that I could do it, no problemo.

This time Dad has good reason to be pissed. Not to mention actually fucking enraged. We're in Dad's house (not Mom's, nobody would dare call it Mom's house, or even *their* house), in Dad's study, a recent addition. I could have predicted the decor. Dad's taken the many animals he's killed over the years, including the fish, and scattered them across the floor and the walls. His favorite is a wolverine he shot from a helicopter. He tells everyone that he likes to run his fingers through fur dense enough to endure fifty-below nights.

"I got to the motel at eight o'clock this morning," I tell him, "right on time for the meetup. Only the cops were already there. Six or seven cruisers, an EMS truck, the coroner's wagon, and maybe a dozen uniformed cops. The cops were searching the area around the entrance to Room 909."

"Cabin 909, right? The Skyview don't have rooms. They have cabins." Dad scratches at his left ear, the one missing a lobe. "Try to get it right, Connor."

Between the two of us, father and son, we manage a family business. We middle drugs and lend money at high interest. Call them payday loans, without the paperwork. We also put the arm on the hookers working nearby truck stops. The whores pay for protection, and they get it. We keep the pimps away. The girls are also an outlet for yours truly, whose wife left him a year ago. I've never blamed Trudy. In fact, I only wish she'd taken Mom with her, that the both of 'em escaped. This life I'm leadin'? It runs in only one direction.

Dad likes to think of himself as the king. Sitting on his throne, whispering orders to his son, the prince. That's called plausible deniability. See, I'm the asshole who passes those orders to our crew. That way, if one of our boys turns rat, which sooner or later is sure to happen, it won't come back on Dad. Unless, of course, I'm the boy who rats.

"I was pretty far away," I continue. "Parked on the street at the other end of the motel. I couldn't get too close because I didn't wanna be asked what I was doin' there. But I could see that our guy was there, too."

"Doin' what?"

"Standin' around."

"He wasn't in charge?"

"Nope. The bitch was in charge. Lieutenant Mariola. Our guy looked to me like deadweight. Like he wanted to be somewhere else."

I pause, but Dad waves me on.

"I texted our guy and met him a half hour later in the Kroger parkin' lot. Bradley Grieg's dead. He took one through the top of his skull, they're thinkin' while he was asleep. Like he never saw it coming."

And for good reason, given the heroin and paraphernalia the cops found in the unit's bathroom. For now, I'm keeping this to myself. I thought Brad's junkie past was behind him. If I knew he'd relapsed, I would never have sent him up north. But convincing Dad is about as likely as either of us going to heaven.

"What about the money?" Dad has a tendency to repeat himself when he's stirred up, and he does it now. "What about the fuckin' money?"

"I couldn't really ask that question. Not directly."

"Get to the point, Connor." Dad's tone hardens, another trick that leaves me unimpressed. "What about the money?"

"According to our guy, Mariola's thinkin' the motive was robbery. They found a fancy bag in the room, like a gym bag, only made of snakeskin." I enjoy pushing Dad's buttons, and I hesitate long enough for him to raise his eyebrows and tighten a mouth already as tight as a clenched fist. "The bag was open. Open and empty. The only money they found in the room was the hundred bucks in Brad's pocket."

The door opens and Mom walks in, bearing a tray with mugs of coffee and a plate of glazed doughnuts. The doughnuts, when I grab one, are still warm from the fryer.

"I thought you might like some coffee."

There are those who think that Mom's slow. Me, I'm not buyin'. I think she's afraid, but of what I don't know. What I do know is that she'll do just about anything to avoid conflict. Like she's phobic. As for Dad, I've never heard him utter a harsh word to his wife. Or a kind word, either.

Dad nods at his desk, and Mom puts the tray down. I take a second bite of my doughnut as she leaves the room.

"The doughnut's great," I tell her.

Mom offers me a quick smile, a young, almost girlish smile. She's as slim and graceful as dad is thick and clumsy. You'd never take them for husband and wife if you laid eyes on them for the first time.

When I turn around, Dad's standing by the window. He staring into the backyard, with its border of roses. The blossoms present a bloodred wall that extends from one side of the property to the other. It's Mom, of course, who cares for them.

"I'm thinkin'," Dad says, "this is better for us."

"How so?"

That provokes a baleful glare. What horrible thing did he do in life to be burdened with an idiot son? That's all right. Let him think I'm an idiot. Let him live with his delusions, as he'll have to live with the consequences.

"If the cops had the money, it'd be gone forever. This way, if we can find the asshole who offed Bradley, we still got a chance to get it back." Dad lifts a coffee mug and almost drains it. "And speakin' of the dead, I told you Bradley was deadweight. I told you he was a complete fuckup. But he was your buddy, and you fuckin' vouched for him. Am I wrong? Tell me."

The job couldn't have been simpler. First, I give Bradley seven hundred little green pills with the number 80 (for 80 mg) on one side. Second, Bradley carries them to a buyer in the northern part of the state. Third, Bradley carries back the eighteen thousand dollars the buyer gives him, going to the Skyview Motor Court before anyone knows he's in town.

The Skyview was my idea—just in case the cops were set up on Bradley's house—but it was pretty much routine.

When it comes to drugs, our rule of thumb is simple. Here and gone before anybody knows what happened. That said, the virus was good for us, what with just about every cop busy and the newly unemployed with nothin' but time on their hands. True, I got sick, Mom too, but we both recovered after a couple of weeks. Not Dad, though. He isolated himself early on while his wife, even sick, left his meals by the door to what used to be their bedroom.

"How can you blame Bradley?" I ask. "The guy's dead. He paid with his life."

"I thought you said he was asleep when he bought it."

"The cops think he was asleep, okay? What's the difference? You don't get deader 'cause you see it comin'."

Dad picks up a doughnut and bites off half. I watch him chew for a moment, watch his Adam's apple bob as he swallows. I'm wondering what it would feel like to run a straight razor across his throat.

"I want that money, Connor, or I want my pound of flesh. I can't let myself get ripped off and do nothin'. Somebody, somewhere has to pay. You're gonna make that happen." He hesitates, then repeats. "You're gonna make that happen by yourself. I don't want no one else knowin' I'm out eighteen grand."

I don't mention the obvious, that the cops will also be looking for whoever took Bradley off the count. Or that my interest might catch their attention.

"Look, Connor, you know the jerk, right? His friends, where he hangs out, what he likes, what he don't like? So ask around. Bradley musta told somebody he was gonna be in that room. You find that somebody, you'll find our money."

I think I'm supposed to respond, but I don't. I just shrug and reach for my coffee. The rip-off isn't do-or-die. The eighteen hurts, but we'll be okay. I gotta figure Dad already knows that. He has something else in mind.

"Try hard, Connor. Try real, real hard. Because we wouldn't be in this mess if you hadn't recommended that asshole." He smiles. Here comes the punch line. "If you don't find that money, it's gonna come out of your end of the business."

# CHAPTER SEVEN

## DELIA

Felice Gaitskill is several inches taller than my five-six and big-boned as well. But she's not as formidable as her son. Richard Gaitskill's as tall and thick as Vernon Taney, who seems unimpressed. Vern's pulled a chair up before a monitor in the back office. He offers me the chair, which I take, then waits for me to nod. Vern will conduct most of the interview, as usual. My job is to close the deal.

"I wanna thank you, Felice," Vern begins, his tone amiable, "for accommodatin' us on such short notice."

Felice sneers, her eyes narrowing. "Just do what you gotta do, Vern. Get it over with."

"Now, Felice, no need to get testy. This is murder we're talkin' about." He hesitates, but Felice, though her mouth moves, holds her peace. "First, did you know Bradley Grieg before he registered last night?"

"Why would I know him?"

"That's actually my second question. The *why* part." Vern lifts his head to look into her eyes, his expression still friendly. "So, you did know him, right?"

"Uh-uh, not the way you mean. Grieg was a regular, checked in maybe three times a month. Usually had a woman in the car. Different women."

"Hookers?"

Richard answers this time, his voice surprisingly high-pitched. "I think Bradley was a . . . a ladies' man. I think he liked to show off, at least to me. Whenever I was workin' outside the office—collectin' trash, cuttin' the grass—he'd stop and talk for a minute. The women he was with, a lot of 'em were older than he was, and most of them wore their wedding rings. Like they weren't ashamed, ya know? Like knockin' off a quickie was routine."

"What about yesterday? Was he alone when he registered?"

"Yeah."

"You sure, Richard?"

"He parked his car out front when he came into the office. There was nobody else in it."

"Okay. So far, so good, and I appreciate the cooperation." Vern pulls a chair up beside me. "Anybody object if I work this?" Nobody does, and we're off and running.

Drawn from an external hard drive, the video's grainy and blurred, pretty much as I expected. It's that privacy thing again. Don't see, don't tell. According to the desk register,

Grieg checked in at 6:20 P.M., and Vern fast-forwards at high speed from early morning, through the afternoon to evening. At 6:15 he slows it down, then slows it further when an Audi pulls onto the lot and drives up to the office.

Richard Gaitskill wasn't lying. Grieg was alone when he registered. What's more, the time/date stamp at the bottom of the screen reads 6:21, which jibes with the desk register. So far, so good.

Bradley Grieg leaves the office eight minutes later, at 6:29. He drives to his cabin, pops the trunk, and carries the suitcase and the smaller bag into the cabin. Then nothing.

Vern taps a key, and the footage rolls on at high speed until 9:03, when the door opens and Grieg pops out. He's carrying the small bag, which he lays on the front seat before driving off. Other guests appear, unloading mostly, as Vern works through the video. The cabins they occupy are all at a distance from Cabin 909. By chance? Most are on the other side of the office.

Vern pauses the video and turns to the Gaitskills. "Grieg brought women to his room from time to time. We've established that much. But did Grieg ever have a male guest in his room?"

"A male guest?" This from Felice Gaitskill. A question for a question.

"Yeah, did he ever have a man in his room?"

"Not that I ever seen."

"How 'bout you, Richie. Did you ever see a man enter Grieg's cabin?"

"Can't recall I have."

"But maybe it happened, right? Maybe?"

"Maybe," he concedes.

"Like Connor Schmidt?"

Richard's too young and the name too unexpected. Now he's asking himself what we know and what we don't. He's cooked. Not his mom, though.

"What are we now," she asks, "suspects?"

Vern slides his gaze from son to mother, taking his time, the gesture almost lazy. "You live on the premises, Felice, and you were home last night. So, yeah, you could've killed him." Another smile, this one less amiable. "Nobody's eliminated until they're eliminated. Now, do either of you know Connor Schmidt? Or his father, Carl? A simple yes or no will do here." Neither Gaitskill volunteers a reply, and I step in to close the deal.

"Think about it. A man was murdered in one of your cabins, only the second murder this year. Do you really want to impede my investigation when Mayor Venn is personally involved? Use your heads. If you don't cooperate, I gotta ask myself why. And me, when I have a question, I keep turning over those rocks until I find an answer."

I nod to Vern, and he fast-forwards until Grieg returns at 10:42, his Audi followed by a midsize sedan I can't identify. Mitsubishis, Hondas, Toyotas, even Fords and Chevys? From this distance, they could all be poured from the same mold. If I didn't know that Grieg drove an Audi, I wouldn't be able to identify his car either.

A woman exits the second car. Average height, average weight, a blur actually, the video worthless as far as identification goes. I can see that she's wearing a hat, but it's the only detail I can make out.

Neither hesitates. Grieg holds the door open as she passes, then follows her into the room. Thirty-three minutes later, at 11:15, the woman exits, walks to her car, and drives off.

Please be it, I tell myself. Let there be nobody else on the video until Richard Gaitskill discovers the body. Let it be the woman for sure, without doubt, the only card on the table. Identify her, and I close the case and the chief says, "Attagirl."

It begins to rain a few minutes further into the video. The rain gradually becomes more intense, until Cabin 909 is reduced to a vague outline that finally disappears altogether. It doesn't reappear until sunrise. Anybody might have exited or entered in the intervening seven hours. Not likely, true, but maybe enough to create reasonable doubt. It only takes a single juror.

Richard Gaitskill enters the video at 7:47 A.M., driving an electric vehicle the size of a golf cart. He steers the cart from cabin to cabin, picking up trash, skipping the currently occupied cabins. At 9:10 he stops in front of Grieg's cabin and peers at the door for a good thirty seconds before hopping down. I watch him approach the cabin, push the door open, then quickly back away. Within seconds he's on his cell phone.

"That call you're making?" I ask. "To 911?"

"Yeah."

"You sure? Because every call to 911 is time-stamped to the second. So if you're lying to me, I'm gonna find out."

Richard's eyes narrow slightly. "Look, you asked if I knew Connor or his dad. Well . . ."

"Don't tell him nothin'."

Richard responds without glancing at his mother. "We run a clean shop here, Lieutenant." He points to an aluminum baseball bat leaning against the wall. "No whores, no pimps, and if I think somebody's dealin' from one of the cabins, they go, too. But Carl Schmidt and his kid? That's a whole other game. So, yes, I know the Schmidts, in the sense that I'd recognize them on the street, but not so good that I'd say hello when I pass 'em. As for Connor, he's been here a couple of times with Bradley. What they did in the room I couldn't say. I don't know now, didn't know then, and don't wanna know in the future. You fuck with Carl Schmidt, you could end up dead."

It comes too fast for me, too glib. Like he'd rehearsed it in his head, word for word, before he let the words go. And yes, Richard could have killed Bradley. His mom, too.

"Okay, that's enough for now. But listen to what I say, and listen carefully. You really need to preserve the video. That's because, if anything happens to it, I'm gonna charge you with obstruction of justice."

Richard's quick to respond. "I got a better idea, Detective. Why don't you take it with you? That way, if somebody else should wanna take it . . . well, I won't have it to give."

"Somebody like Carl Schmidt?"

"Or his kid."

# CHAPTER EIGHT

## GIT

Charlie's just completed second grade, earning an E for excellent in every category. In the comments section, Mrs. Taney wrote, "Charlotte is reading and doing math well above her grade level. She is an outstanding student."

Mrs. Taney didn't add, "And a beautiful child." She didn't have to. I know that beautiful children sometimes trace the route of the ugly duckling in reverse, but Charlie, at age eight, is a beautiful child. No doubt about it, not in anyone's mind, not even Mom's, and maybe that's no surprise. My marriage didn't work out, but not because Sean was hard to look at.

Charlie's a generally cooperative child who passed her terrible-two phase without throwing a tantrum, though her vocabulary at times was limited to a single word:

Why? *Why* became her chant, and my explanations, no matter how detailed, only led to a demand for more explanations.

Mom insisted that I put an end to Charlie's curiosity with the kind of spanking that resolved all questions. My response was equally emphatic. If she ever laid a hand on Charlie, I'd rip her head off and shove it so far up her ass it'd end up back where it started.

Charlie was through with her questioning phase before she reached her fourth birthday. Not that her curiosity waned; my daughter studies on her own simply because she wants to learn. That's all to the good—right?—a self-motivated child? Meanwhile, I'm the kind of mom who checks her child's homework, her teeth, the dirt behind her ears after she washes up, and what she's been doing while I'm at work. I even check her wardrobe.

What I am, I think, is afraid. Afraid that I'll fall back, that I'll drag Charlie with me. I spent my puberty dodging drunks, including Mom's boyfriends. I gave up at age fifteen. I want more for Charlie, so much more. And why not? My heart beats for both of us.

Within the next hour, I receive very good and very bad news, the bad news coming first. I'm sitting next to Charlie on an autumn-red love seat that I've turned around to face the room's picture window. Our house is flanked on the east by another, even smaller (if you can imagine that) house. But to the west, a short, semi-overgrown lawn gives way to an acre of hardwood forest. I've positioned the love seat so that Charlie and I can watch the trees and shrubs as they transition from season to season.

On this day, we're sitting with our backs to the TV, reading a book, or rather Charlie's reading, with me defining unfamiliar words. The book I've chosen (yes, *I've* chosen) is *Charlotte's Web*, hoping that hearing her own name in the title will keep her interested. We're at the point where the main character, a pig named Wilbur, arrives at a new barn, when Mom's voice pierces our comfortable bubble.

"Hey, would ya take a look at this."

I glance over my shoulder to find Mom seated before our TV, a medium-size flat-screen that's at least two generations behind the smart sets now on the market.

"What, Mom?"

"We got ourselves a murder, right here in Baxter. Second one this year."

The news footage on the screen is familiar enough to be part of a network crime drama. Yellow tape stretched across a driveway, official vehicles parked at weird angles, cops standing around, coffee containers on the hood of a cruiser. Then the parts come together, and I realize that I'm looking at one of the Skyview motel's cabins. Cabin 909.

It takes everything I have to maintain control. I have to because I know that Mom can't be trusted to keep her mouth shut. Even now, she returns every couple of days to Pearl's Beauty Parlor and her old friends in the Yards.

"Okay, so what's the big deal?"

"It's the Skyview, right? The place is a . . . a whorehouse."

Mom was about to say *fucking* whorehouse, but she knows I won't stand for that kind of obscenity when Charlie's around. And the Skyview's not a brothel, either, but a mid-priced motel catering mostly to families. I look from the TV to Mom, at the protruding cheekbones and the yellowed eyes. It's as if the ugliness that rules her soul has invaded her body, a cannibal of an evil spirit run amok.

"What are they saying? About . . ." I almost say his name, Bradley, just catching myself at the last second. "About the killing?"

"Nothin' yet. Gotta wait until the next of kin's been notified. But you can pretty much figure what happened. Some workin' gal decidin' to get herself a tip whether the john liked it or not. Then again, it could be the john took somethin' he didn't pay for and she collected on her own." Mom snickers. "Anyways, I've been knowin' the woman who owns the Skyview—that would be Felice Gaitskill—since we was in high school. The woman ain't no better than she has to be."

For just a moment, I close my eyes. This isn't the time to get into it with Celia Graham. I reopen them just as two men dressed in white coveralls push a gurney loaded with a gray body bag through the cabin door. A second pair, a man and a woman, emerge from the room as the gurney's loaded into a fire department ambulance.

Mom points to the screen. "That'd be Vern Taney. Vern was a hotshot football player in high school, and everyone thought he was headed for college. Then his dad got sick and he had to go to work. Maybe that's why he's got that reputation. Quick with the hands if you get in his face."

"And the woman?"

"Gotta be Taney's boss. Don't know her name, though. Lieutenant something."

The video's running on a loop, and the sound is too low for me to make out the reporter's words as they play in the background. But I can't focus anyway, and the scene has to repeat several times before my thoughts settle down, before a sentence from a time when I was young enough to believe that church and prayer would save me drills its way into my brain. Here to stay.

*For the thing which I greatly feared is come upon me.*

Most of the kids where I grew up in the Yards—the little rats, like me, who scuttled between the trailers and the shacks—gave up early on. And why not? By the time they reached high school, they were years behind in their studies, and the only people they feared were the junkies in that shooting gallery around the corner. Loser was their fate—that's what they told themselves—and there's no escaping your fate. Survival would never come by way of a paycheck.

I said no to that way of thinking. I said if you work hard enough, you can make a decent life for yourself and your family. I waited too long to get started, true, and I kept making mistakes, like marrying Sean and trusting Franky Belleau. But there was this bottom-line truth to my dreams, a truth I took the trouble to name. I called this bottom line my bootstrap plan and told myself that willpower was the only requirement. Luck would play no part.

If the cops connect me to the body in that cabin, they'll put the murder on me. That's the way cops have always operated in the Yards, and I can't make myself believe—or even hope—that anything's changed. I turn back to Charlie, but I'm thinking about Vern Taney and his boss.

"What's happening, Mommy?"

Charlie stares up at me, her clear blue eyes reflecting her curiosity. I don't pull my punches, but I do censor myself. I'm about to say a man's been murdered. But how would I know the victim's a man and not a woman?

Going forward, I'll need to be careful. Very careful.

"Someone's been murdered, honey," I tell my daughter.

"Like in *Watership Down*?"

"That's right."

Charlie raises a finger and smiles her ah-ha smile. "But not a rabbit. A person."

"Yes, a person. You got me."

My little girl's delighted laughter enchants me, but my brain resumes its spinning a moment later. I have to get rid of the hat and the dress, but wouldn't that be proof that I did it? Dumping evidence? There's DNA, too, and I must have left some behind. But at least we never made it to the bed. And Bradley took a shower and I put that sixty dollars back in his pocket instead of leaving it on the floor. Maybe the cops'll look at the paraphernalia in the bathroom and decide that Bradley was killed in a drug dispute. But what about security cameras? I never thought to check. For all I know, there could be cameras in front of every cabin. And maybe someone in Randy's Tavern recognized me. It's not like I'm a hermit. Also . . .

"Mommy."

Charlie's voice jolts me back into the present. So much at stake. Her life, as well as mine. "Yes, honey?"

"What's a whorehouse?"

# CHAPTER NINE

## GIT

An hour later I'm on my way to my second job at Zack Butler's—one eye on the rearview mirror as my paranoia blossoms—when I get the good news. Zack's four-bedroom house is in Mount Jackson, Baxter's most expensive neighborhood, proof positive that he's made it. Exactly how, on the other hand, is still a mystery. But I'm not thinking about Zack or his fortune when my cell rings.

The number and the 732 area code are unfamiliar, but I lean forward to flick the little green arrow to the side. The phone's mounted on a dashboard vent and set to speaker.

"Hello."

"Good afternoon. May I please speak with Ms. Bridget O'Rourke?"

Mom would confront directly: Whatta ya want her for? And it's true that I half expect the caller to be a cop investigating the death of Bradley Grieg. But I make it a habit not to go with the first words that pop into my head. Better to stall until you get a fix on the situation.

"May I ask who's calling?"

"My name is Madison Klein. I work in human relations at Short Hills Medical Center in New Jersey. Am I speaking to Nurse O'Rourke?"

"Yes."

"Well, I'm sure you're busy, so I'll get right to the point. Our medical center won't open its doors for a month. We're brand-new, and we're hiring personnel for every division, from janitorial services to radiology. I'm what you call a recruiter. It's my job to fill the empty slots."

Madison has one of those breathless speaking styles, every sentence running into the next, as if a supervisor were timing her sales pitch. When she comes to a sudden stop, it takes me a moment to get my bearings.

"You're recruiting on Sunday afternoon?"

"That's when most working people are home."

"Okay, but I hope you know that I'm a long way from New Jersey."

"True, but you applied to one of our affiliates in Jersey City a couple of months ago—we're part of the Galvers Medical Group—and we're wondering if you're still interested in making a change."

The McDonald's parking lot is almost empty when I pull in. I find a space away from other cars. As if I'm about to share some dark and dangerous secret.

"Yeah," I tell the recruiter, "I am."

"Well, our Jersey City affiliate—that would be Knowles Trauma Center—checked your employment record when you submitted your résumé. First, you've been working two jobs almost from the day you received your license. Second, your private patient, that would be Mr. Butler, raved about you. Third, the manager at Resurrection described you as 'reliable and efficient.'" She finally pauses. "Frankly, you're the kind of committed nurse Short Hills Medical Center needs."

Slow down, I tell myself. Madison's flattering you. That's nice, of course, but she's trying to sell you something. If it's too good to be true . . .

"When I looked a little closer at Jersey City," I finally say, "I realized that I could never afford an apartment in any decent neighborhood. Even small apartments rent for more than I can afford. A lot more."

"Not to worry. Short Hills is in Essex County, thirty miles from New York. Housing is still relatively affordable out here. Also, we're adding a small dormitory to help our people relocate. You'd be eligible to stay there for up to three months."

Madison's trying too hard. Tomorrow, when I get home, I'll go online and check out the medical center. For now, I'm happy to keep the conversation moving.

"May I call you Madison?" I ask.

"Of course."

"I have a child, Madison, an eight-year-old girl. Dormitory doesn't work for us. Too much like a shelter."

"No biggie. We also work with real estate brokers. May I call you Bridget?" She doesn't wait for an answer.

"Look, Bridget, why don't we set a date for a second interview, hopefully on Zoom or Workplace. If we're all on board after that, I can make you this promise. We won't risk losing you because you can't find a place to live. And by the way, Short Hills is an upscale community. The schools are marvelous."

"And the pay?"

Madison laughs, but doesn't hesitate. "We're paying twenty-four fifty an hour to start, with overtime available. Benefits include seven holidays, two weeks' paid vacation after a year on the job, and medical insurance. Tell me, are you interested in furthering your education? Because we're opening our own nursing school, fully accredited. Short Hills employees will be entitled to a fifty percent reduction in tuition costs. You'd make a lot more as a registered nurse."

Zack's left enough room behind the Lincoln in his driveway for my little car. I pull in but don't open the door. And yes, I'm going to make myself available for that second interview. I've been trying to get out of Baxter for the past three years, sending my résumé to hospitals as far away as Seattle. I've gotten a few offers, but they were dependent on a face-to-face interview, and I wasn't willing to relocate on a maybe. Even when I did set up an interview at a Chicago hospital, I ran into the same problem with insanely expensive housing. I don't want to move into a big-city version of the Yards.

This offer is different, or I'm hoping it's different. Madison was very persuasive. If I'm ready to pull up stakes—and she advised me to think about it carefully—Short Hills Medical Center will make it happen. The physical part, at least.

On another day, I would have brought a bottle of wine to Zack's, would have shared it with him. We do that now, on holidays, though his doctors have taken alcohol off the list of pleasures Zack can still enjoy. But there's no wine, not now, and I can't make myself pretend that Bradley's murder won't come back to hurt me. I was in a nightclub with Grieg on the night he was killed. I left with him, for Christ's sake.

No, I didn't leave with Bradley. I may have followed him out the door, but I never actually spoke to him inside the bar. And we didn't leave in the same car, either. I followed Bradley to the Skyview. If . . .

Enough with the bullshit. I open the door, get out, and walk up to Zack's door. Miranda opens it before I ring the bell. Zack suffers from fairly advanced emphysema that'll eventually kill him if he doesn't get a lung transplant. At this stage of his disease, he's able to breathe on his own with the aid of a trach tube and supplementary oxygen, at least while awake. Just as well, because Miranda's not a nurse or even a certified health aide, and she can't handle a ventilator. Meanwhile, she's indispensable. The woman helps Zack dress, bathe, and keep his doctors' appointments. She cooks his breakfast and his lunch, makes sure his meds are refilled, and takes him for short walks, following behind his walker with a wheelchair. She does his laundry.

The nights are different. Zack can't breathe on his own while asleep. When he tried—over my objections—his oxygen-saturation level suddenly dropped to sixty-four percent and he turned blue. I had him on the vent within seconds, and his stats came back up, but later that night, he told me that he'd felt his life being drawn from his body.

"I can't bullshit myself anymore. I know there's a God out there." His look was imploring as he added, "Now what the fuck am I gonna do?"

# CHAPTER TEN

## GIT

With her daughter home sick, Miranda's out the door almost as soon as I walk inside, so Zack is left to my tender mercies. But there's to be no mercy tonight.

"We have to do this, right?" Zack pleads. "It's a hundred percent necessary?"

Zack's trach hasn't been changed in two months, and it's beginning to stink. He should be used to the drill by now. Five years ago, a surgeon cut a hole in his throat and the trachea beneath, then inserted a curved plastic tube into the hole and secured it with a trach collar, a strip of fabric that's merely tied off. At the same time, a bulb on the end of the tube inside the body was partially inflated. The bulb prevents the trach tube from popping out, even if the collar loosens, yet still allows enough air to flow around the tube and over his vocal cords to sustain ordinary speech.

As I said, from the patient's perspective, changing the tube is unpleasant. It can't be done without activating the gag reflex. Zack will cough and choke when the old trach comes out, then again when the new trach is inserted. But that's another thing I like about Zack. He's not a whiner.

"I smoked three packs a day for more than forty years," he once told me. "I'm lucky I'm not breathin' dirt."

Ten minutes later I attach the oxygen converter to Zack's trach and we're done. He's in one of the four recliners in his living room, watching the news on a TV big enough for a theater while I head for the kitchen. Nurses don't usually do housework, but as Zack's willing to feed me as well as himself, I usually throw something together when I arrive.

Not tonight.

"Whatta ya say to pizza and a salad?" Zack asks.

Sal's Pizzeria is on my starred contact list. It's my go-to restaurant when Mom's out and I'm too tired to cook for Charlie. I'm on the phone within a minute.

"You heard about this?" Zack asks.

"The killing?"

"Yeah." Zack's speaking voice is fairly soft, but the effort to push enough air over his vocal cords to be heard often leaves him gasping as he draws breath into his lungs. "I know this guy. I mean the victim."

The doorbell rings, allowing me time to think. It's the pizza and salad. I pay for both with Zack's money, then head for the kitchen. Zack loves to talk, and I'll let him go on until it's time for baseball. He's a St. Louis Cardinals fan and bets every game.

"Say that again," I call over my shoulder.

"This guy, Grieg. I know him."

"Did I ever meet him?"

"I mean I know *about* him." Zack pauses, his breath coming fast. I'm used to it, and I simply wait. "But I never done business with him."

Carrying a tray large enough to fit across the arms of Zack's chair, I come back into the living room. Dinnertime.

We eat for a few minutes while I watch the same footage I watched this morning, the gurney wheeled out, the cops following. Only this time the footage cuts to an afternoon press conference held by our chief of police, Harry Black. The chief ducks and dodges most of the questions but does admit that the cops have no suspects and robbery was a likely motive. This is standard stuff, and Chief Black's matter-of-fact tone gives that away. But my attention's focused on the two cops standing behind the chief. I recognize Vern Taney, but I still don't know the name of the woman next to him. She's wearing a navy-blue pantsuit that does nothing to soften a blocky frame, thick at the waistline, wide at the shoulders. Her thin mouth is turned down slightly at the corners. With disdain? I'm sure her dark eyes are sharp and focused. And I can only hope they won't, in the near future, be focused on me.

Zack wipes his lips with a paper napkin, then looks up at me. "The victim, Bradley Grieg? He runs with Connor

Schmidt. Him and Connor, they're good buddies. Or they were."

Though I don't recognize the name, I mumble an uh-huh.

"Connor Schmidt is Carl Schmidt's kid," Zack continues. "You heard of him? Carl Schmidt?"

"Can't say I have."

"Carl's a pimp and a drug dealer. Really old school, Git. You don't shake in your boots at the sound of his name, he starts to worry. Maybe he's losin' it. Maybe somebody's comin' for what he's got."

Back in the kitchen, I refill our plates and return to the living room. "You haven't touched your salad," I tell Zack.

"I'll get to it." He waves me to my seat. "Point I'm makin' here is that if the chief's right, if Bradley got robbed, there's gonna be trouble. The way Carl Schmidt's brain works, he's already tellin' himself that he's gotta do something about it. The robbery, I mean. He's gotta balance the scales."

"That's crazy. Even if the victim was robbed—Grieg, or whatever his name is—how can you be sure the money belonged to Schmidt?"

"You're innocent as a baby." Zack laughs. "You see, a certain class of people around here connected Grieg and Schmidt the minute Grieg's name was released. Now our police chief's sayin' robbery was the motive. This class of people I'm talkin' about, they're not deep thinkers. They're gonna assume the obvious. They're gonna assume that Carl Schmidt got ripped off and he's out for blood. Literally, Git. Bruises ain't gonna do it."

I consider this for a moment, but can't find anything to add. "What about the cop," I say. "You know her?"

"By reputation alone. Name's Mariola, from somewhere further east. Word out there is that she's sharp. And Vern Taney, he's nobody to mess with either. In fact, I gotta believe it'll be a race between the two of 'em and the Schmidts, father and son. See who gets to the shooter first."

# CHAPTER ELEVEN

## DELIA

First thing after we finish working the crime scene, I send Vern Taney in search of Connor Schmidt. I want Connor down at headquarters long enough to get his statement on the record. I'm gonna connect them, Bradley and Connor, once and for all. (You believe those names? When you think of Bradley and Connor, you imagine a pair of towheaded kids in a 1970s sitcom. Not the vicious predators I know them to be.)

With Vern gone, I head for Cindy Sherman's last known address on Claymore Road in the Yards. Cindy's the victim's ex-wife, the one Bradley Grieg put in the hospital. She's also the victim who refused to testify. Supposedly, Cindy and her ex avoided each other. Supposedly. But Cindy can still help. She can fill us in on who he hung out with and where he hung out. Other names will emerge over time, but she's the logical starting point.

The weather's still damp, but I roll down the window anyway. Lately, days have been taken up by administrative detail. I've got a real case now, and I hope to work it until I have a suspect in custody. Illusion or not, closing the cuffs around a perp's wrists feels like finality. It feels like success.

Most Baxterites imagine the Yards to be one long road flanked on both sides by dilapidated campers and tar-paper shacks. They imagine appliances in every yard, rusting cars stripped of every usable part and half-buried in mud.

As a cop, I know the Yards to be uniformly poor, but not the cesspool others believe it to be. Yeah, there are trailer parks with no trailers. Only a collection of rusting campers inhabited by alkies, junkies, and tweakers. But I also pass trailer parks with cared-for double-wides on straight, well-maintained roads. I see flowers and shrubs out front. Planted by men and women who are as addicted to respectability as tweakers are to meth. They fight an uphill battle, these families, and I admire the effort. Their children are subject to just about every temptation known to man. And that's only when the kids aren't being coerced.

Cindy's home fits the second category. It's a nicely kept single-wide trailer with a border of newly planted impatiens. There's even a lawn between her trailer and the next in line. Still lush this early in the year, the lawn appears soft and springy as I approach the trailer's small porch along a flagstone path.

There's no bell, and I knock hard on the screen door. I hear movement inside, and a man calls out, "Coming, honey." My unexpected appearance earns a double take out of a silent movie. The man on the far side of the screen is middle-aged, with a pronounced paunch and an artificial leg made painfully obvious by the cargo shorts he's wearing.

"Lieutenant Mariola." I flash my badge. "Looking for Cindy Sherman."

"Yeah, well, I'm her father. That'd be George Sherman. Cindy's out to the grocery store. Fact, I thought you was her, needin' help with the groceries." He pauses to rub at the stubble on his chin. "This here about Bradley?"

Cindy chooses that moment to drive up to the trailer. She steps out of a battered Ford pickup and looks at me for a long moment. "Been expecting you," she finally says.

The girl's beautiful, simple as that. Honey blond hair rolling to her shoulders, eyes as blue as they are confident, dimples she can't hide, even when she's not smiling. A far cry from the first and only time we met in the past. On that night, one side of her face was the color of an overripe plum, and a line of sutures crawled from behind her ear to the edge of her jaw like ants in a line. The doc had shaved part of her scalp before he stitched her up. That made the side of her head appear even more lopsided.

I follow her through the living room and into a spotless kitchen.

"This about Bradley?" She lays the groceries on the counter. "I hope you're not thinkin' I had something to do with . . . with killin' him."

"No. That's not why I'm here."

"Don't bullshit me, Lieutenant. I'm not a fool, not anymore." She turns her back on me, leaving me to sit while she puts her groceries away.

"Cindy was home last night," her father says from the doorway. "Me and—"

"Hush, Dad. I'll handle this." Cindy runs a finger along the scar behind her ear, the gesture seeming unconscious, a habit. When she speaks, she looks directly into my eyes, no longer the naïve child who married Bradley Grieg. "I used my cell phone to find a recipe for pulled pork last night. That was about ten o'clock. I made a call before that, to my girlfriend, Lea-Ann Cowpers. I don't remember the time exactly, but we were on the phone for almost an hour. Lea-Ann's gettin' married, and we spoke about the hall she wants to hire but can't afford."

The unidentified female in the video entered Cabin 909 at 10:42. Cindy's alibi isn't an alibi at all, but it's too early to go there. Just now, I need cooperation. "I'm not here because you're a suspect. I'm after background information. Bradley's friends and associates, where he hung out, maybe his current girlfriend. Anything you can tell me about him will help. There's a killer out there. A killer free to kill again."

The look in Cindy's blue eyes remains skeptical. Still, she has to answer, and she knows it. "Look, after the

73

attack . . . after what happened, I was all set to cooperate. I wanted to see the bastard behind bars for the rest of his life. I wanted revenge."

"She ain't the only one," George says. "I started cleanin' my shotgun soon's my girl come back from the hospital. I was gonna kill the son of a bitch, but then Connor Schmidt showed up and . . ."

I motion for George to continue, but Cindy's the one who speaks first. "Connor, he was . . . sympathetic, that's the right word. He was so sorry for what happened to me. He even agreed that Bradley deserved to spend time in jail. But he needed Bradley—for what he didn't say—so I'd have to back off. If I did, he'd guarantee that Bradley wouldn't come anywhere near me. Ever again, Detective. What Connor said, exactly, was, 'If the shithead so much as speaks to you, I'll put him in the ground. Me personally.'"

Cindy stops long enough to draw a breath. "Only thing about it, the deal worked both ways. I couldn't come anywhere near Bradley. Couldn't call him, either. We were done with each other."

"And it held up?" I ask.

"I don't know what Connor said to Bradley, but it scared him straight. I haven't seen or heard from him since."

The lie-detector alarm in my head's not goin' off. I think the girls tellin' the truth. If she was out for revenge, she could have gotten it a long time ago. "But you do know people who have contact with Bradley? You have friends in common?"

Her pretty blue eyes narrow slightly and draw together. Lie or tell the truth? Finally, she decides to answer a question I didn't ask.

"I never talk about Bradley with my friends."

"Try again, Cindy."

"Look, I don't need trouble, not with the Schmidts. I just wanna live my life in peace."

"Cindy, you don't cooperate, you're trading problems with Connor for problems with me. I'm not asking for the moon here. So who was Bradley seeing? Did he have a current girlfriend, someone special? How 'bout enemies? Anybody you know? Any rumors out there?"

George picks that moment to become protective. "Cindy ain't committed no crime, Detective. You got no call—"

"No call? Tell me, George, where were *you* last night?"

"Never left the damn house."

"You make any phone calls? Go online? I mean, you just told me how you were preparing to kill the bastard. Maybe you bided your time. Maybe you waited for Bradley to forget about you."

Now it's Cindy's turn, and she finally gets it right. "What do ya wanna know, Detective? Let's get to it."

I manage a relatively encouraging smile. "Bradley's friends and enemies. Who he hung out with and where. Anything you know about your former husband, any rumor, any crimes he might have committed. Look at it from my point of view. You're either cooperating or you're hindering. And if you're hindering, I have to ask myself why. Considering what he did to you."

# CHAPTER TWELVE

## CONNOR

I spend most of the day with Violet Arabella. She works out of a truck stop north of Baxter and she's a major coke junkie. When I dangle a little baggie holding a gram of decent powder in front of her nose, she hops into the car, snuggles up, and says, "Game time."

I don't do any of the coke. In fact, outside of an occasional beer, I never use drugs or alcohol. My old man busts my balls about it, but he busts balls about everything I do. In his world, drinks with the boys—on the house if the barkeep's properly intimidated—are mandatory. But like I said, I stopped carin' about what Daddy thinks a long time ago. Our relationship, from his point of view? It's user-usee. Like I was born to be used, and no two ways about it. That's my purpose. There was no other reason to bring me into the world.

Over the years, I've seen a bunch of movies with dominating fathers and cringing, creepy sons. But I'm not the cringing type. I'm more the time-biding type, and Daddy's time is coming soon. I'm already putting the pieces together.

Violet's as generous with her body as I am with the coke, and the day passes quickly. We're in a motel far from the Skyview Motor Court, and Violet's talking a mile a minute. Me, I'm watching the TV, watching our police chief's press conference. Deliberate or stupid, I can't tell which. But when Chief Black tells his audience that robbery was the most likely motive for Bradley's murder, he's pouring gasoline on the fire. He has to know that, right?

"My mother kicked me out of the house when I was thirteen and I got pregnant," Violet tells me.

"What happened to the kid?"

Violet slides a rolled-up twenty over a line of white power. "I got beat up a couple months later and had a whachacallit. A mis-something."

"How old are you now?"

"Sixteen."

"You got a pimp on the outside?"

"I'm stayin' with a guy."

"How many whores he runnin'?"

Violet's eyes drop to her naked lap. "Three."

"So, you're payin' him and you're payin' me, too? When are you gonna stop bein' a jerk, Vi?"

"Everybody," she tells me, "needs somebody."

"Speak for yourself."

I'm back in town again a little before seven. I know the cops are gonna come to me at some point, and I want to put that point as far into the future as possible. I'm on my way to an abandoned strip mall on Baxter Boulevard, one of many. I'm meeting Augie Barboza. Augie and his crew service the assholes who borrow money from Dad, mostly degenerate gamblers who bet their mortgage money and lose. They approach me for a loan because they can't face their families. That's fine as long as they pay up at the end of every week. If not, they get to play with Augie.

The two of us have a job to do tonight. My old man was right on target when he said that somebody else had to know Bradley was gonna be at the motel on Saturday night. Me and Augie, we're gonna talk to that somebody. This is not a problem I couldn't handle on my own, but Augie . . . Augie's got the look, the shovel jaw, the broken nose, a pair of deader-than-dead eyes the yellow-brown color of dog shit on the bottom of your shoe. I'm not forgetting that my old man told me to handle this on my own. I just don't care.

In a way, I get lucky. The cop lights me up while I'm still a few blocks from the strip mall. If he'd caught me and Augie together, it'd be a lot worse. The only thing bigger than Augie's bicep is his mouth.

I let the window down and put my hands on the steering wheel. I don't want any misunderstanding. The cliché is that cops like to shoot black people, but you can count the number of black families in this town on your fingers. So when it comes to cop shootings, it's white people or no one. Me, I wanna be counted among the "no one," and I'm not exactly cheered when Vern Taney climbs out of the unmarked Ford. Me and Taney played football together in high school. I was only a freshman that year and barely got to play. Taney was a superstar offensive guard, strong enough to intimidate whoever lined up across from him. Word on the street is that his laid-back attitude is purely for show.

Taney's dressed in street clothes, including an unbuttoned jacket pulled far enough back to reveal the automatic tucked below his left armpit. I'm also armed, my gun as legal as his, but I don't want any misunderstandings, and I keep my hands where he can see them.

"Reach through the window and open the door, Connor," he says, putting the emphasis on my name.

"I'm carrying a gun," I tell him as I comply.

Taney pulls his own weapon at that point, the movement smooth and quick, but his expression doesn't change. He's looking at me like I'm something crawling across the floor that he wants to crush. I tell myself not to react, but I can't help it. When someone puts a gun in your face, cop or no cop, you pay attention.

"Get out of the car. Keep your hands where I can see them." He waits until I'm out and standing. "Now turn around and put your hands on top of the car, palms down."

Taney puts his gun away before treating me to a thorough shakedown. He takes my gun, cell phone, and wallet, then runs his hands along my body, gripping hard. I've been through this drill before, and I don't react, not even when he puts me in handcuffs. At this point I'm supposed to ask him why he's arresting me, but I won't give him the satisfaction.

"We're gonna take a little ride," he tells me. "There's somebody wants to talk to you."

I can't help it, I lose my cool, which is not my style: "Your dyke boss maybe?"

He slaps me in the face, and I eat the pain. We're standing on the sidewalk in front of a drugstore, which is closed at this hour. But I have to figure the security camera hanging above the front door is operating.

"Hit me again, asshole," I tell him. "I can use the money."

# CHAPTER THIRTEEN

## DELIA

T he shithead's been cooling his heels inside one of our interrogation rooms for the past two hours. No phone calls, no trips to the bathroom, no food, nothing to drink. This isn't New York or San Francisco or even Des Moines. Plus, for Mayor Venn, it's strictly see-no-evil. And Chief Black's not much better. Black wants results, methodology be damned. Find the killer and do it quick.

Bottom line: there's nobody looking over my shoulder.

As it turned out, Cindy Sherman was eager to help once she got going. She provided me with a list of clubs that she and Bradley visited regularly back when they were still courting. She also named several women Bradley cheated with. Referring to them as "Bradley's whores." But there was bad news, too. The list includes eight clubs, and it seems that Bradley dumped his conquests almost as fast as he took them to bed. Still, Vern and I had spent most of the afternoon visiting the clubs, showing Bradley's picture to the mostly uncooperative help. Nobody would admit to seeing him last night, which didn't surprise me. His connection to the Schmidts is well known. Just as you don't speak ill of the dead, you don't speak ill of people who can make you dead. Tomorrow I'll try a few of the individuals Cindy named, but I really doubt that gentle persuasion is going to produce results. It'll take something more, but exactly what, I don't know.

There was a notification to make, as well. Grieg's parents left Baxter ten years ago for warmer pastures in San Diego. Somebody had to track them down and deliver the bad news. I assigned this task to Detective Meacham. It took most of the afternoon, and several reminders, but the Dink got it done. Personally, I hate notifications. Like most cops, I've learned to put my emotions to the side, empathy be damned. You wallow in that pain, you end up eating your gun.

"This prick, he's not gonna give us shit." Vern bites into a roast beef sandwich, his lunch and his dinner both. "He's gonna play the tough guy."

"Do I look like I'm expecting a confession?" I pick at a slice of apple pie with the edge of a fork. I should be hungry, but I'm not. I need to get home to Danny. He's old enough to stay by himself, and he's almost surely asleep by now. Meanwhile, I can't stop worrying. Or feeling guilty.

"Then what are you expecting?"

"Best case, he gives us an alibi that doesn't check out."

"You're thinking he did it? What about the woman?"

"If we find her, we'll have to hold her." I find myself wishing we had a real medical examiner instead of Arshan Rishnavata. The coroner's estimated the time of death between nine o'clock at night and two o'clock in the morning. A true professional would have been a lot more precise.

"C'mon, Delia, where's that devious brain of yours going with this?"

"Muzzle flash."

When you fire a gun, the exploding gunpowder produces a gas hot enough to burn. This burning gas exits the weapon through the barrel, blinding you for a few seconds if you happen to be looking directly at it. I'm speaking from experience. Only a year ago I was part of a nighttime drug raid that went bad. Real bad. "I'm gonna review the video from the Skyview's camera again, but I didn't pick up any muzzle flash while the woman was inside the cabin."

Vern doesn't come back with the first idea that pops into his head. That's not his style. But when he finally gives his opinion, it doesn't surprise me.

"The cameras at the Skyview are for shit, Delia. They're also far away and it was rainin' and the drapes are thick, and we know the muzzle was jammed into a pillow. Maybe the flash was just too dim for the security cams to pick it up."

"Exactly what a prosecutor's gonna tell a jury if we find the woman and charge her. That doesn't make it true."

Connor's sound asleep when Vern and I walk into the room. Then Vern slaps him in the head, and he wakes with a start, his hands balling into fists. They open quickly when he finds Vern towering over him.

"Hi, guys, how's it goin'?"

"Never better."

"Glad to hear it. So, what can I do ya for?"

Connor's sitting behind a small table with his back against a windowless wall. I sit across from him, place a digital tape recorder on the table, and turn it on. Good to go. "First, let me say that I'm sorry for the long delay. I was conducting interviews in the field. But that's no excuse, and I'm sure you want to get home. So let's make this as painless as possible. Answer my questions and you'll be out of here in an hour." I pause for a fraction of a second, then say, "First, tell us how you'd describe your relationship with Bradley Grieg?"

"Grieg?"

"Cut the shit."

Connor's a good-looking boy, blue-eyed with a full mouth. I watch him lean back in the chair. Despite the smirk, I know he wants to tell me to go fuck myself. I can punish him if he does. I can walk out of the room and leave him to stew overnight. Another mutt, trapped behind the same table, might voice his resentment. Not Connor. He's not going to give us the satisfaction.

"We run into each other from time to time. In the bars and clubs."

"Which bars?"

"I don't know. Palacio, the Dew Drop, Randy's, the Black Sheep, Underground. And don't ask me for a time and date. I go clubbing three or four nights a week."

"And you had no other contact with Grieg?"

"Like I said, I see him around."

"But you were buddies in high school?"

"That was a long time ago."

"You drifted apart, did you?"

"Yeah, you could say that."

"When was the last time you saw Bradley?"

"I don't exactly remember. Maybe sometime last week." He glances at the ceiling as though searching his memory, the pose so theatrical I want to laugh. "Yeah, last week. I think it was Thursday or Friday. At Randy's. Brad likes Randy's. He claims the women he meets at Randy's ain't that complicated. Like they know what they want and it's not a long-term relationship."

Connor laughs at his own joke, but stops abruptly when I say, "*Liked*, Connor. Not *likes*. Grieg's dead. No more relationships for the man, long-term or short-term." I smile. "Now, have you ever been to the Skyview Motor Court?"

"Where?"

"The Skyview, Connor. You ever been there?"

"Is that where Brad . . . got whacked?"

Vern speaks for the first time. "Answer the question, asshole. Yes or no."

"No."

I jump back in. "So you didn't visit the Skyview last night?"

"Nope."

"Then tell me where you were."

"At what time?"

"Say from eight o'clock."

"I was at the Underground at eight o'clock. I stayed for another hour, then went home."

"And you were home all night?"

"Yup."

"Alone? Or did you have company?"

"Just me."

# CHAPTER FOURTEEN

## DELIA

An hour later, his statement on the record, Connor's out the door and I'm finally home with Danny, who's somehow stayed awake. I feel pretty good about my day, especially Connor's interview. I got him on tape lying about his relationship with Bradley and about never visiting the Skyview. And his alibi is no alibi at all. Not that I've convinced myself that he's involved. Or that the woman on the tape is somehow innocent. At this point I'm willing to entertain other possibilities. Including the possibility that Connor and the woman are somehow connected.

Danny's sitting next to me on the couch, waiting for me to make good on my promise to discuss the case. We've grown incredibly close, me and Danny, closer than we've ever been. Courtesy of the virus, Covid-19.

Dodging the virus was never on the table. As a first responder, I walked into homes where every member of the family was sick, half of them coughing their lungs out, and not a mask to be found. So I'd get sick for sure, and my son, in all probability, as well. But I didn't worry about Danny all that much. I just assumed that his illness would be short-lived.

Viruses don't read probability charts. That's what it boiled down to. I was only sick for three days and my symptoms were mild. Not my son. At one point Danny ran a fever of 103.2 that persisted through the longest night of my life. He complained of headaches, broke into sweats that soaked the bedclothes, had chills that all the blankets in the house couldn't warm. His harsh, dry cough quickly became constant, and he cried out for me at times, even as I sat on the edge of the bed holding his hand.

"Mom, Mom, Mom."

The theory shared by most cops is that human beings have only three responses to a threat: fight, flight, or fright. Me, I was a fighter, always ready to throw that first punch, especially as a child, when boys and girls are close to the same size. Not this time. This time an uncontrollable fear seized me and held on day after day. I could barely force myself to leave Danny's side to use the bathroom or to gather the boxes of food left at my door by Vern and Lillian. And I finally understood the power of love, a truth I'd resisted throughout my life. The thought of losing Danny was simply unbearable, yet I felt utterly helpless. Yes, I tried cold compresses and Tylenol to bring his fever down, and I practically force-fed him liquids to keep him hydrated. But his fever returned night after night after night until time lost all meaning, until there was only the present and my son lying in pain on the bed.

Danny recovered, obviously, with no sign of any permanent change except with our relationship. Our ties go unspoken now. There's no need to speak them aloud, because there isn't any room for doubt. There's no distance between us, no considerations to be considered.

Danny eagerly scrutinizes a series of photos I took at the crime scene with my cell phone. Including a few of the body. And, yeah, I'm guilty enough to swear him to secrecy. On the other hand, he loves to watch high-body-count movies with his friends. Movies where human beings are torn apart by everything from knives to death rays to flesh-eating zombies. A little reality won't hurt.

"Was he a bad guy?" Danny wants to know.

"Very."

"Then he got what he deserved?"

Danny's not being flip. He really wants to understand why I'm making such a fuss when the world's better off without Bradley Grieg.

"In a way, he did," I admit. "It's like justice, right?"

"Yeah."

"But in this country, regular people aren't allowed to get justice for themselves. Not unless they're defending themselves against an immediate threat. If people want justice, they have to call the police and let the government find justice for them."

"That's not fair."

I know better than to continue discussions when Danny retreats into fair mode. In his mind, he's the chief justice of what's fair and what's not. Like this morning, when Barry called me a dyke. Punching Barry in the face was fair, even necessary.

"Fair or not, this particular killing wasn't about justice. We're pretty sure the motive was robbery."

Danny mulls it over for a minute, then surprises me by asking a truly important question as he points to a photograph. "Was he dead?"

"Before he was shot?"

"Yeah."

This is a possibility Vern and I discussed. Given the drug paraphernalia in the bathroom and the frequency of fatal overdoses, you have to figure it's a possibility. If Grieg was already dead when he was shot, the only crime was illegal discharge of a firearm. You can't murder a dead man, try as you might.

I glance at the photo on the coffee table. Grieg's lying on his belly, legs stretched out behind him. One arm's extended alongside his head, the other's curled along his side with the palm up. His face is concealed by the blackened pillow and the blood. Just as well, because there isn't all that much of it left.

"Our coroner's doing the autopsy tomorrow morning. We'll know for sure afterward. But it's an excellent question. Grieg was a junkie. He might have OD'd before he was shot."

Danny beams. This is a kid who loves to be praised. And the truth—I admit that I'm prejudiced—is that he mostly deserves the praise he gets. I put my arm around his shoulders and pull him close. We've moved three times since Danny was born, forcing him to make new friends and forge new alliances. Having a dyke for a mother didn't make the process any easier.

"I love you, kid," I tell him.

Danny responds immediately. "I love you, too, Mom."

I'm still at it an hour later when I receive a phone call from Vern. Vern's still at it, too, but he's actually working.

"Bingo, Delia. Bradley Grieg was in Randy's last night."

"How do ya know?"

"Well, it was Connor got me started. You remember, he said the last time he saw Bradley was at Randy's . . . then he said that Bradley liked Randy's because the kind of women he meets at Randy's are uncomplicated."

"C'mon, Vern, out with the story."

"It ain't that complicated, Delia. When I got outta my car at Randy's, I smelled weed. Strong, right? So I followed my nose to the back of the club and found a busboy suckin' on a joint. The kid hit me with 'No habla Inglés,' but I speak enough Spanish to get by, and I convinced him to cooperate. That or go to jail and most likely find his ass deported. It wasn't much of a choice, truth be told, and he recognized Grieg's photo right away. Told me Grieg comes in a couple of times a week and that he was in the bar last night."

"Anything else? Did he leave with a woman?"

"The kid didn't notice. He thinks Grieg left after ten, but he's not even sure about that."

"You think he was being honest? The kid, I mean."

"A hundred percent. When I let him go, he was so grateful, I thought he was gonna kiss me." Vern pauses a moment. "Should I go in? They've got a dozen security cameras inside. I could ask to see the data."

The offer's tempting. Get the case rolling, maybe identify the woman tonight. But I'm not big on gambling, not if I have an option. Suppose whoever's in charge at Randy's says no. Suppose the footage goes missing overnight or accidentally gets deleted. Better to take the sure thing.

"Get out of there, Vern, without being seen. Tomorrow morning we'll find a prosecutor to sign off on a subpoena for the data. Then we'll serve it before the club opens."

# CHAPTER FIFTEEN

## GIT

I t's eight o'clock, an hour after I leave Zack's. I'm in the living room with Mom, eating a breakfast of scrambled eggs and toast. Charlie's in her room, watching *Charlotte's Web* on her tablet, both the 2006 version and the animated 1973 version. She's already read more than half of the book.

Charlie's skills can't be allowed to erode over the summer. She's only finished second grade, but she reads on a fifth-grade level. Better still, she's willing to use an online dictionary to define words she doesn't know. Just now she's comparing the novel to the movie versions made from it. I didn't ask her to make the comparison, didn't even suggest it. Charlie's curious in ways that never crossed my little mind when I was her age. Maybe I was too busy surviving.

On most nights, Zack sleeps peacefully and I get to catnap. But the arthritis in his knees kicked up last night and the old man had a tough time. I spent most of it next to his bed, listening to him talk about his first wife, the only woman (according to Zack) he ever really loved.

Sleep's calling out to me, but I'm determined to pass some time with Charlie. I'll join her in her room as soon as I finish breakfast. Meanwhile, I have to put up with Mom.

"Katie Lowe dropped by last night," she tells me. "You remember Katie?"

"Yeah, sure." Another lowlife.

"Well, she's tellin' me that the one who shot Bradley's a woman."

"How does she know?"

"Her cousin, Ellie Norton? She's goin' out with the dispatcher works out of the police station? That would be Austin Flint? Anyways, Austin told Ellie, and Ellie told Kate. The killer was definitely a woman."

"Well, that proves it." I add a little salt and pepper to my eggs. "Austin told Ellie and Ellie told Kate."

Mom looks confused for a moment. She never reads newspapers and only watches the local news to catch the weather report. The grapevine provides all the information she needs to guide her life. Experts piss her off.

"Don't come as no surprise," she says, ignoring my sarcasm. "That Bradley Grieg was a son of a bitch from the get-go. Same for his daddy, Big Jim. The man's wife spent more nights alone in her bed than with him for company. In fact, far as Big Jim was concerned—this goes for his son, too—the women in his life didn't mean no more to him than one of them love dolls."

Thankfully, Charlie's door is closed. The girl has big ears, and I'm tired of apologizing for Mom's foul mouth. The woman says whatever comes into her mind, then accuses me of putting on airs when I complain. But this time she's right on the money. I was no more to Bradley Grieg than a love doll. Whenever I close my eyes, I see those twenties fluttering to the carpet. I hear his voice, too, hear the contempt thick as vomit: "Fuck off."

"Hate to imagine," Mom adds, repeating herself, "what ol' Connor Schmidt's gonna do when he catches up with the one killed his buddy. Though it likely ain't but a slap on the ass compared to what his daddy's got planned. I knowed Carl Schmidt growin' up and the man wasn't nothin' but mean."

Mom drones on, but I tune her out. I work at Resurrection tonight. That means I'll have thirty patients instead of one, most in poor condition. But that's nothing compared with what I dealt with only a year ago, when the virus finally invaded Baxter. I should have seen it coming. No, I did see it coming. I worked, after all, in a nursing home located in a city economically dependent on a meatpacking plant. At the same time, as the virus slowly closed in on the country's heartland, the danger seemed unreal. The coasts went first, California and Washington on the west; New York, Massachusetts, New Jersey, and Virginia on the east; Florida, Louisiana, and Texas on the south. Nestled in the belly of this beast, we somehow believed that the infection would spare us. Then hundreds of workers at Baxter Packing tested positive. My patients began to die. Then my turn came.

Harold McCarthy got sick in late April. Harry was ninety-two, and his legs were gone, but he was a relatively cheerful man who'd retained his faculties. He used to read me letters from his grandson while I dressed a bedsore on his lower back that refused to heal. Harry woke up with a fever one morning, usually the first sign of infection, and died forty-eight hours later in the hospital. This was before the virus overwhelmed Baxter Medical Center.

We didn't mourn Harold, neither the staff nor the residents at Resurrection. We didn't have the chance. Within a few days, thirty of the home's fifty-two patients sickened. Initially we turned to Baxter's volunteer ambulance corps for help. Our patients were transported to the hospital, where they received treatment, including ventilators. Then there were no more ventilators; then so many paramedics sickened that ambulances couldn't be had; then my patients began to die in their beds.

Two weeks after Harold's passing, Charlie and I both came down with a fever and chills. Not Mom, though, despite all her risk factors. I don't know whether she was one of the many who remained asymptomatic, despite being infected, or whether the virus never touched her. I do know that her continued good health was very fortunate for our little household.

Charlie's slight fever lasted all of two days. She had no other symptoms, no cough, no body aches, no chills. Me, I was sick enough for both of us. For the next two weeks my temperature rose above 103 degrees in the evening and never fell below 101.5, even at daybreak. My whole body ached, nose to toes, and my blood oxygen saturation level dropped to ninety-three percent from its normal hundred. At times I sweated, at times I shivered; my cough overwhelmed me whenever I lowered my head, and my chest burned with every breath. I had trouble walking across the room.

My room became a little prison, which I left only to use the bathroom, the trip an ordeal that exhausted me. Food was left outside my door, but I had to force myself to eat and couldn't get beyond the first few mouthfuls. Charlie was seven at the time, and frightened, obviously. I tried to reassure her by sitting on one side of my bedroom door while she sat on the other, reading me a story as I sometimes read to her in bed. At times, even that was too much for me. At times I became delirious.

My delirium, at least the episodes I can remember, took on a dreamlike aspect. I was a nurse, and supposed to heal my patients, but I couldn't get to them. I tried. I started over and over and over again, only to have some obstacle block me. A car that wouldn't start, a closed street, a cop issuing me a ticket. Then I'd find myself in my room, back where I started.

At the end of the second week, I had an especially bad night. My patients were dying and it was my fault. They needed my care, but I couldn't get out of this room. Of course, I might have opened the door and walked out. It wasn't locked. But the thought never occurred to me. No. I wept, I moaned, I cried out against this injustice, but I never tried to leave.

Propped up on pillows so that I was sitting upright, sleep finally came to me. As always, my fever retreated toward daybreak, and I woke up at first light, so weak that it was some minutes before I realized that my daughter had crept into the room during the night. She was now lying in my bed, one arm thrown out, her head on my lap. I should have reacted, should have shaken her awake, should have given her a stern lecture as I led her from my room. I didn't, not for many long minutes, my need to be close to her overwhelming. But then my door opened and Mom walked into the room. She didn't berate me. In fact, the hard lines of her mouth softened and I found a measure of compassion in her eyes. Nevertheless, she picked Charlie up and carried her, still sleeping, out of the room, leaving me to my tears.

After eight long, hard weeks, I returned to Resurrection. To the living and the dead, to empty beds and patients who never became infected. The living welcomed me home with hugs and tears. I mourned those gone. I went to work.

My bed calls to me as I finish my eggs, drop my dishes in the sink, and walk into Charlie's room. Charlie will pass most of the day outside with the local kids, but I always spend a few minutes with her in the morning. Then, in the evening, we'll have supper together before I head out to work.

This morning I stand in the doorway for a moment. Charlie's sitting in her little blue chair, absorbed in her tablet. She seems especially small to me. Especially small and especially vulnerable. I'm all she has, all that keeps her on this side of the Yards—or, worse, from foster care. And I could be gone in a heartbeat, one minute safe, then the knock on the door. Police, open up.

Because the more I learn about Bradley Grieg, the more likely it seems that the cops will track him to Randy's on the night he was killed. They'll commandeer any footage from the security cameras, and there I'll be, loaded with makeup, in my broad-brimmed hat. My one consolation? Nobody at Randy's knows my name, and I didn't use a credit card. I'm not a regular, either, and I didn't recognize any customers in the club.

Enough, enough with useless speculation. Charlie's right here, right now, and I can't take my outing back. I glance around the room at the purple walls, the gold curtains and pink bedspread. As usual, I allowed Charlie to choose the decor, then saddled her with a lecture on compatible colors. But this time she was adamant, and I let her have her way, accepting even the metallic thread in the curtains.

Charlie finally looks up. "Hi, Mom."

"Hi, honey. How's the book going?"

"I think it's too sad."

Guilt washes through me, as it always does when I see my daughter unhappy. After all, I chose the book.

"Why?"

"I didn't want Charlotte to die, Mommy. I don't see why she had to. If I wrote the book, she would've lived."

"But didn't Wilbur save Charlotte's babies?"

Charlie won't be distracted. "But Charlotte's my name, too, Mommy."

I run my fingers along the side of my daughter's face. Charlie's asking me if she's going to die. After my own battle with Covid-19, this is a subject I prefer to avoid, mainly because I have no good answers. The possibility that I might have died isn't, I'm certain, lost on Charlie. I stifle my daughter's fear by taking her in my arms and holding her tight.

# CHAPTER SIXTEEN

## CONNOR

It's after ten o'clock when the bitch lieutenant kicks me out of the precinct. I head straight to my home, a two-room cottage on my father's property. I might have gone to Augie Barboza's place, but Augie's got two kids and a wife with a tongue almost as sharp as Mariola's.

I call Augie from inside on my house phone. He comes on a few seconds later, and I can already hear Donna in the background, her mouth going a mile a minute.

"I got picked up," I tell him, "which is why I didn't make the meet last night." I'm too wiped out for a long explanation. "I'll come by tomorrow morning. Say seven."

One thing about Augie, he never argues. "Got it, boss."

I'm up early, at six o'clock, in the kitchen with Mom. As often as possible, we have breakfast while the scumbag's still asleep. Mom's wearing a terry-cloth robe over her pajamas this morning. The robe's brand-new and thick. It makes her appear even tinier and more vulnerable.

The air in the kitchen is saturated with the odor of bacon and Mom's homemade rolls, still in the oven. I draw a long breath through my nose, remembering that I never did get to eat last night. My little cottage lacks a kitchen, and Baxter was pretty much closed down by the time I was released. I suppose I might have driven out to one of the truck stops on the interstate, where meals are served 24-7, but I was too tired. Now I plan to make up for lost time.

I kiss my mother's forehead, then take a seat. Mom's at the oven before I can lay the napkin in my lap (which she insists I do). She's pulling out a small baking tray that she lays on a trivet. A half dozen rolls, still steaming, form two rows on the tray. She makes these rolls from scratch, as she makes her own pasta, a source of pride.

I drive a fork into one of the rolls and bring it to my plate, then a second. The butter I slather on melts as quickly as my mouth fills with saliva. The rolls are still too hot to eat, and I have to drink from a glass of cold orange juice before nibbling at one end.

"Unbelievable," I say, more to myself than to Mom.

We don't speak much as I work on my breakfast. Instead of words, I show my appreciation by finishing everything she lays before me, the bacon, the eggs, the little cubed potatoes fried up with onions and garlic. I show it again when I carry my plate to the sink. Mom needs to know that someone cares for her, even if that someone is a dope-dealing asshole like me.

Mom hugs me for a minute before I leave. "You take care, Connor. Don't do anything foolish. Your father's very angry." She hesitates long enough to look over her shoulder. "I think he suspects you for whatever . . . happened."

As I turn to go, I suddenly remember Violet Arabella and what she told me about her pimp: "Everybody needs somebody."

Turns out the whore was right.

Me and Augie pull into the Skyview a few minutes before nine. There are no cars parked in front of any of the rooms, but Richard Gaitskill's electric cart is parked outside one of the cabins. There's also a cleaning crew working in a cabin at the other end of the lot, Mexicans who refuse to speak English. Richard brags about paying them six bucks an hour. That's below the minimum wage by more than a dollar.

"If I make a phone call," is the way Richard puts it, "they're on a plane back to Mexico."

This is good for me and Augie because these workers are sure to keep their mouths shut, no matter what goes down. They might even join the party if we decide to give Rich a good beatdown.

Rich is in the cabin's little bathroom when Augie and I come through the door. He's bent over the sink, a monkey wrench in his right hand. Rich is a big kid. He could do a lot of damage with that wrench, but that's not who he is.

When he catches our reflections in the mirror, he turns to face us.

"Hey," he says.

"Come out here and talk to me." I don't tell him to put the wrench down. I don't have to. He lays it in the sink, wipes his hands on a towel, and walks toward me, stopping about five feet away. He's scared, and for good reason. We've got a deal, me and Rich. He gets to buy a small piece of whatever dope we're runnin' at ten percent above my cost. In return, he keeps the rest of his guests—and there ain't that many—away from my and Brad's business. That and a heads-up if the cops come around or set up a surveillance, which before last night they hadn't.

"Talk to me, Rich."

"What could I say? The cops are all over Bradley's murder."

"Which cops?"

"The broad was in charge. I think she said her name's Mari-something. She was with Vern Taney."

"And?"

"They wanted to know when Bradley checked in, did he go anywhere. I gave 'em the time he registered. It was in the book, anyway. But if he left his room, I told 'em I didn't know about it."

"Nothin' else?"

"Yeah. I dummied up. Told 'em Grieg was just another traveler in search of a bed."

Augie's something of a mind reader, and I only have to glance in his direction before he steps forward and slams a fist into Rich's ribs.

"Whatta ya tellin' me, Rich? The cops didn't look at the video from the surveillance? Huh?" I don't do anger as a rule, not in my head, but I can fake it well enough. I step forward and put my finger in Rich's face. He's dropped to one knee and is showin' exactly no sign of tryin' to stand up again. "Don't play me, man. I'm not in the fuckin' mood."

"Okay. You could just ask, Connor. Sure, they watched the video. It showed Bradley drivin' off somewhere. That was a little after nine. He came back about ten thirty with a woman. She had her own car . . ."

"Didn't you just tell me you didn't know if he left his room?"

"I meant what I told the cops when they first asked."

Rich's answers are coming too quick. "What'd she look like? This broad?"

"You couldn't tell, really. She was too far away. You couldn't even tell what kinda car she was drivin'." He hesitates. "But she was definitely wearin' a hat. Ya know, like with a brim that covered her eyes."

"That what the cops said? They couldn't make an ID?"

"The cops didn't say nothin'. They just watched."

"And that's it? They saw a woman and nobody else?"

"Not exactly. See, it started rainin' a little later. After that, you couldn't even see Bradley's car—or the cabin."

"For how long?"

"All night."

I take a minute to think it over. The cops probably think the broad killed Bradley. They have a motive, too, robbery, which they've already announced to the world. Or at least to Baxter. Plus, if it started rainin', like Rich says, and you couldn't make anything out, the cops'll have to put it on the broad. She's the only game in town.

Of course, they gotta find her first. But maybe that'll be easy. Maybe it'll turn out to be one of Bradley's girlfriends. He's got enough of them, and more than a couple of 'em will do just about anything to get the price of a fix. For eighteen large, they'd kill their own kids.

"So let's have a look, Rich. At the video."

I don't surprise easy, but this time Rich catches me off guard when he steps back and says, "The cops took it."

"What?"

"The cops took it with 'em. The video. It was on a thumb drive."

"Did they have a warrant?" I don't wait for an answer. They couldn't have had a warrant, not that early. "The cops didn't take that video, Rich. They got no right to take it. No, you gave it away. Why would you do that?" Again, I'm not waitin' for an answer. I look over at Augie and say, "Hurt him."

It doesn't stop until Rich is doubled up on the floor, gripping his sides. I don't blame him. We've left his face alone, but he'll be pissin' blood for a couple of days. The cracked ribs probably won't feel all that good, either. Rich doesn't fight back—he's too smart for that—but I'm thinkin' that he knows too much about my business. I mean for a guy who's basically straight. He knows too much, and maybe I have to do something about that.

"What else you do, Rich? Did you mention my name?"

"No. I swear, Connor."

He's lying and it's fucking obvious. The cops know that me and Bradley were close. Mariola made that clear last night. "So what else did you tell them? What else did they want?"

Rich brightens suddenly. Something he's remembered, most likely.

"When Bradley registered, he told me he might go out for a while and I should keep an eye on the cabin. I asked him where he was goin' and he said Randy's. To pick up a woman, right? He told me he's been runnin' around for the last few days and he needed a little relief. Randy's was the place to find it."

I have more questions, but they're not gettin' answered. Not today. That's because Rich's mom comes through the door holding a sawed-off 12-gauge in her hands. I'm not scared exactly, but I'm not about to make a move. No, I'm looking into Felice Gaitskill's baby blues and thinkin' my old man's the only reason she doesn't pull the trigger to protect her little boy. What I heard, Felice came up hard. She understands consequences.

Felice steps to the side as I walk past and through the door, Augie trailing behind. Neither of us speaks until we're in the car and driving away. Augie's behind the wheel.

"So what now, boss?"

"We're gonna pay another visit to Rich and his mom, Augie, but that's for later. First thing, we gotta find the woman who stole from me."

"Randy's?"

"Randy's doesn't open till six. They won't even start settin' up until four. So I don't know. Maybe I should drop you, then hang out at the Black Sheep. You can pick me up this afternoon."

My phone goes off before Augie replies. My burner. The incoming number has been blocked, and I answer before it rings a second time.

"Hey, C, it's Waylon."

"What you need, Waylon?"

"A couple of pounds."

I don't have to ask pounds of what. Waylon and his crew deal ice out in the countryside. They've been at it so long, they take turns going to prison. "You're lookin' at around twenty-five," I say. "You got that kinda money? Last time, you held me up for two days. I can't have that, Waylon. You know my game."

"I got it, Connor. Swear on my mother."

Waylon's mom has been a tweaker for thirty years. She hasn't got a tooth in her mouth.

"Gimme a couple of hours, Waylon. I'll get back to you this afternoon."

# CHAPTER SEVENTEEN

## DELIA

I start my day with an early-morning call to my mother in Centralia. Mom was the rock that anchored my childhood, and I reached out for her comfort whenever life became too much for me. I loved my daddy, too, but he worked at a factory that manufactured replacement windows and grabbed every opportunity to work overtime. At home, he tended to veg, except on Sunday morning, when we attended church. Mom worked, too, part-time as a bookkeeper at Centralia's library. She often took me with her when I was young, maybe hoping I'd pick up a love of learning. Instead, she got a female Action Jackson. Disappointed? If so, she never complained.

"Hey, baby, how are you feeling?"

"Good, Mom."

"And my grandson?"

"Your adorable grandson lost his temper on Sunday and punched a kid in the mouth. For calling me a dyke."

We go on for a good ten minutes, back and forth, until the conversation finally shifts to Bradley Grieg's homicide. Mom reads the *Baxter Bugle* online every morning, and the murder's grabbed her attention. Call it prurient interest. On some levels, she's worse than Danny.

"I think I've wanted the woman, the one in the hat, to be a lone suspect from the beginning," I tell her. "Easy-peasy. Find her and close the case."

"But you can't make that work?"

"No, I can't."

"Then what are you going to do about it if you have to arrest the woman?"

"Damned if I know."

Our conversation continues for another fifteen minutes, until Danny wanders into the kitchen and I suddenly become redundant.

"Is that Grandma?"

"Is that my grandson?"

As they talk, grandma and grandson, I rummage in the refrigerator. Baxter's just a bit over four hundred miles from Centralia, close enough for visits on Thanksgiving and Christmas, plus a weeklong stay during the summer when I'm on vacation. That'll be six weeks from now, in mid-August.

My workday begins with Bradley Grieg's autopsy, performed at Baxter Medical Center, a second-rate hospital I hope never to need. The interior of Bradley's abdomen, emptied of his organs, has the texture of old leather.

"I'm listing the cause of death as a gunshot wound," Rishnavata tells me as he saws away.

"No chance of an overdose?"

"If his heart hadn't continued to beat, there'd be less blood. And by the way, given the bleeding, I'd have to say he lived for a couple of minutes after he was shot."

"Is that possible?"

Arshan surprises me. "A small caliber bullet, say a .22, will fragment as it pierces the skull, sending splinters of lead in every direction. A higher caliber round, a 9mm for example, cuts a straight path, with unpredictable results. It depends upon which regions of the brain are impacted. One can live for some time, or even survive. In this case, I'm finding blood in the victim's nasal passages and trachea, blood he most certainly aspirated."

We're in Baxter Medical's basement pathology room. Rarely used, the room smells only slightly of decayed flesh and antiseptic. Grieg's lying faceup on a stainless-steel table, his organs removed. Rigor mortis has deserted his body, and he's lying unnaturally flat. Every curve, his lower back, his buttocks, even his neck, is flattened. The gaping hole in his abdomen has rendered him hollow, empty, unreal.

Coming into the autopsy, I still clung to the living Bradley Grieg who deserved what he got. At least according to Danny. No more. Bradley Grieg is gone. There's nothing left to blame.

Vern's waiting for me when I finally walk out of the building. He's in his Ford with the wipers running. "You convince Arshan to narrow it down?" He puts the car in gear and pulls away from the curb. We're on our way back to the station. Chief Black wants an update.

"Yeah, but the prick made it worse. If you could believe that."

Vern's asking about the time of death, originally set between nine and two.

"How so?"

"Now it's between eleven and three."

Vern's too laid-back to vent, but I'm sure he's as frustrated as I am. Grieg's female companion left the cabin at eleven fifteen. That puts her close to the earliest estimate of time of death. In the hands of a defense lawyer, even a bad one, it's ammo. In the eyes of a jury? If we can't develop any forensic evidence?

Ten minutes later, Chief Black has no trouble reading the bottom line. "Any chance our beloved coroner will reverse himself, Delia?"

"He can't, Chief. He's committed his estimated time of death to paper. It's now part of the autopsy report. That leaves fifteen minutes for the woman to kill him."

"And the next three-plus hours," Black observes, "for somebody else."

"There's good news, too," Vern announces. "The bullet, the one recovered from the mattress, is only slightly flattened. If we get our hands on the murder weapon, it'll make for an easy match. And we've found the nightclub Grieg visited. Randy's. Given that a woman followed him back to the hotel, it's likely that he met her there."

"Have you been to the club?" the chief asks.

"Not yet, Chief," I tell him. "Just now, we're headed to the courthouse. I want a subpoena for the club's security tapes. That way there's no chance something will happen to the data before it's surrendered."

"What about Bradley's drug works. You find DNA?"

"I called the state crime lab this morning. Don't hold your breath is what they basically told me."

Chief Black favors me with a nod. I've given him a line of attack if he needs to hold another press conference. Blame the state. "Better get on with it, then." He taps the table with a forefinger. "And good work, Lieutenant. Excellent."

We're still inside the precinct when Vern speaks for both of us. He has a habit, Vern does, of reading my mind when it comes to policing.

"We need to reenact the sequence," he tells me. "You're not gonna be happy until we do."

The conditions are perfect. The light rain and drizzle that began early this morning will continue through the night. All we need is a bag of rice and a pillow. My own weapon is a 9mm. I can fire it through the pillow into the bag of rice while Vern watches the video from the office. But the way I'm thinking, my interests are best served by abandoning the whole business. That's because Vern had it right.

"The cameras at the Skyview are for shit," he told me. "They're also far away, and it was raining, and we know the muzzle was jammed into a pillow."

# CHAPTER EIGHTEEN

## DELIA

Vern and I spend most of our day interviewing women on the list supplied by Cindy Sherman. The term of art these days is person of interest. But to me, and probably Vern, these are suspects. Any one of them might be the woman who entered Grieg's room at 10:42 and left at 11:15.

The ladies recite the same basic story. Their affairs were brief enough to be called hookups, and they haven't seen Bradley Grieg in months. What's more, despite running in the same circles, they don't know anything about his current life. They don't know his friends or his lovers. They don't know about his relationship with Carl and Connor Schmidt. So sorry.

If nothing comes of the video from Randy's, we'll ferret out the liars and use their lies against them. But that's for later. For now, I just want them on the record.

It's three thirty when we finish with the last of the group, Candy Gowen. She bursts out laughing when I mention Grieg's name.

"He pretended that we were beneath him, but it was a cover-up," she tells us. "The asshole was a complete dud in the sack. Too quick on the trigger. I spent the month after we hooked up avoiding him."

Our timing is perfect. The busboys are setting up the tables when we stroll into Randy's. The waiters, all female, are huddled with the cook. Two bartenders are rolling an aluminum keg into place. The only bouncer leans against the door to the kitchen.

The workers continue about their business when Vern and I come through the door, not even looking up. All except the boss, Mason Cheat.

The surname works well for Mason, who passed his mid-twenties in prison after a credit-card scam fell apart. The assumption, these days, is that he managed to hide a chunk of his ill-gotten gains. Enough to open the bar. His actual claim, that a silent investor supplied the capital, is universally rejected. But now that he's found the light, Mason's become an asset. Twice in the last year, he's informed on drug dealers working his club.

Mason Cheat's a short, broad-shouldered man with dark brown eyes that bug out of his head, a wide mouth that usually hangs open, and a receding chin. To this cop, he seems to be perpetually pleading. The reality, on the other hand, is that nobody fucks with Mason Cheat, not even

Carl Schmidt. That's the word, anyway, and I've yet to see it disputed. Having been in prison once, Mason doesn't care to have his liberty threatened.

Mason's gaze fastens on me as I approach. I can almost see the questions rushing through his brain. Then he blinks twice, and I know he's come up with the answer. I won't have to waste my time explaining.

Mason nods to my partner, who returns the gesture. "How do, Vern?" Then he turns to me. "You here about Bradley?"

"Sure am, Mason."

"He was in here for a time on Saturday." Mason's wearing a brown sport coat over a white shirt. He runs his finger along both lapels of the jacket as though adjusting body armor. "I was gonna call ya, sure as hell. Just ain't got around to it."

I don't dispute the claim. There's no point. "Were you here on Saturday, Mason? Did you speak to him?"

"I was in my office. Never laid eyes on the man."

"Then how do you know he was here?"

Mason's mouth is very wide, and his responding smile reaches almost to his ears. I got him, but he's not holding a grudge.

"One of the waitresses, Maureen, served him. She told me right after the killing was reported."

"And Maureen would be?"

Mason points to the waitresses, still huddled around the cook in his white apron. The girls wear black T-shirts, scoop necked and tight enough to pass for a second skin.

A single word, Randy, is printed across their breasts. Not Randy's. Randy.

"Which one?"

"The blonde."

I take the subpoena from my bag and pass it over. Mason's hands pull away at first, but then he accepts the document.

"What's this?"

"A subpoena, Mason. For all the video shot by your security cameras between 9:15 and 10:45 on Saturday night. Every single frame, Mason. You hold out on me, I'll bust you for obstruction. Think I'm kiddin', try me."

Mason leans back in his chair and shrugs. I'm taking that to mean we got to the club before Connor.

"No problemo, Lieutenant. Only thing, I can't cut ninety minutes out of the data. We're digital now, and our data's broken down into whole days and recorded on flash drives, one for each camera. I can give you everything for June twenty-fourth, and I'm glad to do it. I don't like the idea of Bradley's killer running free any more than you do."

I wave off his reply. "How many cameras, Mason? Show Vern where each camera is placed and what part of the club it covers. Please."

Mason doesn't argue, but he's not about to play guide for a hick cop. He turns and motions to the bouncer, who snaps to attention. Is it kick-ass time? If so, he's roid-rage eager. I watch him approach Vern, the greater threat, his fingers curling, only to stop suddenly when his boss speaks.

"This is Detective Taney," Mason says. "He's gonna check out our security system and pick up the drives from Saturday. Make sure he's taken care of. Understand, Mark? We're cooperating."

"Got it, boss."

"You could've just asked," Mason tells me as Vern and Mark walk away.

"Sorry, but I'm not the trusting type."

"I can see that, but look here, I hope you don't suspect me or anyone in the club . . ." When I don't answer, he continues. "I know about Bradley, about the game he runs with Connor Schmidt. Swear on my mother, Lieutenant, they don't play that game in my club. I got two more bouncers comin' in later. I pay 'em well."

Mason's too eager, and I'm pretty sure he's holding back. That's okay, like the bullshit fed to me by Bradley's former girlfriends. Maybe later I'll follow up. For now, I want a few words with Maureen while my partner collects the video.

The waitresses peel away as I approach. Their movements are synchronized, a kind of water ballet on terra firma. I dutifully show my badge. As if they didn't make me for a cop the minute I walked through the door.

"Maureen? Can I speak with you for a moment?"

Maureen shoots a glance in her boss's direction, then says, "Sure, why not."

I lead her to the end of the bar and give her a second to adjust. I'm a cop and I'm confronting her, but I'm not dangerous. Meanwhile, the woman's in her mid-twenties, with teasing green eyes and the most erotic smile I've ever seen.

"I understand you served Bradley Grieg on Saturday evening. Is that right?"

"Yeah."

"You know him?"

"He comes in a couple of times a week. Usually takes a table in front of the bar. That's where he sat on Saturday."

"When did he arrive?"

Maureen opens up at that point, rambling on without prompting. She tells me that Bradley showed up around nine thirty and left an hour later. He had two drinks, Maker's Mark on the rocks, but nothing to eat. And no, she didn't see him talk to anyone. That was unusual in itself because Bradley usually hit on every woman in the club, starting with the youngest.

When she finally rolls to a stop, I'm faced with a choice. I'm tempted to ask if she remembers a customer that night, a woman wearing a hat. Quick, right? Directly to the point?

But I can't be sure the woman wasn't a regular, and I don't want her warned. "All right," I finally say, "and thanks for the time."

I turn to go, but Maureen puts a hand on my forearm, holding me back. I look down at her hand, but she leaves it right where it is, the touch of her fingertips featherlight.

"I just remembered something," she tells me. "About Bradley."

"What's that?"

"Bradley had this bag with him. Like a gym bag, only too expensive for the gym."

"Describe this bag." I find myself disappointed when her hand falls away from my arm.

"I think it was made out of snakeskin . . . Hey, wait a minute."

I watch her take a pad and a pencil from the pocket of a mini apron that drops from her waist to the crotch of her yoga pants. She scratches away for a minute, then tears off the top page and hands it to me. Maureen's drawn a reasonable representation of a gym bag, but that's not where my eyes are drawn. No, my eyes are drawn to the phone number at the bottom of the page.

"If I can be of any more help, call me," she says.

# CHAPTER NINETEEN

## CONNOR

I can't believe what Cully tells me, so matter-of-fact I wanna punch him in the mouth. Cannot-fucking-believe. Cully's a bouncer at Randy's. When we come up to him, he's standing outside, blocking the door. Filling it, really. The guy's a giant.

"The cops are inside," he tells me.

"Are you kidding?"

"Wish I was, Connor." He shifts his weight from one foot to another. "I come to work around twenty minutes ago, open the door, and see 'em with Mason. The lieutenant and Vern Taney. Right away, I back off. I'm way behind on my child support, and I'm thinkin' I got a warrant on me. At least that's what my ex claims."

I look at Augie. Augie looks at me. I wanna hit someone, which Augie recognizes right away. He shakes his head.

This ain't the time and it ain't the place and Cully ain't a man I need to be hittin'.

"Richard Gaitskill, boss," Augie says. "That's gotta be how."

Yeah, Richard Gaitskill. Bradley told Rich where he was goin' on Saturday night, and that prick told the cops. Him or his mother. Me, I got a thing about hittin' women, but in this case I could make an exception.

Augie turns to Cully. "You know what they're doin' in there?"

"When I opened the door, the one cop, the woman, was handin' Mason some papers. Don't ask me what was on 'em, but Mason didn't look happy."

That's enough for Augie. He lays a thick hand on my shoulder and says, "We should really go, boss. Like before the bitch catches us out here. I mean she already pulled you in once."

Good point, but I continue to stare at Randy's lacquered double doors.

"C'mon, boss," Augie continues. "I got a line on Rink Meghan. Let's take care of a little business."

Rink Meghan's a deadbeat who's into us for two-and-a-half large. Not a huge amount, but after makin' regular payments for six months, he vanished three weeks ago. Word on the street is that he picked up a dope habit that's accounting for every penny in his pocket.

I shake off Augie's response. "How'd ya find him?" Someone I can hit, at last. "Forget that. Where is he?"

I'm afraid Augie's gonna say Portland or San Diego, but Rink's not that smart.

"On the west side, at his aunt's."

Rink's standing outside his aunt's garage on Baker Street when we pull up. I'm expectin' him to rabbit. He doesn't, though his expression turns glum. Rink's not meant for the life. He's only about five seven, and he can't weigh more than 150 pounds. Next to Augie, he's a mosquito.

"Hey, guys," he says. "I got somethin'. For the loan, right?"

Augie comes close enough to stand on Rink's toes. "Somethin'? Not cash?"

"No, but it's good. I swear. Come inside, I'll show ya."

He starts to raise the garage door but stops abruptly when Augie pushes him aside. "There anybody else in there?" Augie wants to know.

"Nah, it's my aunt's house. She's at work."

Augie shoves Rink toward me and opens the door to reveal a banged-up Crown Vic covered by a thick layer of dust. The car hasn't been on the road in years.

"Open the trunk. Go ahead." Rink's tone is upbeat, and I know we're gonna find something reasonably valuable inside. I also know he's convinced himself that he's escaped a serious beatdown. That remains to be seen.

The open trunk reveals two items, a pump shotgun with an etched barrel, and a wooden box.

Rink points to the box. "Check it out."

Augie looks at me, then lifts the lid to reveal a full set of polished cutlery. Only the handles are visible, but they gleam as if they've been waiting for enough light to show themselves off. Augie removes a dinner knife, checks it out for a moment, then hands it to me. I turn it back and forth until I find a set of stamped figures on the handle. There's a running lion and a crown, good signs, plus the knife is too heavy to be junk.

"So what am I supposed to do with this, Rink?"

"C'mon, you're lookin' at antique British cutlery. You couldn't buy a set like this for less than six grand."

Probably true, I'm willing to admit. But that doesn't mean I can sell it. The set is heavily engraved. Most likely it's already on a list of stolen goods posted in every pawnshop from here to Chicago. So what am I lookin' at? The melt value? Or what I can get from a fence like Frankie Lapaglia, which won't be a whole lot more?

"Take the silver and the shotgun," I tell Augie. "Put 'em in the trunk."

Rink's eyes reflect the truth as it settles over him. Bye-bye, dope money. Better than a beating, though. It begins to drizzle, as it has been on and off all day. Augie opens the trunk of my Lexus and drops the silverware and the gun inside. As he closes the trunk, my phone begins to ring.

My father.

"Do what you gotta do," I tell Augie.

I let the phone ring out, then jump into the back seat and redial. Where's the money? That's what he wants to know, all he wants to know. It's been two days, and he's still out eighteen grand. What the fuck's wrong with me? Why can't he trust me to do the least little thing?

And what am I gonna tell him? The cops beat me to it? Beat me to the data from the Skyview? Beat me to Randy's? And if I don't catch a fuckin' break soon, they're gonna beat me to the broad who stole his money?

This—the truth—is not what he wants to hear. "Did you speak to our guy?" he demands.

"Yeah. He's only sure they're after a woman. Mariola and Taney."

"Are they close?"

"He doesn't know from nothin', Pop. They got him workin' burglaries in Oakland Gardens."

Augie slides behind the wheel as I hang up. "That enough?" he asks. Rink is lying on the ground, blood streaming from a cut in his brow. Somehow, I don't think he'll miss his next appointment.

"Yeah, Augie, that'll do. Let's move."

"Where to?"

"Hell and back."

# CHAPTER TWENTY

## GIT

It's been gloomy all day, but now it's starting to rain for real. I call to Charlie: time to go. She's with her park friends, kids she gets to see only when I take her to Baxter Park. We're on the fancy edge of town, me and my little girl, or what passes for fancy in Baxter. Charlie and her friends are still too young for snobbery, but they'll learn. The other mothers in the park are gathered on benches to either side of me. They don't even glance in my direction. Me, on the other hand, I can't stop looking around, like I'm expecting to see Connor Schmidt walking toward me with a pistol in his hand. I saw Connor's photo yesterday when a local newscaster linked him to Bradley Grieg. The man seemed nondescript except for his mouth. Connor's lips turn down at both corners, and I sense a calculating ruthlessness. This is a man with no stopping point. At the same time, he's not stupid. He won't act on impulse. Does that mean he can be manipulated? At this moment, I have no desire to find out.

"Coming, Mommy."

Baxter Park has been thoroughly rehabbed despite the economic slump. Teeter-totters, slides, swings, monkey bars, even a geodesic dome made of aluminum tubes. Instead of blacktop, the surface of choice in Baxter's other parks, this one's of padded rubber in case one of the darlings should fall from the top of the dome.

Charlie waves to her pals as she settles into a booster seat she hopes to outgrow in the near future. In fact, I plan to strap her down until she's eighty.

On the way home, I stop at the Dairy Queen on Baxter Boulevard for ice-cream cones. I know the only healthy choices for children lie somewhere between a stalk of celery smeared with sugar-free peanut butter and a carrot dipped in plain yogurt, but Charlie and I pass so little time in each other's company that I can't resist. Charlie displays her appreciation with a happy grin as she nibbles at the edges of the cone. That's enough for me.

"Charlie, what would you say if I told you that I've decided to leave Baxter?"

We're in the car, me in the front, Charlie in her booster seat, the strap loose. Charlie's not grinning now; she's looking at me, her blue eyes narrowed. What's Mommy up to?

"Where would we go, Mommy?"

The plaintive tone—the one that makes me want to give her anything she asks for—usually draws a smile. Not this time. Late this morning I got a call from Madison Klein at Short Hills Medical Center. Madison woke me, but I pulled myself together real fast when she asked if I'd be up for an interview tomorrow morning.

"We'd move to New Jersey, a place called Short Hills."

"Where is that? Will I have friends there? Will Gramma be coming?"

I gobble up the last of my cone and wipe my fingers on a paper towel. "Let me show you where New Jersey is. How'd that be?"

No response necessary. I shift to the back seat and slide in beside my daughter. Charlie has a tablet, one of the benefits of working seventy-two-hour weeks. It's on the seat next to her, as usual, and I turn it on. We're getting an unlocked signal in the parking lot and it takes me only a couple of minutes to produce a map of Baxter.

"Okay, baby, this is Baxter. This is where we are."

"I know that, Mommy."

Charlie loves her tablet, and she loves maps. She pulls up a street view of our house and the houses of her friends several times a week.

"Now, pull back. A little more, a little more. Stop." I drop a finger to the screen. We've got most of the country in view. "This is New Jersey. See if you can focus on it."

Charlies fingers work until the state fills the touch screen.

"And this is Short Hills."

Again, Charlie fingers work their magic, and we're soon traveling down a residential street, taking short hops from one colonial home to another. The homes are large, the lawns meticulously cut, the shrubbery trimmed. Summer flowers gleam in weeded beds.

"Will we live here, Mommy?"

I usually don't lie to my daughter, but I'm not always frank either. Now I merely smile as I get out of the car. Maybe one day she'll live in a neighborhood like this, but the best her mom can hope for at this point in time is an apartment over a two-car garage.

My bedroom's a place of refuge this afternoon. Mom's been going on about Carl Schmidt and what he's gonna do to the "bitch who ripped him off." Bradley Grieg's no longer part of the story, or at least he's been reduced to some kind of prop, future bloodshed apparently more interesting than past bloodshed.

If my mother was the only one, I'd probably be able to hide from my fears of attack. I get enough stress from imagining cops knocking on my door. But the Schmidts, father and son, now dominate the Baxter grapevine and my mother's conversation. Mom's repeated the most current rumor three times. According to her, the Schmidts are offering a big-time reward to anyone who can name the woman who killed Bradley and stole his money. That means they're hearing from every strung-out junkie in Baxter, naming their sisters, mothers, nieces, aunts, or children.

What's the word? Counterproductive?

Still, I have to take the threat seriously. I didn't even know who Carl Schmidt was before yesterday, but now

I do. At the very least, Carl and Connor will transform parts of my body into an object lesson for others. If they can find me.

Charlie's outside playing and Mom's in the kitchen when I pull a small metal chest from beneath a pile of shoes and discarded hangers on my closet floor. The chest's lid is secured by a padlock with a keypad, and I quickly punch in the code, unhook the padlock, and open the box. There's a gun wrapped in a cotton cloth. Not the one I used on my ex-husband, this is a smaller pistol, a .32 caliber CZ 83 manufactured in the Czech Republic for the Browning Arms Company. The gun's far from new, but the price was right and a trip to a gun range confirmed its reliability.

Purchasing the little .32 required no more than a trip to Baxter Guns & Ammo. I walked in, submitted to an instant background check, and walked out with the weapon in my purse. As for Sean's 9mm, I sent it back to him through a mutual friend. I didn't know who owned it before Sean or what it was used for.

The CZ 83's a bit heavier than most .32s, but still lighter than Sean's Glock. I bought this model because it has a double-stack magazine. Most .32s hold only six rounds, this holds twelve.

Annie Oakley I'm not, but I'm not afraid of guns, either. And I know something about them. My .32 isn't powerful enough to stop a man determined to hurt me, not with a single shot. But twelve bullets will stop anybody, and the

CZ 83 will fire as fast as I can pull the trigger. With only minimum recoil.

Like I said, I'm not the victim type. That doesn't mean I'm not afraid, or that I'm dismissing the threat. Too many people are saying really bad things about the Schmidts for me to minimize the danger. It's just that I'm not going down, if I have to go down, without taking somebody with me.

With only fifteen minutes before I leave for Resurrection, I'm content to sit quietly. No such luck. Mom comes through the door to Charlie's bedroom bearing a glass full of clear carbonated liquid. Mom doesn't complain when I come close enough to make sure there's no alcohol in the glass. She's dropped off the wagon more than once.

"Charlie tells me you're leavin' town."

Charlie doesn't look away from the pad, but a flush creeps up her neck. The girl has a big mouth, true, but she's eight years old, and I never swore her to secrecy.

"There's a job opening back east, Mom. I'm lookin' into it."

For sure, Mom wants to ask if she's invited, but that's all the explanation she's getting for now. I haven't made up my mind about her. On the one hand, I wouldn't mind saying goodbye to my past, especially to my childhood memories. On the other hand, I can't make myself believe that child care is less expensive in New Jersey.

With other things on her mind, Mom drops the subject. "Spoke to Katie on the phone a couple minutes ago. Guess what she told me, Git?"

"That she's marryin' the mayor?"

"That ain't funny, and Mayor Venn's already married. Been married for near thirty years." Mom sips at her drink, a familiar smirk gradually dominating her face. "Nope, Katie tole me the cops was over to Randy's this afternoon. Servin' Mason Cheat with papers. According to Katie, Mason was in a cooperatin' frame of mind."

# CHAPTER TWENTY-ONE

## CONNOR

The club's up and running when me and Augie pull into the parking lot. Cully's at the door, ready to check IDs, but it's still early and the parking lot's almost empty. He straightens as we approach.

"Cops are gone, Connor."

"You know why they were here?"

"Askin' about Bradley. That he was in the club on Saturday." Cully pokes at a small dent in his forehead above his left eye. Courtesy of a pool cue. I remember when it happened, and that the fool who wielded the cue disappeared a couple of weeks later. Two rumors sprang up to explain the vanishing act. That he left town in a hurry. That he never made it past the city limits.

"Mason inside?" I ask.

"Last time I looked."

"He in a good mood?"

"No idea, Connor. With Mason, you can never tell."

I don't like Randy's, though I have to spend time here. Business, mostly. The business of connections. I have to be available. What's up? Whatta ya need? You make yourself hard to find, people forget you.

But the club's too sleek for me, like it's tryin' too hard. Like it's the right place for cheating wives and husbands who wanna believe they're real sophisticated when they're just out to get laid.

On the other side of the room, the club's bartender, Shiloh, is restocking the shelves. He looks up, waves, and says, "In the office."

Mason Cheat's office is as comfortable as his club is hard and slick. A wooden desk and matching file cabinets, a worn swivel chair, an even more worn leather couch. But there's no window, and the room stinks of cigarette smoke despite a vent fan humming away.

My father and Mason Cheat are about the same age. They knew each other growing up, and rumor has it they worked together from time to time before Mason went to prison. They're not partners anymore, not that I know of. But they still respect each other, which means I can't play the tough guy.

"Evenin', Connor." He nods to me, then to Augie. "Be better if it was just the two of us, Connor. No offense, Augie."

Augie waits for me to shrug, then leaves the room. Funny thing about Augie, if I told him to shoot Mason, he'd do that, too. The man likes his work.

Mason takes his time after the door closes behind Augie. He lights a cigarette, blows the smoke toward the ceiling, flicks the match into a glass ashtray. The ashtray's blue and looks more like a candy dish, what with its rolled egdes. Me, I'm the beggar at the table. I don't say anything.

"Had a call from your old man," Mason finally says. "Asked me to cooperate. Said you'd tell me what's goin' on."

"Not much to tell. Bradley had something with him that belongs to me and my father. It's gone missing, and we want it back."

"What's that have to do with me?"

"Bradley was in here an hour before he was offed. After he left, he went straight to the Skyview. Had a woman with him, Mason. Did he pick her up here? You got cameras everywhere inside. Probably outside . . ."

"Lemme correct you right there, Connor. We got no cameras in the parking lot. The inside cameras? They're about preventin' a robbery before it happens. But who gets into whose car is no business of ours. We respect our patrons' privacy."

"I guess that's where the favor comes in." I don't think Mason likes it, but I'm not in the mood to spar with him. Yes or no, you'll help me or you won't. "I need to see whatever those inside cameras picked up. And I need to talk to anyone who remembers Bradley bein' in the club."

Mason taps his cigarette, dropping the ash into the ashtray. "There's a flash drive for every camera," he tells me, "and they left with the cops. Mariola had a subpoena. If I didn't turn over the video, she'd call in backup and take it."

"So what are you tellin' me? You got nothin'?"

"Nope. The flash drives are backup for our main computer. I've still got every second of the time your boy was in the club. But I got a problem, too. If it should get out, say to Mariola, that I helped you? She wouldn't like that, Connor, me helpin' a known criminal. And bein' as I need a license to sell liquor, what she don't like, she can do somethin' about."

Mason wants me to think he's not gonna let me see the video, but I'm not fooled. If he was gonna say no, he would've said it to my father. And tough guy or not, he hasn't got the balls. Mason's reached a stage in his life where he only wants peace. I don't blame the man. I could use a little myself.

"I'll owe ya, Mason. Me, personally. And the last thing I wanna do is talk this up. This bitch who took me and my father's property? I wanna keep running into her, if it should happen, completely private."

I'm sitting in another small room, Mason's security room, staring at a computer screen. Augie's sitting right next to me, at my insistence, and Cully's standin' behind us. That's at Mason's insistence. But Mason's not there. He doesn't wanna know.

We're starin', the three of us, at a woman sitting on a bar stool. She's wearin' a green minidress, the skirt pulled up to within a few inches of her crotch. The dress has sequins sewn into the fabric. They're catching the red light from a sign on the wall behind her and splashing it in every direction. Her arms are bare except for a stack of bangles, and there's a wedding ring on her finger.

"Jesus Christ," Augie says, "that's gotta be her. Look at the fuckin' hat."

I'm thinking the hat's white, but it catches so much of the red light I can't be sure. I'm also thinkin' the broad's beautiful, but I can't be sure about that, either. The hat she's wearin' is made of what looks like stiff lace. It's got a wide brim that curls down in front, and for the most part, she's sitting with her chin lowered. I'm getting only glimpses of her face, of green eye shadow, of a dark line curling from the corner of an eye, of glossy lipstick over a full mouth. Shiloh's serving her some kind of drink in a martini glass, his eyes occasionally flicking to the low-cut armholes of her sleeveless dress. Truth be told, if I'd run into her that night, I would've been all over her. Like the two guys she rejects as the video rolls on. As it is, I find myself waiting for an upskirt view.

It's not happening. I'm watching the video recorded by camera number four. The camera's positioned high on the wall to her left, and it's looking down at her hat and shoulders. There's another camera, too, camera five. This one's dead center over the bar, and what it shows is Bradley Grieg sitting at a table. The snakeskin bag is on the table beside him. I'd told him not to let it out of his sight, coming or going.

Bradley's facing the woman at the bar. He's got the good view, and I can't shake the feeling that she's puttin' on a show for him, even while she's rejecting the other guys.

And I'm still wishing—and I know Augie's wishing—it could have been us.

At ten thirty on the dot, Bradley gets up and walks out the door. The woman says something to Shiloh, then follows. She's as graceful and sexy goin' out as she was comin' in forty-five minutes earlier. But I'm still not gettin' a good look at her face.

"I gotta talk to Shiloh," I tell Cully. "Unless you can tell me who she is."

To his credit, Cully doesn't pretend he doesn't know what I'm talking about. He mutters, "Never seen her before." A few minutes later, Shiloh walks into the office.

He nods to me and Augie. "Whatta ya say, guys?"

"Evenin', Shiloh." My voice doesn't reveal a hint of my frustration. "You know this woman?" I've stopped the video at a point just after Bradley gets up to leave. The woman's turned to Shiloh, obviously saying something.

"Know her? Nope. But I remember her. She's the woman left with Bradley on Saturday night."

"Left at the same time? Or left with?"

"Left at the same time, Connor. I'm sure because she asked me if he was all right. Like was he safe or bad news. I told her . . ." Shiloh looks up for a moment as he searches for the right words. "I told her that he's a regular and he's never caused trouble at the club. That was enough, and she followed him out the door."

"You ever see her before Saturday night?"

"Once, about a month ago. And maybe once before that, only I'm not sure. A real beauty, though. The clothes, the makeup? I do love me a woman who knows what she wants. Fact, if she hadn't trailed after Bradley, I was gonna offer myself as a substitute."

"Very good." Now for the big question. I cross everything, my fingers, my toes, even my eyes. "Did she pay with a credit card?"

"Sorry, Connor. She put a twenty on the bar." He scratches the top of his head and smiles. "The broads who come here wearin' their wedding rings? They never leave a paper trail."

I eventually walk out of Randy's with something half-assed decent to show for the effort. A printed screenshot of the woman. She's in profile, with her forehead and most of her eyes blocked by the brim of her hat, but it's the best I can do.

Augie follows me out of the bar. He's been keepin' quiet, but now he lights up a cigarette and sucks down a lungful of smoke. "I'm thinkin' that I almost know her," he says.

"Know who?"

"The woman offed Bradley. Like I'm not gettin' a name, but I can't shake the feelin' I seen her before. Growin' up, ya know?"

"And where'd you grow up, Augie?"

"The Yards."

I show my appreciation with a nod. A place to start, which is good. Meanwhile, I got another appointment to keep.

"Whatta ya say, Augie? Let's go have us a talk with Richard Gaitskill and his loving mom. I could use the exercise."

# CHAPTER TWENTY-TWO

## DELIA

The alarm bells in my head won't stop ringing. Don't do this, don't do this, don't do this. But I'm doing it anyway. I can't help myself. By now, Vern and I have reviewed the video from Randy's. We've isolated the woman in the hat, watched her blow off two men, watched her follow Bradley out the door. But the full-face likeness we needed wasn't there, and we eventually settled for a series of photos that reveal bits and pieces of her mouth, jawline, and the corner of one eye.

The chief's gone by the time we quit, but we leave copies of the photos on his desk, then clock out. We're off duty now. On our own.

Fifteen minutes later we're approaching the counter in the Skyview's office. Richard and Felice are behind the counter. They're sifting through a pile of bills, probably deciding which have to be paid and which can be post-poned. Matching their needs to their checkbook.

The Gaitskills are skeptical when I explain what's about to happen. Felice points out that we have no authority to conduct this little experiment. No court order, not even a note from Chief Black. We're acting on our own, and we plan to kill a pillow and a sack of rice, both of which I've brought with me.

Earlier, I offered to let Vern off the hook, but he declined. "Fuck it, Delia," he said. "I wanna know, too. But you understand, as evidence, it's useless."

There's no denying the observation. We haven't reproduced the conditions exactly. We're close, what with the drizzle, but close only holds up in court if the experiment's conducted by a forensic expert. And even then, a judge might exclude it.

"We have guests staying here," Felice tells me.

Vern picks that moment to step in, his tone reasonable, as usual. "Now, Felice, you have exactly one occupied cabin, and that's at the opposite end of the property. The people inside won't even notice."

"What if they hear a gunshot? After what happened on Saturday, they'll go out of their minds."

"Did you hear a gunshot on Saturday? I mean, you told us, the both of you, that you didn't. And knowin' you as I do, I believe you were tellin' the truth."

"We were, but—"

Vern dismisses whatever she planned to say with a wave of his hand. "Look, it'll only take a couple of minutes. Then you can go back to whatever you were doing."

Felice doesn't like it, but I have the feeling she doesn't like much of anything. On the other hand, Richard seems indifferent. He knows we're not going anywhere until we get what we want. He's the one who hands over the room key. He's the one who leads Vern to the Skyview's computer.

A twenty-pound bag of rice cradled in one arm, a pillow in the other, I walk from the office to Cabin 909. I'm telling myself there's no other way. Insisting, really. I can't let this slide. I have to know.

Inside, I find a room that's been cleaned by professionals. Every drop of blood, every chunk of brain, every bone shard removed. Not the smell, though. The air-conditioning's off and the humidity's at a hundred percent. Try as I might, I can't escape the faint metallic odor of blood.

There's a new mattress on the bed, and I know there's a chance that I'll put a hole in it. But not a good one. I'm counting on the twenty-pound bag of rice stopping the single bullet I intend to fire. The way it did on the YouTube video me and Vern watched just before we set out.

The bed's aligned as it was on Sunday morning when we responded to the scene. But the drapes, though closed over the room's single window, have a slight gap at the top. Was it there on Saturday night? The drapes close with a pair of rods at their leading edges. I open and close the rods. No difference. I try it again, this time snapping the rods together. Same result.

I place the bag of rice on top of the Skyview's pillow, place the pillow I brought with me on top of the rice, finally bring out my Glock. I don't give myself a chance to change my mind. I push the Glock's muzzle into the pillow and pull the trigger.

The muzzle flash is bright enough to blind me for a few seconds, and it's only afterward that I notice a tiny fire around the bullet hole in the pillowcase. I put the fire out with the edge of a blanket and check the rice bag. The bullet's contained inside. The mattress is undamaged.

Score one for YouTube.

I'm hoping the camera above the office won't pick up the muzzle flash. That would make my life easiest. But what asshole said life's supposed to be easy? Vern's waiting for me as I approach the office, and I don't have to ask the question. The answer's written on his face. I find it in the soft smile and the apologetic tilt of his head. I march past him without speaking, through the office to the small room holding the computer.

"Run it."

It's faint, the flash, but it's undeniably there. Not only in the gap at the top of the drapes, but the drapes themselves appear to glow.

"She didn't shoot him."

This doesn't come from me or Vern. Richard Gaitskill's first to state an obvious truth that my brain doesn't care to process. Talk about buyer's remorse. I'm telling myself the experiment was bullshit. That I was only guessing about how hard to press the muzzle into the pillow. Maybe she pressed it a lot harder. And maybe the mist and drizzle between the office and the cabin was thicker. It wouldn't take much. The flash in the window of Cabin 909 is very faint.

"Can you copy this out?" I ask.

Richard takes a step toward the computer, then stops abruptly. He draws a sharp breath, his right hand going to his side. Vern asks the obvious question. "You hurtin', Richard?"

"I fell."

"Yeah?" Vern's not buying. "The Schmidts, right? Or one Schmidt? Connor?"

Richard makes his way to his desk and the motel's single computer. He takes a flash drive from the center drawer of the desk and inserts it into an open port on the computer. He doesn't speak until his fingers begin to work.

"Whatta ya wanna do, Lieutenant? You wanna kill us? Just take your shit and get outta here before somebody sees us together. Somebody who ain't supposed to."

I'm sympathetic. No way do I want him to get hurt. The man's had enough. But we don't leave until I drop the flash drive into a labeled evidence bag.

"Anything else you want to tell me, Richard?" I say. "About your relationship to Connor Schmidt and Bradley Grieg."

"Like what?"

"Like who else had a key to Cabin 909?"

"Nobody, Lieutenant. I swear."

# CHAPTER TWENTY-THREE

## CONNOR

"You fuckin' believe this shit?"

It's Augie who speaks first. We're parked on the eastern end of the Skyview Motor Court. We've been here for a good fifteen minutes, ever since we drove up to find Mariola's black Toyota parked in front of the office. Now I'm watching the bitch walk from the office toward Cabin 909 on the other end of the lot.

"You see what she's carryin?" Augie asks. "My eyes ain't that good."

"It looks like a pillow in one arm and a bag in the other."

"What's that mean, Connor?"

I'm not mad. At least not crazy-mad. I know the Gaitskills fucked me. And when you fuck Connor Schmidt, you fuck Carl Schmidt. There's no way I can let that go. Especially given the circumstances.

Mariola's in no hurry—like she knows I'm watchin', like she's rubbin' it in that she's not takin' the easy way out. What she should do is grab the woman in the hat and lock her up. But I'm thinkin' that Mariola doesn't want the woman. Mariola wants me.

What I know for sure is that Mariola puts the squeeze on every mutt she picks up, especially the junkies. What do you know about Connor Schmidt? What do you know about Carl Schmidt? Why don't you do the smart thing for once in your moronic life? Set up the Schmidts and win a get-out-of-jail-free card. Or maybe you prefer kickin' your habit in a jail cell instead of a treatment center.

How do I know this? First, our guy. That would be Detective Meacham. Not that Mariola lets the jerk get anywhere near the druggies she works on. But she can't hide the fact that they're in the station house and she's questioning them.

Me, I don't deal with all that many people, not when it comes to drugs. The sentences are too long, and most junkies will rat you out in a heartbeat. No, I have a hard-and-fast rule. You get busted, I don't give you a chance to set me up. I stop doing business with you.

And if you're too persistent? If you won't let go? In that case, you end up as fertilizer in some farmer's cornfield. Prison's not on my bucket list.

Mariola strolls through the parking lot, both arms full, never lookin' back, never lookin' right or left. Like she's got a purpose and there's nothin' else in her life, not for now.

She has to set her packages down to unlock the door, but she still doesn't hesitate, so far away now I can only see her outline. And maybe I wouldn't see her at all if I hadn't watched her cross the lot.

I'm still wondering what the fuck she's doing, but then the cabin's window lights up. Not bright, but definitely there.

"What's that?" Augie asks.

I say the first thing that comes into my mind. The only thing. "A camera flash."

"Yeah, okay. But whatta ya think she was doin' with the pillow?"

"Don't know exactly. Some cop bullshit."

My brain's already shifting gears. Whatever Mariola's up to, there's nothin' I can do about it. Meantime, I got other problems. Like Richard gave me a key to Cabin 909, which I still have. Like I'm keepin' Richard supplied with high-quality product almost at cost. Like I've done too many deals with too many people in that cabin. Like Richard and his mommy are just too fucking friendly with a cop who hates my guts. If Mariola can put Bradley's murder on me, she won't hesitate.

"So what now, boss?"

"I'm gonna take you home, Augie. Enough for tonight. I got business tomorrow morning, but I want you to carry the photo down to the Yards, ask around. Not hard, Augie. Keep it polite, as least for now. Let 'em know we're prepared to show our gratitude to anyone who identifies her. Me, I'm gonna head home now. It's been a rough couple of days."

# CHAPTER TWENTY-FOUR

## GIT

I t's two o'clock in the morning, finally quiet, and I'm trying to prepare for my interview with the recruiters at Short Hills Medical Center. That's happening in eight hours, at ten o'clock, and I'm not ready, physically or mentally. The whole night's been completely crazy, and my adrenals are as empty as popped balloons. The open book in front of me might as well be written in Egyptian hieroglyphics.

I dealt with the usual collection of routine duties and mini-crises when I first got to work, the chores nonstop until ten o'clock, when our patients began to settle in for the night. Virtually all our residents are on some form of sleep meds, and I distributed them quickly, hoping for a quiet night. It was not to be.

Resurrection has several patients (eleven, actually) who should be in a psychiatric facility. And I'm not talking about dementia, which is always a problem. These patients are diagnosed psychotics. They're living in a nursing home because Resurrection's board of directors decided they had to fill beds after the virus killed thirty of the home's residents. Either that or close the doors permanently. They had to fill beds and these patients were available.

The directive from the administration was unambiguous. Deal with it or find another job. Deal with Josie Brown, for example, who tries to kill herself at least once a month despite being paralyzed from the waist down. And Frank Granger, who talks to his imaginary friends (Frank's term) from the moment he wakes up until he falls asleep. But these residents have never posed a threat to the staff, unlike Lester Powell, a diagnosed schizophrenic with paranoid delusions.

Lester is prescribed massive doses of phenobarbital, enough to keep him rooted to a chair on most days. But even then, he positions the back of his chair against a wall and never takes his eyes off the staff, as if he's only waiting for the attack to begin. Which it inevitably does.

Lester has an episode every couple of weeks, despite the pheno, despite regular doses of antipsychotics that also sedate him. His demons can be contained for only so long before they rise to the surface.

The good news is that he generally begins slowly, barking like an animal, crawling on all fours, pounding a massive fist into the tile floor. It's fear that drives him, that much is obvious, but so what? Fear, hate, confusion, what matters is that the man's dangerous. He's hurt other patients in the past, and I've got no reason to believe that he won't hurt me.

There's a plan in place, the Lester strategy, to handle his outbursts. A massive dose of a drug called Ativan, enough to put even a man Lester's size out of commission. But if that sounds easy enough, it comes with a big-time problem. The Ativan must be injected directly into a muscle, and that means getting within arm's length of a violent psychotic.

The alternative—call the cops and let them handle it—doesn't work. Lester's rage builds fast once he gets going, and the cops would be at least ten minutes responding. And that's even if the few cops on the street at night aren't busy elsewhere. Meantime, the Ativan's prepared in advance, always at the ready, but not left out where any patient can grab it. The syringe is kept in a locked cabinet in the meds room, which is also locked. I've got keys to both on a chain around my neck, ready to go, but the meds room is at the end of a long hallway on the other side of the unit and I'm not the fastest girl on the planet.

As I said, usually we get a warning. Not tonight. I was in Mrs. Knowle's room changing the dressing on the massive bedsore that covers her lower back. It was a little after nine, and I was rushing things because I wanted a chance to review vent procedure before my interview tomorrow. That's when I heard someone running in the hallway, coming toward me really fast. A second later, the face of the only other employee on the floor, a porter named Cesar, appeared in the doorway.

"You come, nurse. Lester go crazy."

Instead of going directly for the Ativan syringe, I decided to assess the situation. A big mistake, as it turned out, because Lester had taken crazy to a new level. I found him in his room, standing in front of a broken window, a six-inch shard of glass in his right hand, blood flowing from both hands, flowing hard enough to drip onto the floor. He was grunting incoherently when I appeared in the doorway, but his eyes instantly fixed on me. They fixed on me, and he smiled.

"Hello, Nurse—"

Lester never completed the sentence. Fully galvanized at last, I yanked Cesar out of the room and slammed the door.

"Keep him inside."

Again, I didn't wait. I ran the length of the hall faster than I've ever run in my life, yanking off the chain with the key as I went. I couldn't evaluate Lester's intentions, didn't try, because his own life was on the line even if he didn't intend to hurt anyone else. The blood flow from his hand and arm had to be staunched, and quick. A pool was already spreading around his feet.

The keyhole, the one on the locked cabinet that held the loaded syringe of Ativan, looked impossibly small when I entered the meds room. I must've fumbled away for a good ten seconds before I finally inserted the key, before the lock retracted, before I had the syringe in my hand, before I flew down the hall toward Cesar, a small fireplug of a man who stood with his back against the door, every muscle straining.

"Get away, Cesar," I said. "Let him out."

Cesar stepped off to the left, his eyes flicking from me to the door, but they settled on the door when it opened and Lester came through. This time, when Lester's dark eyes found mine, they seemed confused, as though he didn't quite understand how he came to be in this situation, a shard of glass cutting into the palm of his hand, blood running down his arm and onto the floor.

"Nurse . . ."

Psychiatric nurses are specially trained to handle psychotic breakdowns. Not me, though, not this LPN. I had to figure it out for myself, how to get close enough to administer the Ativan without having my throat cut in the process.

"What happened, Lester?"

"They came again, Nurse, all of them."

"And you had to protect yourself?"

"Yes, yes. I knew what would happen if I let them take me. I couldn't."

"That was smart, Lester, holding them off. But they're gone now, right?"

He looked around, his eyes settling on Cesar for a split second before he nodded and said, "Yes, I scared them away."

"Very good. You did what you had to do. But see how you're wounded? You need medication, soldier." I held up the syringe. "Let me fix you up."

"Well, I didn't mean to, only they got real close this time."

"But they're gone now and you need your medication. Can I give it to you?"

"Okay, Nurse. I'm sorry."

"Then put down the glass, Lester, because I'm afraid you might accidentally cut me with it."

Lester nodded once, then again, then dropped the shard of window glass, revealing the deep cut in his palm. He opened his mouth, but I didn't wait for him to speak. I stepped in close and drove the syringe into his thigh. Five seconds later he was unconscious.

Despite the adrenaline, despite a heart rate better suited to a canary staring at a house cat, I stayed calm. I had to stop the blood flow, and quick.

"Call 911, Cesar. Get an ambulance here."

I was already running for the blood-pressure kit dangling from the handle of a meds cart. The cuff was useless, I'd never get it tight enough before the Velcro straps gave way. But the rubber tubing that led to the gauge was a different matter. I yanked it free of the cuff, wrapped it around Lester's arm, and tightened down with all my strength.

Beyond unconscious, he didn't react to what must have been extremely painful as the blood flow died off to a trickle. Only then did I look up to find the hallway crowded with patients, who suddenly burst into applause.

# CHAPTER TWENTY-FIVE

## DELIA

I drive Vern back to his car, still parked at headquarters. We have an appointment tomorrow morning with Chief Black and an aide from Mayor Venn's office. What will we say about tonight's experiment? Do we mention it at all? Before I head out to work, I'll compare video from the day of the murder with the video I took last night. I'm pretty sure what the comparison will reveal. In fact, I'm more than sure. But I'm also sure about the chief's reaction if we tell him. Vern sums it up as he gets out of my car.

"We're fucked," he says. "Hope you're satisfied."

I'm supposed to go home now, but I pull to the curb three blocks from where I dropped Vern. A few seconds later my cell's in my right hand, Maureen's phone number in my left. I'm horny and have been for a week. Should I call her? I'm certain that she was coming on to me when she gave me her number. No doubt at all. But I don't know her. Don't know that she won't brag to her coworkers or, worse, to Mason Cheat.

I began applying to police departments in major cities throughout the state of Illinois within a week after landing the job in Baxter. This fear in my chest is a good part of the reason. You can drive from one end of Baxter to the other in twenty minutes. Most of the families have been living here for generations, and gossip spreads at the speed of light. The one time I did begin an affair, two years ago, I found myself in Chief Black's office. Folks were talking, influential folks, and I needed to be more discreet.

"Delia, you're the best officer this department's had in years," he told me. "But there's people above me holding those puppet strings. From where I'm sittin', Caesar's wife is your best bet."

The affair petered out before the string holders forced the chief's hand, leaving me to long for the day when I can separate my personal from my working life. Not today, though. I crumple Maureen's note and jam it into my pocket, thinking that, dutiful citizen that I am, I'll recycle it when I get home.

Before I reach the first traffic light, my thoughts have turned to Danny and whatever snack I can dredge up for us. No more than a daydream, as it turns out. My phone rings, and I know it's gonna be a long night as soon as I hear our night dispatcher's voice. No choice, though, bodies being bodies.

"Don't think she knew what hit her," Vern tells me.

We're looking at Felice Gaitskill, who's sitting in a padded swivel chair behind the counter in the motel's outer office. She's wearing a white blouse, and the parallel bullet holes in her chest remind me of the eyes of a monster in a low-budget horror movie.

"The chest wounds most likely came first." Vern leans back. He's always seemed comfortable in his own skin, and tonight is no exception. "Probably as soon as the shooter walked through the door."

There's a third insult to Felice Gaitskill's body. Another bullet wound, the one that instantly killed her. This entry wound is in her forehead. A small, neat puncture caused by a bullet that exited through the back of her skull.

"Take a look at the chair behind her," Vern continues. "The slugs from the chest wounds are buried in the padding. I didn't dig 'em out, but I gotta believe they're in good shape. Also, check this out."

Vern leads me to a door behind Felice, the door leading to the inner office. He points to a bullet embedded in the wood, just the tip, with the rest undamaged. He doesn't have to explain. All three rounds are suitable for comparison with the bullet that killed Bradley Grieg. I think I'm supposed to be happy, but I can't shake the feeling that I'm being played.

"Any spent cartridges?"

"Fraid not, Delia."

Vern opens the door to the back office where the two of us reviewed the video. The monitor lies on the floor, its screen cracked, but the computer's missing, along with any video stored on its hard drive. A shotgun rests atop the desk, its stock facing the outer office. Felice never got to it. In fact, from the way she's positioned, I have to believe the shooter began pulling the trigger as he came through the door.

Or she?

I close my eyes for a moment as I try to imagine a woman murdering Felice. The party girl with the hat, the elaborate makeup, and the sequined dress. I can't.

"They expected trouble, Vern." I point to the shotgun. "They took precautions."

"For all the good it did."

"Yeah, for all the good it did. Who reported the shooting?"

"An anonymous call to 911."

"Male or female?"

"Male."

The lower drawer of a file cabinet lies open, the files pulled back. I can see a small jar of shiny white powder behind them.

"What am I lookin' at, Vern?"

"Meth, probably, about an ounce."

"Was the drawer open when you got here?"

"No. I opened it myself. The meth was behind the files. Hidden, but they could get to it easily enough."

"You think they were dealers?"

"This much, they had to be." Vern closes the drawer. "There's more, Delia. In the living quarters upstairs."

---

A small living room, a smaller kitchen, and two small bedrooms. As far as I can tell, there's not a single new item in the apartment. From the dishes in the kitchen to the worn carpet on the floor to the battered nightstands flanking Richard's bed. Every item might have been purchased thirdhand at a thrift shop. Call it motive. Vern points me to a brown shopping bag in Richard's only bedroom closet. Illuminated by a small LED flashlight, the money inside the bag is clearly visible.

"You count it?"

"Yeah. Then I put it back. That's where it was originally."

"How much?"

"Seventeen thousand, three hundred. In twenties and fifties."

Always choose the simplest explanation? Sometime during the night, one of the Gaitskills, probably Richard, left the office via the back door, where there are no security cameras. He found Bradley still on the nod and decided to steal the money. Did he also kill Bradley? Better yet, would he dare leave Bradley alive to seek restitution? He would if he happened to be in front of the CCTV monitor when Bradley escorted the woman into Cabin 909. If there was someone else to blame.

Vern leads me to the open window in Richard's bedroom. Richard's body lies on the ground, fifteen feet below.

"Most likely," Vern explains, "he heard the shots that killed Felice and knew he'd be next. The window was the only way out."

Richard must have hit the concrete alleyway hard. Hard enough to break a leg, which juts from his body at an impossible angle. Still, he managed to claw his way toward a fence at the back of the property. He was within five feet when the shooter caught up with him. Did they speak? Richard's lying on his back, so he must have rolled over to face his killer. The bullet wound in Richard's forehead mirrors the wound in his mother's.

"The state notified, Vern?"

"Yeah, but their crime scene unit won't be here for a few hours. I called Rishnavata, too. He'll be on-scene in an hour or so, and he requests that we not move the bodies until he gets here."

"What about the chief?"

"He's on his way."

"Shit."

"Yeah, well, something else you need to see."

Vern leads me downstairs and through the rear door. He points as we approach Richard's corpse, but the gesture's unnecessary. Richard's wearing boxer shorts and a T-shirt. The needle marks on his left arm are painfully obvious.

"So Richard's out to get off. He uses the back door because he doesn't want to be caught by the cameras, and he strolls to the end of the lot. He finds Bradley in Cabin 909, completely stoned and . . ." I stop there for a minute.

"Ya know, Vern, I'm pretty sure Richard stole Bradley's money. Money that belonged to the Schmidts, by the way. But I can't picture Richard shooting Bradley. Stealing? The Gaitskills were living day to day, so sure. But taking up the pillow, pressing it against Bradley's head, pulling the trigger? It's too cold for Richard. Way too cold."

It's no longer drizzling, but the air is thick with a mist that settles against my face. Uniformed cops, the first responders, stand at either entrance to the parking lot. Both entrances are closed off by double strips of yellow tape. If the shooter drove into the lot, assuming it wasn't Richard, we'll probably find tire tracks. But I can't make myself believe the shooter was stupid enough to risk being spotted as he made his approach. Not when he had murder in mind. More likely, he would have come down the narrow alley behind the cabins on foot, then circled the office.

Someone calls from a distance, the cop stationed at the Baxter Boulevard entrance to the motel. He's waving us over. Past him, on the other side of the tape, I can just make out the windshield wipers of an SUV as they pass before Chief Black's jowly face.

"At least he didn't drive onto the parking lot," Vern observes.

Chief Black didn't drive onto the lot, as it turns out, because Patrolman Jerome Meeks wouldn't let him.

Meeks did his job, but he isn't happy. "You told me not to let anyone onto the parking lot. No matter what. Only

I think the chief's really pissed off." He looks down at his feet for a minute. "I just had a kid, Lieutenant, and I really need this job. I mean, we're in a damned depression."

The chief's mouth is so tight his lips have vanished altogether. Me, I don't think he's mad at Patrolman Meeks. The chief woke up believing the arrest of Bradley Grieg's killer was imminent. Just find the woman in the video. Now he's got three murders to explain, and we've yet to identify the woman. Worse yet, an election for mayor will be held in November. New mayor, new police chief.

"Talk to me, Delia."

"Two dead, Chief. Executed."

"The Gaitskills?"

"Mother and son. Plus, we found what's probably a half ounce of meth in a file cabinet. That and a little over seventeen thousand in a paper bag."

"That's a lot of money to be lying around."

"Not if one of them stole it from Bradley."

The chief's eyes close for a moment. When they open, I glimpse the relentless detective he must have been. "The methamphetamine, Vern. Did you perform a field test?"

"No, but—"

Black waves off whatever Vern planned to say. "Did you find what you believe to be methamphetamine with the money?"

"The meth was downstairs, in the office." My turn, now. I can't let Vern take the heat. "The money was in an upstairs closet."

"And you think what, exactly?"

"That Richard took it from Bradley. But it's only a theory. Richard had tracks on the inside of his left arm. Not hard-core junkie, Chief. More like weekend warrior. So late that night, maybe after mom's asleep, he takes a walk up to Cabin 909 and finds Bradley nodding out on the bed. The money's sitting there in that snakeskin bag and Richard can't resist."

"Does he kill Bradley?"

"Maybe. But that's not the only consideration. The Schmidts are claiming that Bradley's killer took money that belonged to them. By this time, one of the Schmidts, probably Connor, has checked out the video at Randy's. They've seen the woman in the hat, watched her follow Bradley out the door. Think about where she stands in all this. She can't make restitution if she didn't steal the money, so if Connor finds her . . ."

The chief slaps his palm against the steering wheel, then suddenly turns off the wipers. He watches the windshield mist up for a good minute before he says, "What about the woman? What have you got?"

I bring up copies of the photos I left at the station and offer them to Chief Black without speaking. He slides his reading glasses over his nose and peers at the woman. "This the best you have?"

"Afraid so."

"But she was in the bar for thirty minutes."

"True enough, but we were lucky to get this much. She kept her chin down most of the time, and the hat covered a lot of her face. Plus, the cameras, all of 'em, are located high up on the walls. If there was even one mounted at head height, we'd have her cold, but they all look down."

"Okay, Delia, let's get real for a moment. For all we know, the money you found in the closet might have been there for weeks, or months. You've got no evidence tying the money to Bradley, or even to the methamphetamine you found in the office. If it *is* methamphetamine. More important, you didn't find the murder weapon in their apartment."

"Right."

"So let's stick with the woman. At least she's alive. Later on, if we hit a dead end, we'll pin it on Gaitskill. For now, keep your theory under your hat."

At this point I'm sufficiently pissed to blurt out a description of the muzzle-flash experiment Vern and I conducted a few hours ago. Chief Black is not pleased.

"You did this for what reason? No, wait, Delia, let me ask your partner. What was the point, Vern?"

"We're detectives, we detect."

Chief Black opens his mouth, but nothing comes out. He closes it again, then stares at the streaked windshield for a moment.

"What makes you think you reproduced the conditions exactly?"

The question's obviously directed at me, and I answer truthfully, "I can't be sure."

"And you can't be sure of what happened inside the cabin on the night Grieg was killed. There's no video, not even bad video."

"That's true."

Another pause, this one shorter. "Did you write this up, Delia? Is it in the files?"

"Not yet."

"Then don't." Black leans forward to restart the wipers. Time for his closing argument. "Something I don't get. This business with the money and your little experiment with muzzle flash, both of 'em help the defense no matter who we charge."

"Chief, I don't think she did it."

"Doesn't matter. We need to talk to her anyway." He reaches for the gearshift. Time to go. "As for the money, leave it where it is. Understand? The entire property is a crime scene. Seal it off. Nobody in the office or the living quarters or any cabin. Later, when we know where we stand, we'll do a close search and discover the money. And not a word to anyone in the meantime. Got it?"

"Yeah, Chief, I got it."

"How 'bout you, Vern?"

"Me, too, boss."

"Good. Our meeting for tomorrow morning is canceled. I'll be holding a press conference instead, and I want you there. That a problem?"

"Two things, Chief. First, Danny's home alone and I have to get to him. Second, my son's off to camp at nine o'clock. I won't be seeing him for a month, and it's his first time away from me. I need to be there when he leaves."

"Ten o'clock, then. On the dot. You, too, Vern."

# CHAPTER TWENTY-SIX

## DELIA

Between bites of banana pancake, Danny's examining photos of the woman in the hat. The pancakes are heavy and overcooked. Without the raspberry syrup they'd be as chewy as cardboard. Danny doesn't seem to mind. He's sitting close enough to touch me, and I have to think he's as nervous as I am. This is the first time we've been separated. He'll be all right, though. His best friend, Vern's son Mike, is also headed for camp, and the coordinator promised to keep them on the same team.

"She doesn't look like a killer," he says. The new murders have him super-hyped.

"Why not?"

"Cause she's . . ." He looks up at the ceiling. As he always does when he searches for answers. "She's too pretty."

"Prettier than me?"

"Mom, c'mon. You're not like that."

Danny's smart enough to know that his mother's messing with him. Smart enough to cut off the conversation. I watch him dig into his pancakes for a minute or two.

"Did she see the owners while she was there?" he finally asks. "You know, at the motel?"

"That would be Felice and Richard Gaitskill. I questioned both of them. They swore they'd never seen her before she turned up on the video. Remember, they couldn't identify her, and the video doesn't show her near the office."

"Do you think they were lying?"

"No."

"But someone killed them?"

"Yup."

"Well, if she killed the other one . . ."

"Bradley Grieg."

"Yeah, him. If she killed Bradley for money and she only just met him, why would she hurt the—"

"The Gaitskills?" I haven't told him about the money we discovered in the filing cabinet. We're keeping that to ourselves, Vern and I, as per the chief's instructions. But I can't imagine the woman in the hat killing Bradley, then leaving the money behind.

"Why would she come back to hurt them if they never saw her?"

There's no good answer to that one. If she somehow decided the Gaitskills had to go, she would have done it right after she killed Bradley. Instead of waiting two days.

That conclusion was reinforced when a Mexican family—two sisters, an aunt, and a nephew—showed up at seven, only a few minutes after I returned to the motel. With no choice, I delivered the facts of life. There'd never be another payday at the Skyview Motor Court.

They didn't react to the news. Just took it in stride. Nor did they react when I asked them to examine Connor Schmidt's photo, the one on his driver's license. True, they were hesitant at first, but when the older sister identified him, the others joined in.

Connor Schmidt was a regular at the Skyview. He always stayed in Cabin 909. He had his own key and regular visitors.

By then, a search of the alley had turned up a shoe impression. Very distinct, very fresh, and too big to be a woman's. I personally watched the state's CSU pour a mix of dental stone and water into the impression. I even waited for the cast to dry and be lifted out. Given the stakes, I wasn't prepared to take anything for granted.

Danny's sitting next to me, fiddling with the strap on his seat belt as we approach Roosevelt High School. We're close enough to see the line of yellow buses that will carry the children to camp. Danny's looking more nervous by the second.

"Do you think she did it?" he asks for the second time.

"C'mon, Danny, didn't I already answer that question?"

"Yeah, but . . . like if you don't think she did it, will you arrest her anyway?"

This is a question I prefer not to answer, and I respond with the answer to a different question. "Let me explain how it really works. Detectives gather evidence and hand it over to their superiors, in this case Chief Black. It's his job to pass judgment, not mine. If he orders me to make an arrest, I have to do it. I'm a worker, not a boss."

I don't add, Unless I quit.

Suddenly I'm wondering who I hope to convince. I'm still wondering as I lead Danny to a registration table. After the counselor checks him off, my son gives me an unexpected hug before rushing away. I'm still wondering as I slip behind the wheel and start the car. But then I take a moment to remind myself of the work still ahead.

Meanwhile, I miss him already.

The chief's out to make a statement. Mayor Venn, too. They're both standing on a low platform when I come up. The city's best podium has been placed at center front. It's made of walnut and polished to a high shine that reflects sunlight over the reporters in front. There's an easel as well, bearing something rectangular and flat that's covered with a gray cloth. I know what's underneath, and my heart sinks. I also know that I was right when I told my son that I was only a worker. And poorly paid at that.

I circle the platform but discover that I can barely climb the two steps. Vern doesn't look much better. He shrugs as I join him at the back edge of the platform. We're a pair, the two of us, me five-six, him six-four. Beside Vern, I seem almost a child. I know because I've seen news footage of us together.

Mayor Venn goes first. He's the what-happened half of the presentation. Murder one, on Saturday night at the Skyview Motor Court, a guest. Murders two and three last night at the same Skyview Motor Court. This time the owners. All shot, all executed, finally, with a bullet through the brain. This cannot be tolerated in a low-crime city like Baxter. The perpetrator or perpetrators will surely feel the wrath of the people. Eventually.

In full uniform, Chief Black follows the mayor to the podium. Standing ramrod straight, chest out, head thrown back. There's a comic element here, what with his stomach protruding so much farther than his chest. His fat ass doesn't help either.

There won't be any surprises, not today, but I have to show a modicum of interest while Chief Black recites the history of our heroic investigation. You'd think he was describing a group effort roughly the equivalent of D-Day. I doubt that the reporters are fooled. But they're tolerant enough, and reasonably patient. The show must go on.

Chief Black finally segues into the big reveal as the reporters straighten in their seats. A dozen flashbulbs pop when he yanks the cloth away to reveal the woman in her white hat. Or the lower half of her face, anyway.

"I want to emphasize that she is not a suspect, and there is no warrant for her arrest. She's a person of interest, and we're requesting anybody who recognizes her to call our hotline."

# CHAPTER TWENTY-SEVEN

## GIT

Desperately hoping for a burst of energy, I sit down at our dining table a few minutes prior to my interview. No such luck. My thoughts seem to crawl through my scrambled brain in no particular order. Call it passive resistance, or passive-aggressive. What I need is rest, and my brain doesn't want to hear about anything else. But it's too late to postpone the interview.

Out of nowhere, I recall my Granny Jo telling me about her father and brother returning to the mines after a deadly cave-in.

"Didn't have no choice," she insisted. "It was dig or die." Then she'd laughed. "Or more likely, dig *and* die."

My life isn't at risk, only my future as I set to work. I had installed Zoom on my computer about a year ago, when Sean decided to be a father instead of a deadbeat. His impulse lasted all of a month, during which he had three conversations with his daughter. Followed by nothing.

The only good thing to come out of the episode was that I learned to use Zoom, which I bring into play at ten o'clock, the appointed hour. A moment later, I'm staring at three faces, all female. Madison Klein introduces herself first. She's a middle-aged woman, with red hair bright enough to match her professional smile. Allison Fromm comes next. In her sixties, at least, she's the medical center's nursing director. Her smile is a good deal thinner than Madison's, but I'm not detecting hostility. More like wait and see.

The third woman is much younger, almost a girl, and I assume she's there to reassure me. Her name is Valentina Cepeda, and she's the first to speak after the introductions. "*Hola*, Bridget, how are you this morning?"

My response should be enthusiastic, but I can't work up the energy. I can't screw this up, either. That's because I've reached the point where escaping Baxter is all I can think about. The Resurrection Nursing Home, too. If patients lose it in a hospital, you've got instant backup, including hospital security officers who get paid to handle violent patients. I could have been seriously injured last night or even killed, and I know Lester will lose it again if he returns.

"I'm fine."

Madison picks up on my hesitation. "Are you okay, Bridget?"

"A little tired."

"Did you work last night?"

"Yes, at the nursing home."

"Rough night?"

"The worst, Madison. The absolute worst."

"Did someone pass?" This from Allison, the head nurse. "Did you lose somebody?"

"Yeah, you could say that. Someone *almost* passed."

"Someone close to you?"

"Yeah, I'd consider *myself* fairly close to me." I open up at that point, beginning with Lester's background. If there's any drama, though, it's in the words. My tone remains unemotional. Just the facts, ma'am.

"Lester's kept on one hundred mg's of pheno, four times a day, along with fifteen mg's of Zyprexa. That's enough to induce a stupor most of the time. But every couple of weeks . . ."

Valentina's mouth is hanging open before I even get to the part about the blood, the part about flying down the hall, retrieving the Ativan, confronting a psychotic who has the means to slice my throat in his hand.

Madison's reaction mirrors Valentina's. Her jaw drops so far I can see the back of her throat. But Allison Fromm only nods, and I know she's been there. She reminds me of a Resurrection patient who died a year ago after being infected with Covid-19. Teddy Wright had spent most of his adult life in the military before suffering a massive stroke at age fifty. He'd seen action in first and second Iraq, in Afghanistan, in Syria. Nothing, not even Lester at his worst, could shock the man.

"When I told Cesar to open the door and let him out, my heart was beating so hard I thought it was going to blow a hole in my chest. But I got lucky. Lester was almost through the episode before we opened the door. He was ready to be talked down, and that's basically what I did. I convinced him to drop the shard of glass, then drove the Ativan into his thigh before he could react. He was unconscious a few seconds later, but still pouring blood. I tore the rubber tubing off a blood-pressure cuff and used it as a tourniquet until the paramedics came. By that time, Lester's blood pressure had dropped to eighty over forty."

Madison can't hold it in. She raises both hands as she interrupts. "What about the RN? Didn't you tell me you were supervised by an on-site RN?"

"You mean Lena Proctor? She slept through the whole thing."

Madison and Valentina appear shocked, but Allison laughs until tears form at the corners of her eyes. "Let this be a lesson, Valentina," she says. "Right now, you work in a hospital where there's always help at hand. Later in life, you may find yourself in a situation where you have to rely on your own judgment." She turns her head slightly to look into the camera. "You come work for us, Bridget. We'll put you in our psych ward. That way you can deal with psychotics every night."

Now we're both laughing.

I find Mom outside when I leave the house. She's leaning against my car, puffing away, her gaze sharp enough to chip a diamond. I'm not expecting her to skirt the issue, subtlety being a skill unknown to her, and she doesn't surprise me.

"You kill him, Git?"

"How can you think that?"

"How? Do I have to remind you about trying to kill your husband? Remember Sean? You didn't miss by much, girl. A few inches one way or the other and he'd be over and done with."

"That was different. I was defending myself. Remember the cracked rib? The black eye? I had to make a point, Mom. The scumbag wanted to turn me into his slave."

Mom's always admired women who fight back, and she finally smiles. "Lemme see if I got this right. You didn't kill Bradley, but the cops think you did."

"I watched the press conference, Mom, and they don't even know who I am. They just want to talk to me."

"Then what keeps you from makin' a phone call, lettin' 'em know who and where you are?"

The question's reasonable, but I don't have a ready answer and I don't try to make one up. "I didn't kill Bradley Grieg, Mom. Him or anybody else."

"But you were at the Skyview, where he was killed by someone?"

I can almost see those twenties fluttering to the carpet as I open the car door. I can see the twenties, and I'm glad he's dead. I'm only hoping it hurt. "Yeah," I tell my mother. "I was there."

It's eleven o'clock that evening, and we're watching the local news, me and Zack. Or rather, Zack's watching the news. I'm watching Zack.

"Almost think I know her," he says. "Problem is she reminds me of just about everybody."

"Why do you think the cops want to find her? The chief didn't say."

"Word I got, they think she might've killed him. But she don't look like a killer to me. Looks like she's out to get laid." Zack pauses for breath. "What do they call them things? Pheromones? Feels like I can smell 'em from here."

"Maybe it happened by accident." I'm telling myself to keep my big mouth closed, but I can't. It's like I have to know. "The cops are saying that Grieg was robbed. So maybe what started as a hookup . . ."

No need to say any more. Zack gets the point, but he's shaking his head. "Passion's one thing, Git, but it's no small thing to kill a man cold. You got to have a nose for it. You got to have experience. Stealin'? Yeah, okay. But killin' is another thing. What I heard, somebody put a bullet through the back of Grieg's head while he was passed out. I can't see that girl there bein' the one who pulled the trigger and watched his brains splash against the pillow."

The pressure inside my pressure cooker of a brain finally overpowers me. I have to tell someone. I can't hold it in any longer. "Zack, it's me."

"What?"

"It's me, the woman in the photo." I'm searching for the right words, but the best I can do is repeat myself. "It's me."

Zack starts to speak, then checks himself. I watch his eyes soften. With regret? Sympathy? I only know that I can't stop now. I have to let it loose.

"Listen to me, Zack. I work seventy-two hours a week and take care of Charlie when I get home. On my one day off, I play catch-up, shopping, cleaning, cooking, taking Charlie somewhere special, even if it's only to a movie. This is my life, the life I chose. But once in a while, not even every month, more like every two, I need to get out. The sex is part of the draw, but only part. Mostly, I want to feel a man's eyes on me, a man wanting me. If the situation was reversed and a man—"

"Git, listen to an old fart who's been around. You're more than desirable. You're a fantastic woman, and you should have found a steady man long ago. I can't—"

"Attracting a man's not my problem. My problem's that I keep picking the *wrong* man. My whole life, from my first boyfriend to the last. If Bradley isn't proof of that, nothing ever will be." Suddenly I'm letting it all go. The bar, Bradley at the table, riding to the motel so horny I couldn't sit still, me bent over the dresser, the shower running, the twenties casually tossed in my direction. Then Bradley unconscious on the bed and that snakeskin bag.

"I shouldn't have looked. I even told myself not to look, to go home to Charlie and my real life, but I opened it anyway. I found a gun inside, lying on a pile of money." I turn now to face Zack. "A lot of money, Zack. Enough to change my life, mine and Charlie's."

"And you took it?"

"No, Zack, I didn't. Maybe I should have, what with everybody thinkin' I did. And I wanted to, that's for sure. Only it wasn't mine, and I just . . . Call me stupid, but I have this thing about earning my own way. Earning your own way is how you take charge of your life."

"So who took it? The cops?"

"Does it really matter? Like you said, once the cops went on the record about the motive being robbery, Connor Schmidt had to do something to somebody, and I'm the only somebody out there . . . Not that it matters."

# CHAPTER TWENTY-EIGHT

## CONNOR

'm on the road as soon as I finish breakfast with Mom. Headed for a truck stop ninety miles away on Interstate 80. I'm driving a Toyota Camry instead of my red Lexus, dark blue and three years old. My wardrobe is as dull as the car, a gray polo shirt with a little elephant on the breast, a pair of khaki slacks, and well-used white running shoes.

Anonymity is the goal, the whole, entire point, and a light but steady rain definitely helps. My car is just another hunk of metal cruising down one of the country's many interstates. No need to check this one out. The state troopers who pass me only glance in my direction. Here and gone.

Business is business, and the Schmidt crew stands to clear a cool five grand from the deal with Waylon. Assuming the prick has the money, assuming he's not bullshitting me. One thing sure, I won't accept any delay, not even a minute, and Waylon knows it. Screw me, and we'll never do business again.

Ninety miles is a long way to travel with two pounds of methamphetamine in the trunk, but I have no choice. The time and place were dictated to me last night by the seller. But I'm not really thinking about the job. I'm only a step away from accomplishing what I've wanted to accomplish for a very long time. But in what direction? When you have to involve cops as smart as Mariola, you can't count on trickery. You have to put them in a position where they have no choice except to play your game. You have to outgame them.

At one time, and not that long ago, bulk drug deals involved guns. Guns on both sides of the equation, the whole transaction an exercise in paranoia. That changed when I was introduced to my current suppliers. Outside of being Hispanic and able to supply just about anything I need, they're completely anonymous. I don't know the location of their base, if they have a base, or the names of the men and women who make the deliveries to a different location each time we do business. I place orders via text message through a preprogrammed burner phone they supply. A short time later, I receive a text message on the same phone telling me to be at a certain place at a certain time.

Me, I'm grateful. In the past, you never knew what you were getting, or that it wouldn't be a bullet. Now the price, the count, and the quality are always right. I'll take what

I'm given this morning and carry it directly to Waylon, no weighing or testing involved, a perfect middle. Here and gone.

I'm in the truck stop for less than five minutes. Long enough to spot the gray van, pull in beside it, open my trunk, watch a package that includes a new burner dropped into the well, finally make payment. Then I'm off, headed for a park ten miles from Waylon Longstreet's home. I suppose I should be worried. Waylon's not especially trustworthy, and he's got a big family. But my thoughts have already turned to the girl in the hat. I need to find her, and I think I will if I have enough time. I'm in a race with the cops.

Our guy on the job told me the released photo is the best they have. I find that amazing, but I watched the video myself. Maybe the bitch was inside Randy's for a long time, but she never raised her chin, and the fucking cameras were positioned high up on the wall. That means she was makin' sure nobody recognized her, which also means there were people in this town, people who might show up at Randy's, who knew her. She has to be local.

First things first. I'm driving through farm country, where most of the farms cover more than a thousand acres. Towns are few and far between, with the occasional cluster of small farms and even smaller businesses.

I don't know how Waylon and his extended family accumulated enough money to buy the meth they've been selling for the last ten years. I don't give a shit either. On the other hand, Waylon and his brothers and cousins take turns going to prison, and a rip-off is always a possibility. Which is why I stop a few miles outside of Whitson, the town Waylon calls home, and go into my trunk for the .45 semiauto hidden beneath the spare tire.

Better safe than sorry, but my precautions are a waste of time. Waylon meets me at an intersection, then follows me to a small park. Deserted in the rain, the park's little more than a collection of picnic tables and benches set before the only year-round stream in the county. In the movies, the buyer cuts open one of the bricks with a knife, then subjects the product to some kind of chemical test. But the Schmidts, father and son, play a different game. Our customers have twenty-four hours to return any product we handle. No questions asked. No testing allowed. Here and gone.

Believe it or not, my scumbag of a father is still unhappy. I'm handing over five grand, the take from a morning of work in which my old man played no part. In fact, the cartel, which is how I think of our supplier, has never spoken a word to Carl Schmidt. It's all Connor, all the time. I set it up and I make it work, but he gets the money. You'd think, at the least, I'd hear a thank-you as he peels off fifteen hundred, then drops the rest into a drawer. You'd be wrong.

"I seen that picture," he tells me. "The broad in the hat. Take this to the bank, Connor, somebody out there knows her. The assholes who drink at Randy's don't commute from Chicago. If she was deliberately keepin' her head down, she's gotta be from around here."

I ignore the fact that I've arrived at the same conclusion. "Sorry, but I was kinda busy this morning. I'll get back on it after lunch."

"What about yesterday?"

"I asked around, but I'm thinkin' she can't be ID'd from that photo. Not for sure."

"You didn't get a name?"

"No, Pop, I didn't get a name. But I sent Augie out this morning, and he came back with ten names. That's because you put out the word. Identify the girl in the hat and the Schmidts will reward you."

"Now what, you got an attitude?"

"No. What I have is orders to fill and a list of deadbeats we need to contact. Like, before they overdose."

"Okay, so forget the girl. Forget she robbed and killed your best buddy in the world. Just pay me the eighteen large and go about your business. And by the way, your cut of the deal this morning? Consider it a first payment on the debt."

I'm thinking that should be the end of it. No such luck. My old man's always had a gift for delivering one last punch.

"Them people at the Skyview, the ones got killed yesterday?"

"Yeah?"

"You have anything to do with that?"

"Not a thing, Pop. I was with Augie all night. Takin' care of your business."

# CHAPTER TWENTY-NINE

## DELIA

I t's eight o'clock in the morning, and I'm eating breakfast. Alone. When Danny's around, I cook. Eggs, bacon,
sausages, waffles, something to fill him up. The kid's
always hungry. Now I'm looking at a buttered corn
muffin. Not freshly baked, but dug out of a package I
bought yesterday at the city's only Kroger. I heated the
muffin in the microwave. Which did nothing to improve
its dense texture. At present, it's rapidly cooling on a
paper plate.

What I'm feeling is lonely. Danny's been part and parcel
of my daily life for twelve years. Long enough for some
part of my deluded brain to pretend that he'll always be a
child in need of parenting. In fact, he's showing an interest
in girls while he formulates vague plans for adulthood.
A baseball scholarship to college. A degree in computer

engineering if he's not drafted into the major leagues. A life apart from his mother.

Suddenly I'm watching myself a couple of decades from now. An aging dyke with a butch haircut, wearing a man-tailored shirt and chinos. Living alone.

You've been postponing. That's what I tell myself. Having a kid, working a full-time job? You can ignore lone-liness, maybe not even feel it. There's always something that needs to be done. Always someplace you have to be, a phone call you have to make, a suspect to be arrested. And that day of reckoning? I try not to envy straight people. I tell myself that the grass is always greener and heteros have problems of their own. But now I wonder what it would be like to have three or four kids, a dozen grand-children. How it would feel to bury myself in life for the duration of my own. And I have to ask myself if Danny's wife—and I know he's straight—will want me close to her children.

My phone interrupts this pity party. It's Vern. After the chief's grand revelation, we spent the rest of the day run-ning down the false leads that poured into the hotline. The only good news is that I'll get paid for wasting taxpayer dollars.

"I'm calling from the station," he says. "Where are you?"

I glance at the microwave's clock. It's eight fifteen. "I'm home, Vern, having breakfast. So what's up?"

"A call to the hotline just before it closed down last night. A woman."

"One call?"

"Nope, there were lots more, but this was the only call that mentioned the hat. The woman claimed that the hat looked familiar."

"That the word she used? Familiar?"

"Yeah, and that's as far as it got. She wanted to know if there was a reward. When she heard there wasn't, she hung up. But here's the thing. She called on a cell phone, and we have the number and her name." He hesitates for just an instant. "I thought you'd want to know."

"You're right about that. Give it to me."

"Isabelle Zanos. And she's got a record for petty crimes. Shoplifting, bad checks, like that. She lives in Oakland Gardens."

"Anything else?"

"Yeah. The bullets we recovered at the Gaitskill scene? I'm thinking the mayor pulled some strings, because the state lab compared those rounds with the bullet that killed Bradley Grieg. They were fired from the same gun."

Vern and I are on the way to Isabelle's, driving through a light but steady drizzle. I'm not dwelling on the task at hand. We'll hear whatever story she has to tell. Probably after a mild protest. No, I'm thinking about Bradley Grieg and the Gaitskills, especially about Richard's execution. The man was helpless, one leg shattered, staring up at his executioner. It took a cold heart to pull that trigger, a heart as cold as Connor Schmidt's.

"I still think we're being played, Vern."

"Played how, Delia?"

"Well, there's a big-time question out there. One the killer must've known we'd ask ourselves."

"Why use the same gun twice?"

"Yeah. If it was me, I would have used different guns, and both would be at the bottom of the nearest body of water."

"You think he wanted us to know, one perp for all three?"

"Yeah, I think he wanted us to know. He—not she."

The Oakland Gardens neighborhood where Isabelle resides is a notch above the Yards, but only a notch. And I'm not expecting even that small difference to persist, given the effects of the virus on Baxter's economy. Isabelle Zanos's ranch home nicely illustrates the changing reality. Decently constructed of brick, with a picture window in the living room, it's clearly in need of repair. The small porch sags to one side, and the flagstone walk has been raised in places by the roots of an enormous hickory.

The woman who answers our knock (the bell's broken) knows exactly who we are, a recognition born of long experience. But if I was anticipating an attitude, the woman merely steps back to allow us inside.

"I've been expecting you."

Isabelle's in her early thirties, a trim brunette with a hard-eyed smile that betrays a world of experience. She's not afraid of us, or even impressed. Inside, a manikin stands before a long, humpbacked sofa. The girl's dress on the manikin is pink. A party dress, for sure, with a scalloped collar, puffy short sleeves, and a hem trimmed with white lace. There's a little girl to go with the dress. She's sitting on the couch, staring up at Vern, mouth open.

"Go on outside, Sofia," the woman says, "and let me talk to these people."

Sofia circles Vern as she makes her exit, giving him plenty of room.

"Y'all wanna introduce yourselves?" Isabelle's accent is Southern. Not Kentucky or West Virginia Southern. More like Alabama.

"I'm Lieutenant Mariola, and this is Detective Taney. We're with the Baxter PD. I think you know why we came."

"Yes, ma'am. The call." She sits on the couch, picks up a roll of lace, and measures out a yard. "So how 'bout the reward? Y'all change your mind?"

"Fraid not."

"Then how do you plan to compete?"

"Compete?"

"With Connor Schmidt. Man put the word out before Chief Black showed that photo on TV. Identify the girl in the hat and the Schmidts will see you're taken care of."

Isabelle lured us out here for a reason, and there's nothing to be gained by opening my big mouth before she reveals it.

"I been knowin' Connor a long time, Lieutenant. He's worse than cruel. He's a man who'll hurt ya cold. That's why I didn't leave my name when I called that hotline. Connor told me he had someone in your department. A source, or a spy, take your choice. Anyway, if it ever got back to him that I spoke to you . . ."

Her voice trails away as she picks up a pair of scissors and cuts the lace in her hand. Isabelle's searching for the right words, or perhaps the right order. She looks back to me when she's ready to continue.

"My husband died in Iraq four years ago. An IED. Just now, I'm living on his death benefit and a survivor pension while I try to get my life together." She gestures to the dress on the manikin and nods. The dress is obviously well made, and I assume this is the *together* she's talking about. "I got into a passel of trouble right after Freddy passed, includin' a relationship with Connor Schmidt. It didn't last all that long, not after a court threatened to place Sofia in foster care. But I do have a good idea of who he really is."

"And that would be?" This from Vern.

"Connor ain't naturally mean, Detective. He's like ruthless, but it don't come from his heart. That's why his enforcer is a psycho named Augie Barboza. Augie likes hurtin' people. He'll hurt this woman if he finds her. Bad hurt, if you take my meaning."

"Augie Barboza?" Vern again. "I thought Bradley was Connor's main man."

"Bradley was more like Connor's dog. So, yeah, Bradley liked to strut, but that's all it was. Struttin'. Connor once told me that Bradley had the brain of a frog. He could barely run errands."

"Okay, Ms. Zanos, but why did you call us?"

"Because I'm hopin' you'll get to her first. Way it lines up, that's her only hope." She stops for a moment, long enough to form a soft smile. "Thing about it, and y'all are probably gonna be pissed, but I don't actually know who she is. It's the hat that looks familiar. See, there's a woman lives outside of town makes hats look like the one in the photo. Sells 'em on the internet." Isabelle points to the dress on the manikin. "Like I'm tryin' to sell my dresses. 'Cause times in Baxter are surely hard, and I got me a girl-child to raise."

# CHAPTER THIRTY

## CONNOR

T alk about a waste. Augie and I spend the day bouncing from informant to informant. The story's the same everywhere. Nobody recognizes the woman, but everybody knows someone who does. Or says they do. Or maybe told someone who told someone else they did. I finally give it up around four o'clock.

"This ain't workin', Augie. We have a business to run, and here we are spinnin' our wheels. What we did all day? It doesn't fatten our wallets by a counterfeit dollar bill."

Augie nods agreement, as usual. He's a yes-man, which I sometimes regret. But I'm not in the mood for an argument right now. Or even constructive suggestions.

"I'm gonna drop you off while there's still time to do your collections. As for the broad? I wanna find her, sure, but it won't be the end of the world if I don't. Meanwhile, I'm gonna get something to eat."

Forty minutes later I'm sitting in Maxwell's Courthouse Diner, in a back booth, enjoying one of Max's onion-ring bacon burgers. I'm not an inch closer to finding the girl in the hat, but the afternoon's brought an unexpected reward. A deadbeat lawyer who's been avoiding me for weeks not only paid the interest on his debt, he paid off the whole thing.

Kenny Beaumont likes cigars, the bigger the better. When he waved me to the curb, he was smoking one of them, a cigar that could have been mistaken for a blunt object. A few minutes later, as we drove along the perimeter of City Hall Park, he settled the debt.

"Sorry for the delay," he told me.

I don't ask how he came by the money, because I don't care. Beaumont's a degenerate sports bettor who borrowed from me in order to pay off his gambling debts. I lent it to him because he's a successful lawyer with the income to pay me back. He's also a shyster with connections inside the state CID.

"What are you hearin', Kenny, about Bradley?"

"Heard that he's dead."

"C'mon, man."

"They got just about nothin' in the way of usable physical evidence. It's a motel room, for Christ's sake. People are in and out of there all the time. You wanna talk fingerprints? They recovered dozens."

"So, they givin' up?"

"The hat, Connor. The hat is the egg in the basket, the only egg. You find the hat, you find the woman."

"Maybe, maybe not. Have you seen the photo of the girl?"

"Sure."

"So whatta ya think? You think they're gonna find her?"

"From that photo?" He shakes his head. "Look, I'm a criminal defense attorney. I have plenty of experience with photo IDs. Mostly, witnesses can't make an ID when they review full-face mug shots. And what do you have in that photo? A jawline, the side of a mouth, half a nose? Even if you do find her, you won't be sure."

"So what're you sayin? Give up?"

"Nope." He leans forward. "I'd say find someone who recognizes the hat. Hear me—anybody comes forward, if they don't mention the hat, they're full of shit."

I'm thinking that Kenny Beaumont's a prophet. I'm only halfway through my burger when a woman who looks more dead than alive plops her ass down on the seat across from me. She's thin to the point of gaunt, and her eyes are as yellow as buttercups.

"I know her," she tells me.

I don't ask who. There's no point. "I've been hearin' that for the past two days, lady, and I'm tired of the bullshit. Tell me how you know her."

"Maybe I put that hat on her head."

"Maybe?"

A waiter approaches our table, but I wave him away. I'm not buyin' dinner for this skank. No. I'm lookin' in her eyes and I'm not finding fear. Any fear. It's like she's been there, done that, and she's not walkin' it back.

"What's in it for me, Connor? I want a number."

"How 'bout I smash your teeth down your fucking throat. How'd that be for a number?" I was right. Her expression doesn't change. She's not gonna scare. "Five hundred, right now," I tell her.

I'm expecting a negotiation, but she doesn't say a word until she's on her feet and standing next to the table. "You're never gonna find her without me, Connor. But maybe you don't want to. Maybe I need to talk to your father. Think it over. I'll be in touch."

# CHAPTER THIRTY-ONE

## DELIA

According to Isabelle Zanos, Henrietta Taunton lives on a small organic farm about thirty miles west of Baxter in the town of Charleston. Henrietta, Isabelle insists, participates in a new, entrepreneurial economy, one certain to replace the outdated employer-employee model. I've heard this song before, especially since the virus took its toll on the economy, and I'm not buying the hype. But you've got to pin your hopes on something, and I pay attention when Isabelle describes meeting Henrietta at a class on website design, then hauls out her laptop.

Henrietta's website pops up within a few seconds, and I find myself staring at a page titled *MAGIC WITH LACE*. The hats on the page have been treated with a secret process (patent pending). The process allows them to remain shaped after you adjust them to suit your own sense of style.

No question, some of those hats closely resemble the hat we're looking for. That makes a trip to Henrietta's Hattery more or less mandatory. But not right away. As Isabelle describes Henrietta and her business, I receive a text from a city prosecutor. A search warrant for Bradley Grieg's apartment has been signed by a judge. I need only pick it up at the station.

Okay by me, because I'm pretty sure a trip out to Henrietta's will be a waste of time. Not that I'm expecting much from a search of Grieg's apartment, but it's a lot closer.

Energized, I settle into my work. I'm a cop again, which is all I ever wanted to be. I had a friend in high school, a real bookworm who read novel after novel. Why? Because she just had to know how the story turned out. That's the way I feel about serious investigations, especially when I can't be sure of the outcome. The cliché is that cops hate mysteries. Me, I love 'em.

Grieg's apartment is in a complex of attached town houses a block away from the north end of Baxter Park. Living room, dining room, kitchen on the first floor, two decent-size bedrooms on the second. In the living room (reasonably clean to my surprise), three enormous recliners face a large flat-screen TV. A Formica-topped table that might have come out of a 1950s tract home sits dead center in the dining area. The only decorations are predictably simple—two posters in the living room. Both are of obscure rock bands, Lucifer's Friend and Yesterday's Children. A bookshelf behind the couch holds several dozen heavy metal CDs, but no books.

A plastic box hidden beneath the bed upstairs contains 20-gauge syringes. Taped to the underside of a newish dresser, a full ounce of brown powder that will reveal itself to be heroin when field tested. A snub-nosed Colt, a Police Special, rests atop a manila envelope containing three thousand dollars. A silk robe patterned with birds and flowers dangles from a plastic hanger in the bedroom closet. The robe's exquisite. I'd be tempted to bring it home if it wasn't size XXL.

Vern and I transport the heroin, the gun, and the money back to the evidence room at the station. We're still doing paperwork when I receive a call from our DA, Tommy Atkinson. As usual, his tone is engaging and friendly.

"Hey, Delia, how's it goin'?"

"Slow, but steady."

"You find that woman yet, the one in the hat?"

"No, but finding her isn't what has me worried. It's whether she pulled the trigger."

A pause here. In Baxter, the DA's elected by the people, and Tom Atkinson's a seasoned politician. "You don't think she did it?"

"At this point, I can't clear the woman, but we know Grieg and the Gaitskills were killed two days apart with the same weapon, so it's very unlikely that the woman even killed Bradley. But that she returned two days later to assassinate the Gaitskills? Who swore they never laid eyes on her? Tommy, it just doesn't work. It doesn't work, and I think you know it." I'm talking really fast, but I want to get it all out there. "And there's another problem, too. The chief's already told the public that robbery was the likely motive for Grieg's murder. So what was the motive for killing the Gaitskills two days later, if our person of interest committed the murders?"

Instead of the argument I'm expecting, Tommy laughs into the phone. "You're amazing, Delia, but you don't have to convince me. That's because I've got a woman here, arrested for second-degree assault. Her name's Marjorie Carver, and this is her third strike. She's looking at fifteen years."

"Let me guess. She wants to make a deal."

"Yup, her and her lawyer. And you know what? She's claiming to be Carl Schmidt's mistress."

"Not Connor's?"

"Nope, the daddy, not the son."

# CHAPTER THIRTY-TWO

## DELIA

The district attorney's offices are housed in the courthouse, by far the most impressive building in the city. Its red sandstone blocks are enormous, and its three floors stretch from Monroe to Madison streets, with just enough room for a pitted statue of Thomas Jefferson out front. A central tower rises an additional six stories to loom over this flatland city. It speaks to a past when folks in Baxter shared an unchallenged optimism. The good times would last forever. Progress could not be stopped. Any differing opinion was un-fucking-American.

Maybe progress can't be stopped, but it can definitely take a hike. In earlier days, the courthouse's many offices were the exclusive domain of city workers. That ended twenty-five years ago, when the size of Baxter's government began to shrink. Offices were rented out, mostly to lawyers doing business with the city, but even that wasn't enough to keep the building fully occupied. Today, the two upper floors on the west side of the building are entirely empty.

District Attorney Atkinson's suite of offices, by contrast, reflect the fact that he's one of the wealthiest men in the city. Large wooden desks with scalloped edges dominate his outer office. Oil paintings on the walls depict racing yachts in competitions that took place fifteen hundred miles away. On the floor, stretching from wall to wall, an ankle-deep carpet receives my feet as though preparing to ingest them.

Tommy Atkinson's sitting on the edge of his personal assistant's desk, but he rises and offers his hand when Vern and I come through the door. His grip is cool, firm, and quick, a politician's handshake.

"Quickly," he begins. "The woman in question is Marjorie Carver, age thirty-two. Did a year for a string of burglaries at nineteen, then two years for armed robbery in her mid-twenties. Two weeks ago, she smacked another woman in the head with a beer bottle at the Dew Drop. Knocked her cold, then stomped her."

"Got it. So what's Marjorie asking for?"

"For starters, that we reduce her bail from fifty thousand dollars to a thousand. She wants out immediately, and we can discuss the rest later."

"And she's been inside for what? Two weeks?"

"Yup, that's the deal. Marjorie wants out."

I glance at Vern. He's already smiling. If she plans to snitch on Carl Schmidt, having her bail reduced is the last thing Marjorie Carver should demand. A sudden release is the sure mark of an informant. No, what Marjorie should do is stay in jail while she trades information for years taken off her sentence. And Marjorie's no beginner. She knows the system, knows what could happen to her if Carl Schmidt decides she's a liability.

"Lead on, Tommy."

Marjorie Carver stands up when we enter the room. She has narrow hips and breasts large and firm enough for me to assume they've been enhanced. Devoid of makeup, she appears washed out, her complexion empty and dull. This despite her raven-black hair and brittle blue eyes.

By her side, a protective arm on the back of her chair, Marjorie's lawyer evaluates me through owl-eye glasses. Lorimer Taub's been around for decades. He's the shyster of choice for well-heeled defendants throughout the county.

Tommy introduces me and Vern, a waste of breath. Marjorie's casual glance is purely evaluating. She knows who we are.

Taub nods to me. "Lieutenant Mariola, how have you been?"

"Fine, and you?"

"Never better."

As we've faced off against each other several times when I had to testify, the exchange is formal. Taub returns his full attention to Tommy. "What's said here, it's strictly off the record until we reach an agreement. Right, Tommy?"

"Understood."

"Now, I've heard my client's story, and I'm telling you that it's not only big, there's no way you could have gotten it on your own." He glances in my direction for just a moment. "You and I, Tommy, we've known each other a long time. I wouldn't be sitting here if I didn't believe my client. I have better things to do. So I want you to tell me you'll push for lower bail if I make good on my claim."

Tommy pretends to think about it for a few seconds, then says, his tone suitably solemn, "You have my word."

Taub sits back in his chair, and Marjorie Carver leans forward to settle her elbows on the table. Pinched to begin with, her mouth tightens, the corners pushing inward. Defiance is what I'm reading. Fuck you and your self-righteous judgments.

"I'll come right out with it. I'm Carl Schmidt's girlfriend. I been his girlfriend for the past two years."

"Girlfriend?" Vern jumps in. "Not mistress?"

"What's the difference, Officer?"

"I'm a detective, not an officer. And there's definitely a difference between independent and kept. So, which were you?"

Marjorie returns Vern's steady gaze for a few seconds before caving. "Carl paid the rent and helped me out from time to time. So what?"

Vern merely signals for her to continue. His message is plain enough. Whatever you plan to say, say it plain.

"Carl, he don't usually show up without calling. Like he's jealous anyway, and he thinks he might find me with another man. But I ain't no whore. I got a daughter and a son, twins, and I'm raisin' 'em as best I can. I got a job, too, at Baxter Packin'. Only it don't pay the bills, not when I got to fork out for childcare. Those children are still babies, and I couldn't bring myself to leave 'em with the lady up the street. No, I put 'em in professional childcare, *licensed* childcare, and that costs big time."

Taub lays a bony hand on his client's elbow. You can drop a sad story on a judge and hope for mercy, but not on prosecutors or cops.

"All right, Lori. I got it." Marjorie turns her attention, not to Tommy, but to me. "So that's how it's been these last two years. Couple times a week, Carl pays a visit. But he don't just show up. He always calls ahead, except for last Saturday around midnight, when he knocked on my door without callin'. Well, you could believe me when I say the man was upset. Me too, when I seen that gun tucked into his belt. I said, `What's that?' He said, `That's a Glock.' Then he took it out and showed it to me, but I wouldn't lay a finger on it. I said, `That ain't what I meant, Carl. I mean what's it doin' in your belt?'" Carl, he just laughed. "'You'll hear about it soon enough, but right now I need to work off a little steam. Why don't you slip into the nightie I bought you last week?'"

Marjorie finally grinds to a halt, and I have to admit that the woman's convincing. The nightie detail especially. Now she looks at her lawyer for a moment. Finish or wait for the DA to commit? Taub nods once, then again.

"Next day, Sunday, Carl phones me. He wants to come by. I heard Bradley was dead by then." Relaxed now, Marjorie clears her throat. "I knew Bradley and Connor from around town, knew they was best buddies. So it didn't come as no surprise when Carl said the same thing, that Bradley and Connor was so tight, there was no pryin' 'em apart." Marjorie stops abruptly, her eyes narrowing. She looks at me like I'm supposed to understand. Like we're talking woman-to-woman. "Carl told me that Bradley was soft, a junkie with no future and sure to snitch if he got busted, which, bein' a junkie, he definitely would. Carl wanted to know why his own son couldn't see what was right in front of his face—"

Vern again interrupts. "Did Carl Schmidt tell you that he killed Bradley Grieg?"

"No, but he complained about Connor. Told me he had to handle the situation by himself. Connor, he wasn't good for much, according to Carl. But when it came to Bradley, Connor was a complete asshole. 'There's times,' Carl said, 'when a man's gotta take matters in his own hands.'"

It's ten o'clock, and I'm chilling out with a second beer when my phone rings. It's Danny, calling from camp. "I miss you, Mom," he says right out of the box. "I'm having fun, but I miss you."

"I miss you, too, but are you supposed to be making this call? Whose phone are you using?"

"One of the other kids." He quickly changes the subject. "It's nice here, and I'm learning a lot, but like . . ."

"Like . . ."

"I don't know. I just miss you, Mom. Did you arrest anyone yet?"

"No, but there's big things happening."

"See, that's just it. I wish . . . Shit, I gotta go."

I set the phone down on the table next to my chair. Despite my being a complete asshole, my son loves me. I look at the beer in my hand and realize that I'm grinning like an idiot. I've spent most of my life avoiding dependency. No long-term relationships. No emotional commitments. Hookups, instead. Hookups and a bad attitude.

I stare down at the phone for a few minutes, willing it to ring again. It doesn't.

# CHAPTER THIRTY-THREE

## GIT

An hour after I get home, I put in a call to Madison Klein at Short Hills Medical Center. I tell her, Yes, I'll come if living arrangements can be made for me, Charlie, and my mother. I don't really make a decision about Mom. No, what I do is look into her yellow eyes and admit that she can't survive without help. Nor me, if truth be told, without her. I tell myself that we're locked into a joint child-raising partnership that can't be dissolved. Maybe later, when Charlie's old enough to be a latchkey child. Not now.

"I'm really glad to hear that," Madison says. "Allison Fromm liked you very much."

I thank Allison, thank Madison, then collapse onto my bed.

Eight hours later I'm slipping into the pair of no-nonsense walking shoes, about to head for Zack's, when I receive an email from Madison with a link to an apartment complex in Short Hills. Paramount Village is a basic yellow-brick cube, but its borders are planted with bright red flowers and there are trees between the sidewalk and the street. Better yet, the local schools are rated AAA, at least according to Paramount.

On separate web pages, I explore a pair of model apartments, a two-bedroom and a three. With Mom along, I can surely use the extra space, but the three-bedroom's renting for twenty-four hundred dollars, the two-bedroom for seventeen hundred. That's in comparison with the three-bedroom house I'm currently renting for eight hundred per.

Moving on, I tell myself. That's the whole point. Once the move is made, I'll find a way to iron out the small wrinkles. I fill out an online application for the smaller unit before I can change my mind. True, I don't have a formal offer from Short Hills yet, but I'm not worried about that end of the deal. I'm more annoyed than anything else. If you want to rent an apartment in New Jersey, you have to reveal everything about your life short of when you last trimmed your toenails.

Mom's standing behind me when I shut down the computer. I tell her we'll have to share a bedroom for a few months. I need time to get established at the medical center before we can afford a bigger place. More than likely, even if I start immediately, it'll be a few weeks before I complete orientation and receive my first paycheck.

Mom's not having it. Now that she's sure that she's coming along, her attitude has changed. "You ain't tole me yet what happened between you and Bradley," she says.

"Sorry, Mom. I just assumed you were old enough to figure it out for yourself."

"Cute, Git, but the physical part don't interest me."

"Then what does?"

"Connor's been everywhere, offering a reward for the identity of the girl in the hat. That's the way he's puttin' it. The girl in the hat."

"Is there something new here, Mom? Because I'm late for work."

"Connor's lettin' something else slip, too. He's not just out to revenge his buddy. That's 'cause most likely he's the one killed Bradley. No, Connor's sayin' the woman took somethin' from Bradley, somethin' that belongs to Connor, and Connor wants it back." Mom stops long enough to put her hand on her hips. She hits me with her most aggressive stare. "You steal from Bradley, Git?"

I can see those twenties again, Bradley's twenties. They start for my face, then stop midway, suspended for an instant before making their way to the carpet. Bradley's words follow as they begin their descent: "Fuck off."

"No, Mom, I didn't."

Mom grasps the implications immediately. "Then you can't give it back."

"No, I can't. And don't ask me who took the money. Bradley was passed out, and it was raining like hell when

I left. Zack, by the way, thinks maybe the cops took the money. But it could have been anyone."

"Okay, Git, but Connor ain't lookin' for anyone. He's lookin' for you. And if he can't find you himself, the cops'll do it for him."

Miranda has prepared dinner, and it's already on the table when I walk in forty minutes late. Chicken enchiladas in salsa verde, accompanied by a watercress salad. There's also a bottle of wine on the table, but no glass in front of Zack's place setting. Miranda's a rule-bound caregiver. If the doctor says no alcohol for Zack, there's no alcohol for Zack. Later on, I'll pour him a small glass. For right now, I'm trying to understand exactly why we're celebrating.

We're not, as it turns out. We're conducting a wake. Baxter Packing will shut down a month from now. The announcement came this afternoon, and I'm hearing it for the first time. It's like standing in a courtroom and having a judge announce the city's execution date.

"Mayor went on the air an hour ago," Zack explains. "Told us not to panic. Told us we'd have to reinvent ourselves. We can do it because we're Baxterites and we don't give up." He pauses long enough to laugh. "But maybe it ain't that far-fetched. See, Baxter's been an urban enterprise zone, state and federal, for the past five years. Nothin' come of it so far, but folks I know are tellin me there's money from the state capital takin' a look at property in the Yards. So maybe . . ."

Not even remotely hungry, I barely pick at my food. I want to talk about Connor Schmidt. Now that I've decided to leave Baxter, I realize that my family's escape is about a lot more than money. I want to put miles between Charlie and the Yards. I want her to breathe air that doesn't smell of the killing floor. I want her to grow up in an environment that encourages success, but I'm thinking that Mom's right. We'll never be free as long as Connor and the cops are after the girl in the hat. I can't just wait for the hammer to fall.

Zack mutes the TV. He's watching a Cardinals game, and the Cards are on the wrong end of a six-to-one score. "Heard somethin' interestin' this afternoon," he says. "The cops ain't lookin' at that woman, the one in the hat, for killing Connor and the others. They got their eye on somebody else. You might be off the hook far as the cops are concerned."

"And who would that be? The one they're looking at?"

"Don't know, Git. I'm thinking Connor Schmidt, but it could be anyone."

"Anyone except the woman in the hat."

"Yeah, you could say that, but it don't help her all that much. See, Bradley Grieg was an idiot. He might have said anything to the woman, including who he was gonna meet up with later on."

"But he didn't, Zack. I swear."

"I believe you, Git, but the cops don't know that, and they'll be lookin' for you, innocent or not. You're a loose end, which is not something the cops and prosecutors are prepared to tolerate. The Schmidts, either."

I look over at a glass-fronted cabinet holding a collection of exotic geodes whose names I can't remember. A rainbow of colors, the collection was put together by Zack's wife, Elisabeth. A wedding photo sits on the cabinet's top shelf. Zack looks a bit on the mean side, but Elisabeth's actually stunning. A dark-haired beauty with exotic features that might have been drawn from a runway model.

"Zack, I have to go."

"Now?"

"Me, Charlie, and Mom. We're leaving Baxter, permanently." My tone, I realize with a start, is almost angry. Somehow, love, betrayal, and resentment are whirling around each other, emotions I can neither sort out nor banish. It was Zack's money, after Franky Belleau took off with my bank account, that kept me and Charlie from becoming homeless. "I'm going to work in a hospital. In New Jersey."

Zack looks at me for a minute. "I'll miss you, girl."

"Well, it's your own fault. If you hadn't given me a recommendation, they wouldn't have called me."

"Fault? The last thing I want is for you to stick around and decay with this city. You take your little girl and start over while you're still young enough to pull it off. I'll get along."

"With what? Those assholes from the agency?" I tend Zack three nights a week. The rest of the time his nurses come from an agency. He sees new faces all the time, and most are just out of nursing school.

"Honey, I been takin' care of myself for a long time. So, like I said, I'll get along. And I'll feel better about it knowin' you're movin' up in the world. Lord knows, you deserve a break." Zack reaches out to put a business card in my hand: HAROLD MORTON, ATTORNEY-AT-LAW. "The cops grab you, don't tell them anything. Hear me? Call the lawyer on that card, mention my name, tell him you've been pulled in by the cops. Morton's based in Chicago, but he has connections all through the region, and I throw him a lot of business. He'll have someone down there in a big hurry."

"You think he'll get me out?"

"From what I hear, the cops're lookin' at you as a witness. They might threaten to arrest you, but they won't do it, because that would undercut the case they're building against someone else. But—"

"But there's Connor, too."

"Connor and his old man. As to what I'm gonna do about that?" Zack looks down at his hand for a moment. "Once upon a time I had the right connections to handle problems like this. Now, I don't know."

# CHAPTER THIRTY-FOUR

## DELIA

We ride up to Carl Schmidt's house—all workers, no bosses. Chief Black stays home. Likewise, District Attorney Atkinson. They don't want to be around unless the warrant produces something of value. That's not the outcome they expect.

Marjorie Carver gave us enough information to secure a search warrant for Carl Schmidt's property and vehicles. Good only because Schmidt has no residences or offices anywhere else. But the odds against the man hanging on to the weapon after killing three people are long indeed. That's the reasoning, anyway. Me, I know better. We're playing a game Connor Schmidt expects to win.

It's ten o'clock and already hot. A sneak preview of the dog days to come. By noon, with the sun almost straight overhead, the temperature will be above ninety. If our search was limited to an air-conditioned house, that wouldn't be a big deal. But our warrant includes the two-acre property and its multiple outbuildings.

There are ten of us crammed into a pair of SUVs and a patrol car. The SUVs are G-man black, purchased from the feds with money supplied by the feds. The chief ordered this show of force. We're going to confront a gangster, he pointed out, who won't know our business until we ring his bell. And neither will any subordinates who've stopped in for a cup of coffee.

The precautions turn out to be unnecessary. We ride up a curving driveway and approach Schmidt's two-story colonial without incident. Carl Schmidt answers the door himself. His first reaction at finding ten armored and helmeted cops staring at him is shock. Replaced almost instantly by righteous outrage.

"What the fuck do you want?"

The man's all torso, with broad, tapering shoulders and slightly bowed legs. His eyes are small and bright, and I assume his life is about intimidation. My initial impulse is to smack the outrage off his face. Instead, I respond matter-of-factly. The game's playing out as expected. I can say that because the one thing I'm not finding in Carl's reaction is fear. He's a man with nothing to hide.

"I'm Detective Lieutenant Mariola, and I have a search warrant for the property."

"You have what?"

"A search warrant for the property and your vehicles, sir." I pass him a copy of the warrant, which he reluctantly accepts. "Please step aside."

"What the fuck you think you're gonna find?"

"Sir, if you don't step aside, I'm going to take you into custody for interfering with a police investigation."

I motion with my hand, a gentle wave. Vern moves forward, along with several uniformed officers holding batons. For just an instant Carl seems about to resist, but then he backs into the house. Dashing my hopes.

"I'm gonna call my lawyer," he mutters between clenched teeth.

"Excellent idea."

I step into a large open-plan room with a kitchen at the far end. Off to my left, a middle-aged woman stands next to an enormous sectional couch. The woman is tall and slender, with a willowy neck and a little button of a chin. She's the only other person in view.

"Your name, ma'am?"

"Adele Schmidt."

My squad has already fanned out, two men headed up the stairs, but I still ask the relevant question. "Is there anybody else in the house?"

"No . . . not in the house."

"On the property?"

"Connor, my son. He's in the cottage."

"The cottage?"

"Yes. We have a small cottage on the property. That's where he lives."

"Not here, in this house?"

"He comes over for breakfast sometimes, but he lives in the cottage."

Her tone is so flat, I'm sure the line's been rehearsed. Just like I'm sure the mayor, the police chief, and our beloved prosecutor will be smiling by the end of the day. Mission accomplished.

My unit clears the house while I hang out in the living room with the Schmidts. Then I issue orders I can only hope my men will obey.

"Wait here in the living room until I round up Connor. Don't touch anything, and make sure they stay on the couch." I point to the Schmidts. "By the book, all right? You can expect a lawyer to show up before we finish."

But maybe not. As Vern and I head off to find Connor Schmidt, I hear his daddy shout into the cell phone he's holding an inch from his mouth. "Whatta ya mean you got a conflict of interest? You're my fuckin' lawyer. You have to represent me."

Despite the building heat, the walk across the Schmidt property is pleasant. The scattered trees throw lacy shadows onto the grass and there's a rose garden behind the main house. Even past peak, the red-on-red blossoms are as big as my hand.

We make only one stop along the way. To instruct a pair of landscapers to leave the property. Latinos both, they clear out in a hurry when they see our badges. I watch until they drive off, then lead Vern to Connor Schmidt's door.

Cottage is the right word for Connor's home. White stucco walls, a tile roof with a rounded peak, about the size of a two-car garage. There's even a Dutch door, both halves closed.

Connor answers on the second knock. He's wearing pajama bottoms and scratching at his scalp. He wants us to think we've roused him from sleep, but his gaze is too intense. For sure, his adrenals are pumping.

"Hi, Connor." I extend a copy of the search warrant.

"What's that?"

"A search warrant for the property. You can read it or not. Your choice, strictly. The search is going to happen either way." I skip a beat, letting the message penetrate. "Is there anyone else inside? Girlfriend, boyfriend?"

Connor bristles. I'm disrespecting him, and not for the first time. But he pulls himself together. "No. I been home alone since last night."

"Fine." I nod to Vern, and he goes inside. That leaves me and Connor standing face-to-face. Connor's bare chested. Part of the show? Or is he just showing off? Connor's big across the chest, and his arms are well defined. He appears as powerful as his father, but more in proportion. A ragged scar on his left breast adds character.

"Am I under arrest?"

"Just stay where you are. I'll tell you what comes next when I'm ready."

We stand there staring into each other's eyes until Vern emerges a couple of minutes later.

"Nothing," he says.

"All right. So, Connor, you have anything you want to tell me?"

"About what?"

"About Bradley Grieg. About Felice and Richard Gaitskill."

"I don't know anything about that."

"Okay, then how 'bout tellin' me where you hid the gun that killed them?"

"I didn't hide any gun."

"Fine, tell me where your mother hid it." I shake my head. All part of the game. "Put on something decent, Connor. You don't want your mama to see you this way. She might get the wrong idea."

Back in the house, I set Connor, his mom, and his dad on the big couch in the living room. Then I make their options clear. They can leave the property altogether, though not in the Cadillac or the Lexus parked in the driveway. Or they can remain on the couch to enjoy some family time.

"If your cars are locked," I finish, "best give me the keys. Otherwise I'll have them towed to where a locksmith can get at them."

The keys collected, I point at the Dink. That would be John Meacham, who's holding the video camera. "You come with us, John. The rest of you fan out on the first floor. If you should discover anything of value, don't move it. Lay down a marker and wait for it to be videotaped in place."

Do the assholes understand? Does it matter? I very much doubt that we'll find incriminating evidence on the first floor. That's because anything found, say in a drawer, could belong to Carl or Adele. And that wouldn't do. That wouldn't do at all.

# CHAPTER THIRTY-FIVE

## DELIA

Vern and I find three bedrooms upstairs, two of which appear to be guest rooms created from a catalog. Each contains a pair of single beds, a wing chair, a padded rocking chair, a small bureau, and a closet. Not even used for storage, closets and bureaus are empty.

By the book, leave no wiggle room. I order the Dink to video the rooms anyway, including the empty drawers and closets. Meacham grumbles, even this small job taxing his commitment to the craft of policing. But I'm in a good mood and so is Vern as we head for Carl and Adele's bedroom.

"Hard or easy?" Vern asks.

"Hard enough to make it look good. Easy enough to make sure we find it."

"What are you talkin' about?" This from the Dink.

Vern looks at me and smiles. You could lecture John Meacham for the next year and he still wouldn't get it. Myself, I don't think he has enough nerve endings to feel the itch inspired by a setup. But Vern and I both felt that itch when Marjorie Carver made her little proffer. Unless encouraged by a higher authority—or someone aspiring to higher authority—she would have offered up every deviant known to her before giving up Schmidt.

Of one thing I'm certain, whoever decided to use the same weapon on Grieg and the Gaitskills had a third use for it. And the shoe print in the alley behind the Skyview? Even at the time, I'd thought it a bit too perfect.

Carl and Adele's bedroom has two of everything, including two full-size beds. More important, there are two dressers and two large closets. Women's clothing fills one of the dressers and one of the closets. The other closet and dresser hold only men's clothing.

We begin with Carl's bureau. I don't expect to find anything here, and though I'm not disappointed, I'm intrigued by a rainbow of bikini underpants. I wonder who Carl wears them for, his wife or Marjorie. But the answer is obvious. Marjorie is an earthy woman, fleshy, sensual, and hot-tempered. Adele Schmidt is so distant she might have come down from the moon. Or be preparing to return.

Carl's closet is next on the list—ground zero, or so I'm hoping. I might be wrong, of course. Maybe I'll find nothing. Maybe we'll leave empty-handed. Word on the street is that Carl Schmidt doesn't participate in his operation's day-to-day activities. And while he wouldn't hesitate to eliminate a liability, he wouldn't do it himself. So why would he have a gun, a gun used in three homicides, in his bedroom?

"Video the entire closet, John. Then follow us closely as we do the search. Is the time and date stamp functioning?"

"Yeah."

"Then keep the camera running. No gaps, right? Every second accounted for."

"All right, I got it."

The whiny tone's not exactly reassuring, and I reinforce the message. "You fuck this up, I'm gonna think you were paid to fuck it up. And I know Schmidt has a spy in the department." I watch his head jerk back. Is it him? The question's irrelevant at this point, but I won't forget. "You need to cover your ass, John. That's because everyone's watching, from the mayor on down. So do the job I'm asking you to do. No fuckups, no excuses. I need to account for every second we spend in that closet."

Meacham nods acceptance, and I go to work on a couple dozen shoes paired together on the floor. The pair I want isn't hard to find. Most of the shoes are flat-soled loafers or lace-ups. There are only two pairs of athletic shoes, and only one pair specked with mud. Very common New Balance cross-trainers, this pair well worn. The soles are rubbed almost smooth at the edge of the heels, and the toes are scuffed.

"That's it." Vern points to a diamond-shaped insert on the sole that extends from the heel to the ball of the foot. "The insert. It's on the print."

Good news, but there's still the gun to be found. With Vern peering over my shoulder, making suggestions from time to time, I go through the closet. The process is tedious but thorough. Each garment is taken down and carefully examined. I explore every shoe, jamming my fingers into the toes. I don't stop until the closet is empty except for a set of matching suitcases and a duffel bag on the shelf. There are six pieces altogether, from the duffel bag to a giant, hard-sided case that reminds me of a steamer trunk.

The smaller ones come off the shelf first. I examine each in turn, with Meacham recording every move, until only the largest remains. It's heavy enough, when I pull it down, to slip through my hands and fall to the carpeted floor. The suitcase makes a solid thump when it hits, but the sound isn't loud enough to disguise the scrape of a heavy object sliding across the bottom.

"Bingo." This from Vern. "It just had to be."

The case, when we open it, has an obvious false bottom opposite the handle side. Still, it takes me a minute to find the release—a pair of metal buttons hidden beneath tabs at either end of the case. When I finally press them at the same time, a Glock 26, a subcompact 9mm, pops into view. I examine it carefully, mindful of DNA and fingerprints. The serial number has been filed down, which comes as no surprise, but the weapon appears to be in good working order.

I jack out the round in the chamber, watch it drop to the carpet. The magazine comes next. It holds ten rounds, but when I remove the bullets, I discover only four.

Four in the magazine, plus one in the chamber. Five bullets found, five missing. Three in the skulls of Grieg and the Gaitskills? The fourth and fifth in Felice Gaitskill's chest?

At that point I would have bet Danny's college fund on it. All nine hundred and fifty-seven dollars.

We come down the stairs and into the living room, a little caravan, with Vern in the lead, holding the athletic shoes. I'm carrying a shoebox taken from Adele's closet. The Glock's in the shoebox.

"What the fuck are they?" Carl asks, pointing to the shoes.

But I'm not here to answer questions. I've got other things on my mind. I tell Carl Schmidt that he has the right to remain silent, that anything he says can be used against him, that he has a right to a lawyer. The man's not indigent and not entitled to a state-provided lawyer, but I put the possibility on the table anyway.

"Do you understand your rights as I've explained them to you?"

"Get real, you—"

I don't know if he was going to add bitch or cunt. Nor do I care. I remove the cover of the shoebox and show him the Glock, the empty magazine, and the unexpended rounds.

"Recognize this, Carl?"

"That's not mine. You planted that." Carl Schmidt's eyes travel from the pistol to the Dink and his video camera. Yeah, the weapon was planted, but not by us. I nod to a pair of cops behind the couch, and they lean forward. They've been prepped by yours truly, who anticipated this development. Carl spins in his seat to stare at his wife and his son.

"You're both dead," he tells them. "Hear me? I'm gonna have you skinned alive."

Connor rises. He takes his mother by the arm and leads her to the other side of the room. He's quite calm, almost like he wants me to know it. But I don't have time to analyze the asshole. I signal to the cops behind the couch, and they lean forward to seize Carl's arms. I expect him to resist, but he rises without a struggle.

"Am I under arrest?"

"No, but you're being detained. I'm going to put you in the back of a cruiser outside. You can take your cell phone, but we'll have to search you first. Sorry for the inconvenience."

I'm not sorry for the inconvenience, but I want Carl put away. With the entire property yet to be searched, he'll only be a distraction if left in the house. I instruct the cops holding Carl by the arms, then begin the second phase of the operation with a phone call to Chief Black.

"I've got a gun and a pair of soiled cross-trainers, Chief. They'll be on their way as soon as I get off the phone."

"Where'd you find them?"

"Carl Schmidt's bedroom, in his closet."

"Okay, I'll alert the mayor." He hesitates for a second. "And good work, Delia. You've been a step ahead all along."

---

The State Police Laboratory is approximately sixty miles away. I don't know how Mayor Venn did it, but the lab's agreed to process the evidence as soon as they receive it. Just as well, because we can only hold Carl for so long without charging him. I bag and label the evidence, then hand it to Patrolman Jerome Meeks, the cop who wouldn't let the chief drive onto the Skyview's parking lot. Meeks signs the labels on the separate bags holding the weapon, the magazine, the unspent rounds, the shoes. Then he's off.

Back to work. I organize my remaining cops (minus the Dink) into pairs and assign them to the various outbuildings. Connor Schmidt's cottage and the remainder of Carl's bedroom I reserve to myself, Vern, and the Dink. I find nothing of importance in either place, though I'm amused by Connor's immaculate housekeeping. No joint in an ashtray, not a leaf on the floor. Aspirin and nasal spray and a stool softener in the bathroom cabinet. No oxy, no molly, no fentanyl.

Due diligence established, I finally approach Adele and Connor Schmidt. They're sitting quietly, side by side, on the couch. Adele's wearing a gray skirt and a navy blouse. The skirt falls to mid-shin, the blouse buttoned almost to her throat. Connor's wearing blue sweatpants, a white T-shirt, and leather slippers. No socks.

"Step away, Connor. I want to talk to your mom alone."

Adele Schmidt's a shy, retiring type, notably lacking in self-confidence. She's a woman in obvious need of protection, and Connor should be the one to do the protecting.

He doesn't. He rises to his feet and meekly follows Vern into the kitchen. I sit down next to Adele, in the still-warm spot vacated by Connor.

"I have a few questions for you, Mrs. Schmidt. Very few, but they need to be asked. I want you to think carefully before you answer. No rush, okay? I want your responses to be accurate . . . and truthful."

Adele mutters, "All right, Lieutenant," without raising her eyes from her lap.

"Last Saturday night, were you home?

"Yes."

"From when to when?"

She hesitates for a moment, then says, "I shopped at the Kroger in the afternoon. I'm not sure exactly when I left the house, but I know I was home by four. To watch a baseball game. My husband follows the Chicago Cubs, and we usually watch together."

"And you didn't go out again?"

"No."

"What about your husband? Did he stay in the house all night?"

"I . . . I think. Probably."

"Probably?"

The answer comes faster this time. "I take a sleeping medication most nights. I was asleep by ten o'clock."

"And you didn't wake up during the night?"

"No, I never do. But I'm sure Carl was in bed when I did wake up. That was a little before seven."

"Was he also in bed when you went to sleep?"

"Carl was downstairs watching TV when I fell asleep. He generally stays up late."

I jump to Monday, when the Gaitskills were killed, and get the same basic response. Then I ask her to write her statement on a yellow pad. I'm expecting at least a moment of hesitation. That's because everyone hesitates before putting pen to paper. Not Adele. Her handwriting's a bit on the shaky side, but she creates a timeline for both nights and signs without my asking her. Carl Schmidt is now officially without an alibi.

"Is that okay, Lieutenant?" she asks.

# CHAPTER THIRTY-SIX

## CONNOR

The bitch has balls. Serious balls. Augie-size balls. She sits us on the couch for five hours, don't move, don't complain. You gotta take a piss, a cop escorts you and waits outside the door. In your own home. When you're not even a suspect.

Like I'm gonna do exactly what if I'm not watched every minute? Like my mother's gonna do exactly what? Like you already have the gun and the fucking shoe. Like you already have my old man locked in the back of a patrol car. So what are you waitin' for?

Five hours later, finally released, I'm standin' on the porch with Mom. We're watchin' the bitch cuff my father's hands behind his back, then ease him into the same patrol car she took him out of. Doin' it herself, with the old man's new lawyer watchin'. That would be a second-tier mouthpiece named Jeff Hennessy. Lorimer Taub (who's as top tier as it gets in Baxter) now represents Marjorie Carver.

Lorimer was the last piece of a puzzle that began to assemble itself when I opened the door to Cabin 909 that night at one o'clock, half expecting to find Bradley Grieg asleep. Bradley had a tendency to fall asleep when he was bored, like there wasn't enough going on inside his head to keep him awake. But passed out unconscious in a deep nod isn't asleep. I took in his works spread out on the edge of the tub, the bag open on a dresser, the gun sitting at the bottom of the bag, the money gone.

I wasn't angry, just resigned. A couple of years earlier, I'd found out that my high school buddy was a complete junkie. I'm talkin' about in the gutter, with nothing to look forward to except an overdose. I lifted him up, paid for his rehab, put him to work after his release. My old man told me again and again (the asshole never stops once he gets going) that Bradley Grieg was weak by nature, and natures don't change. I should cut him out of my working life, cut him out altogether.

Well, the time had come. That's the long and short of it. I knew he'd get in the wind if he woke up and found the money gone. And I would bet he couldn't name the individual, surely a woman, who stole the money. That's because only someone who didn't know Bradley or his connections could hope to get away with it. But his utter weakness tipped the scales. Bradley was a dope addict, and he always would be, at least until he finally got busted.

As I stood there listening to the asshole snore, I imagined him in a holding cell, the sickness comin' on fast. How long before he decided to trade Connor Schmidt's time for his? Ten minutes? Fifteen?

I took one precaution, but only one. I stepped outside, into the rain, and checked the security cameras mounted over the office, the only cameras on the property. I couldn't even see them.

I was on my way to toss the gun into Grant Lake, about forty miles from Baxter, when I began to have second thoughts. The Glock stashed in my trunk had been used to commit a murder that my old man had a motive to commit. Maybe I should hang on to it, at least until I felt some heat coming from the local cops. I couldn't exactly hear opportunity knocking. It was more like footsteps approaching my door.

The Gaitskills came next. They weren't part of any puzzle, not at first, but they had to go. First, because they gave that video to the cops, then lied when they told me the cops just took it. Mariola would need a subpoena to seize the video, a subpoena signed by a judge. She couldn't have gotten a judge to sign off two hours after the body was discovered.

I tried to send a really simple message that night. Don't talk to the cops. But when I came back the next day, the cops were back, too. With Richie and his mom obviously cooperating.

When opportunity knocks, open the door.

I took out Felice Gaitskill before she knew what hit her. Bang, bang, bang. Here and fucking gone. But Richie got so piss-in-his-pants scared when he heard the shots that he actually jumped out of an upstairs window. He was lying on his back when I caught up with him, staring into my eyes, beggin' for his miserable life. I felt a little bit sorry for him. I mean, I could've been wrong about him and his mom cooperating. I could've. But they knew too much about me, way too much, and they weren't really committed to the life. If Mariola put the screws to them, which she would, they'd probably turn. Better safe than sorry.

So, it was done. Three dead, the murders linked, the weapon (wiped down with bleach) safely planted in Daddy's closet. Only one step remained—getting the cops to the gun.

Marjorie Carver was my old man's girlfriend, and he did nothing to hide the fact. Took her everywhere—out to dinner, drinking with his buddies, even to movies. Mom knew, of course, but so what? She wasn't about to confront her husband *or* his mistress. Then Marjorie went off on some woman and got herself charged with a third-strike felony. No surprise, my old man dropped her cold. Marjorie who?

Was she scared, facing all those years? Not Marjorie. The woman is almost as tough as Mariola. And just as smart. She wanted out, and she'd do whatever was necessary to make that happen.

Lorimer Taub was the final piece of the puzzle. Taub had been handling our affairs for years, representing any member of our crew who got busted. (And making sure they didn't rat.) I was the Schmidt who dealt with him, naturally. My daddy kept his distance, also naturally. That's why my old man didn't know that I'd been feeding the shyster's coke habit for many, many months. Not with heavy-cut shit, either, but with a grade of blow the lawyer could never find on his own.

I sent Taub to Marjorie with a simple message, which she got right away. She could buy her freedom and my eternal gratitude by telling a simple story. Telling a story and stickin' to it. Which she did. As for Mom? I didn't ask her to plant the gun. I planted it myself when she and my father were off to a christening.

I take Mom's arm. I want to lead her away from the chaos. It's instinct to protect your mother, and I know it's been hard for her. But at least I didn't ask her to make anything up. Mom does take a sleeping pill at night, and she can't supply the old man with an alibi. She told the truth, kept it simple, the fewer moving parts the better.

We're still on the porch when Mariola walks up to us. "Come with me," the bitch says.

This is not a request. This is do it or I'll make you do it. Swear to God, if she ever turns, I'll ask her to work for me. She and Augie would make a hell of a pair.

"Think I don't know?" she asks. "You think I'm a fool?"

We're standing in the shade of a huge maple that has to be a hundred years old, but I'm sweating anyway. The summers out here are brutal.

"You don't know what, Lieutenant?"

"Know you set your father up."

I laugh. "You have a suspicious mind."

Mariola would be something of a looker if she wasn't so obviously butch. It's not just the short hair or the man-tailored suit. Most women, if you look close, you can see how—underneath all the bullshit about women's rights—they're scared. And for good reason. Men are much bigger, and they have all the guns.

Not Mariola. If we were still teenagers, I'm thinking she'd punch me right in the mouth. Just for the fun of it.

"I want you to know," she says, "that I'm taking the deal."

"And what deal would that be."

"Your father for you. A kingmaker's move, Connor, and well executed."

I can't help myself. The praise turns me on. And it's nice to know that she's takin' the deal without me having to put it on the table. Now for the bad news.

"The way I see it," she tells me, "you and your old man, you were a pair. Taking both of you out at the same time was never on the table, especially with your old man laying low. But now you're alone, Connor. It's just you and me."

Balls, like I said. Serious fucking balls.

# CHAPTER THIRTY-SEVEN

## CONNOR

Everybody stiffens when I enter the little room at the Dew Drop. They don't rise, that would be too much, and they don't kiss my ring, either, like they kissed Michael Corleone's ring in *The Godfather*. But the principle is the same. The torch has been passed—or stolen, really, which makes no difference—and it's time to make allegiances clear.

Augie's there, along with Little Ricky, the Murphy brothers, Juan Santos, and Lenny Krone. It's not the Gambino crime family, but this isn't New York or Chicago. What's important is that each of these guys heads a crew. They were my father's lieutenants. Now they're mine.

That's the plan, anyway.

"My father's gone for good," I tell them, which they already know because I told Augie to make the point before I got here. "They found the gun in his closet . . ."

"The gun that killed Bradley?" This from big-mouth Lenny Krone.

"Bradley and the Gaitskills. All three. And my father's not gettin' out, Lenny. They're holding him without bail while the DA decides whether or not to seek the death penalty."

"Pardon my sayin' so, Connor, but you don't seem too upset."

"First thing, Lenny, my emotional state is not your business. Second, Bradley was my best friend goin' back to high school. He was a fuckup, yeah, but that didn't give my old man leave to put him in the ground."

True, right? My father had no right to kill Bradley, and he didn't.

I'm tired by the time we break up. Really exhausted. But I have to get something to eat. There's nothing in the cottage except for microwave popcorn, and Mom's sure to be asleep. So I'm sitting with Augie at the Courthouse Diner, shoveling the pot roast special into my mouth. I want to get home, watch a little TV, get some rest. Maybe tomorrow I'll find an hour for my truck-stop teenie. Tonight, it's my bed and a good night's sleep.

Augie's eating an open-faced turkey sandwich smothered in gravy, some of which now decorates his chin. He's going on about collections, which have suffered over the past week. That's not good. Deadbeats being deadbeats, you have to stay on top of them every minute.

"Oh, yeah, Connor," he says out of nowhere. "Something I almost forgot. I'm in the Dew Drop this afternoon, sittin' at the bar, when this broad walks up to me. Swear to God, Connor, she looks like she just popped out of a coffin." Augie pauses long enough to chase a mouthful of turkey with what remains of his beer. "She marches up to my table and says, 'If your boss is still lookin', I'll be in the Dew Drop tomorrow afternoon. He doesn't show, I'm gonna give up on the whole thing.'"

I'm remembering the skank and how she turned down five hundred for the name of the girl in the hat. She also made a threat. If I didn't up the ante, she'd approach my old man. That's not gonna happen, obviously, but I'm kind of surprised that she didn't let it go. Maybe she wasn't bullshitting after all.

"The bitch wants a loan," I tell Augie. "But it looks to me like she'll drop dead before she makes the first payment."

Augie laughs, then says, "Thing about it, I'm pretty sure I recognized her."

"Pretty sure? Or sure?"

"No, I'm sure. Remember when I was on the basketball team and we won the championship? In high school? Well, she was like the guest of honor at a victory party. We kept fillin' her nose with coke, and she kept goin' all night, her and two other girls. Meantime, she's gotta be ten years older than us. At least."

"She was a whore?"

"A whore for coke, maybe. But no money changed hands, and when I propositioned her a week later, she told me to get lost."

"Yeah, she's got a mouth on her. So what else?"

"I asked around a little bit, and I think I could find her. Her name, which came to me later, is Celia Graham. What I heard, she lives with her daughter."

"Her daughter?"

"Yeah, a real mousy type. Grew up in the Yards, but keeps to herself these days."

"What's that mean?"

"Means she moved out of the Yards when she had a kid." Augie laughs softly. "Means she thinks she's too good for people like us. Me, I can't imagine why. Refined as we fucking are."

The Dew Drop is what passes for a neighborhood tavern in Baxter. That means the rails on the pool table have enough dead spots to fill a cemetery. It means the owner-bartender, Jimmy Santini, encourages patrons to carve their names into the bar top. And though Santini will mix you a cocktail, you'd be a fool to drink it.

It's late by the time I arrive, almost ten o'clock, and I'm thinking the crone will have come and gone. But she's there, off by herself at a table near the end of the almost deserted bar. I nod to Mary-Jo and a couple of patrons, but walk directly to the crone's table. She's waiting for me to take a seat, a glass of what looks like tea on the table in front of her.

"We'll talk outside," I tell her.

I don't wait for an argument. This is not a negotiation. I walk back out and cross the parking lot to my Lexus. When I turn around, she's following, so skinny I'm thinking that if she falls, her bones will shatter like glass. I wait until she reaches me, then toss an envelope onto the Lexus's hood.

"Three grand, Celia. First and final offer. Start talkin' or don't come back. I don't need any more bullshit in my life."

If using her name catches her by surprise, she doesn't show it. She looks me straight in the eye and says, "I know you got taken for a bunch, Connor. Thousands, right? But I don't know exactly how much . . ."

"Eighteen grand, Celia. Eighteen thousand fucking dollars."

"I thought it was less, but—but I don't know where it's stashed."

"This I can believe. If you knew where it was, you'd have stolen it long ago."

"Why does a man with no time for bullshit talk bullshit? I know the woman who took your money. If you want it back, you're gonna have to deal with her."

"Trust me, I'm prepared. Why don't you pick up that envelope and give me a name?"

I watch her snatch the envelope as she says the magic words: "Git O'Rourke."

"And who is she to you?"

"My daughter."

"You're giving up your daughter?"

The woman actually snarls, unleashing a mass of wrinkles that crisscross the ones already there. "She's leavin' town, headed east to a wonderful new life. Takin' my granddaughter with her."

"And leaving you behind?"

"Leaving me behind to fucking die."

"So when is she leaving?"

"Two weeks."

"That doesn't give me a lot of time."

"Whose fault is that? I been tryin' to reach you all week."

Truth be told, the crone looks ready to drop dead on the spot, and I can't see her lasting very long on her own. No. Most likely, she'll burn through every dime on her way to a coffin. How long will it take? A month?

"You can't hurt that child," she tells me. "I won't have it."

"I don't hurt kids."

"And you won't kill my daughter, either."

"No killing, Celia. I only want what she stole."

This is a lie. Kill her, no. Hurt her, yes. That's what the boys expect. Anything less would show weakness, at least in their eyes, even if she returns the money. I can't afford to appear weak. Not now.

"She ain't like me," the crone says. "The girl scares easy, so you shouldn't have much trouble convincing her. Anyways, tomorrow morning, around ten, she's gonna take her kid to Baxter Park. Charlie's goin' away to camp for the weekend. That done, she'll be alone."

"What about friends? Anyone I should know about?"

"Nah. The girl runs around with her nose in the air. Thinks she's too good for trash like us. But if you wanna worry about somethin', you should worry she'll run to the cops."

# CHAPTER THIRTY-EIGHT

## DELIA

The mayor's not wasting any time. Chief Black, either. They schedule a press conference for six o'clock, when the nightly news kicks off. Me, I don't argue. I have enough to do getting Carl booked and locked away. Tomorrow morning, when he's arraigned, his lawyer will ask for bail. It won't be granted. Judge Eric Dunn's hang-'em-high attitude has gotten him elected and reelected for twenty-five years. Bail at any price is not on the table. Not for accused murderers. If Carl Schmidt wants out, he'll have to escape.

So I'm busy supervising everything from the paperwork to the handling of the mostly irrelevant evidence we seized at the house. The incriminating material is already in the hands of the State Police Lab. Vern's with me, copying the memory card from the Dink's camera, when I feel a tap on my shoulder. It's Chief Black's aide, a patrolwoman named Bea Thatcher.

"You're wanted," she tells me, "in the chief's office."

The mayor's sitting to one side of the chief's massive wooden desk when I enter the office. Vern's after his share of the credit, par for the course and no surprise. But the presence of Gloria Meacham, president of the city council and sister of John Meacham, catches me off guard. She's sitting on the other side of the desk, the chief between them.

The first thought to enter my addled brain? I've ridiculed the Dink one too many times and I'm about to get canned. Or at least seriously chewed out. I look directly at Gloria Meacham, a short woman who grew up on a farm and maybe spent too much time in the sun. Her face and neck are heavily wrinkled, and she appears far older than her forty-odd years. But there's nothing old about her manner. The woman's blue eyes are intelligent, penetrating, and fixed on mine.

After a moment's scrutiny Meacham nods to me and clears her throat. She even smiles. "May I call you Delia, Lieutenant?"

"Sure."

"What I tell you now, Delia, has to be kept under wraps for another week or two. Understand? It's really important."

"You have my word."

"As I've said, Baxter's been an enterprise zone for some years. Federal, state, and local. Well, it's finally paid off. Nissan is going to open an assembly plant here in Baxter. It'll start turning out cars three years from now. Be a lot of construction before then, too. Work for anybody who wants a job."

Baxter? No fucking way, is what I'm thinking. The country's halfway in a depression. But Gloria Meacham looks most of all proud. Chief Black and Mayor Venn, too. Perhaps that's because their families settled the territory shortly after the Revolution. The city was never a way station for them. Never a stepping-stone. Its collapse had to be like a death in the family, its revival a resurrection.

"What about the recession? New car sales are in the dumpster."

"Corporations like to think ahead. Nobody's buying cars right now, but the first Nissans won't roll off the Baxter assembly line for three years. Hopefully, the economy will be on the mend. Hopefully, there'll be a lot of pent-up demand. In any event, Baxter Packing's decision to leave the city was the final piece of the puzzle. With the plant shuttered, the industrialized sections of the Yards will be completely empty. That works to our advantage because the infrastructure's already there, the power grid and the roads. With a little tweaking, they can be made to service Nissan's individual needs. At the same time, Nissan can place their factory where there's room to grow."

Mayor Venn chimes in after Gloria finishes her last sentence. "I won't bore you with a list of concessions the state had to make. I'll just say the competition was intense. Fifteen states wanted the factory, and they all put in a bid. The way it stands now, our taxpayers will pay a high price for the new jobs, and they'll be paying for a long time.

But even heavily automated, the plant will provide more than five thousand jobs. There'll be support businesses, too. Everything from precision machine parts to interior fabrics." Venn's shoulders finally relax, as if he's relieved himself of an obscure burden. "The feds are supplying start-up money, fifty million dollars for demolition. All the empty factories will come down, roads will be widened, new businesses will spring up. Baxter will live, Delia."

It's Chief Black's turn, and he swivels his chair to face me. "Or they will if we can deal with our drug problems. We have to produce a sober workforce. Workers ready and able to give a day's labor for a check at the end of the week. We're talking about jobs that pay sixty-five thousand a year, with benefits. No slackers allowed."

Not being one of the slackers, I'm having a little trouble here. I'm happy for the city, sure, and it looks like I'll keep my job, which is also good. But I'm still not sure why Meacham's telling me any of this. What was it that Ben Franklin wrote? Three people can keep a secret if two of them are dead?

"You're probably wondering why we called you in, Delia." This from Chief Black.

"Yeah, I am. I'm glad, of course, about the Nissan factory, although I'm a little worried about you prematurely counting your chickens. But why are you telling me this?"

"About a year ago," Black continues, "I started having trouble with my balance. Not every day, but more and more often as time went by. A couple of weeks ago I fell. For no reason. I wasn't drunk or tired or anything. I simply went from normal to the rug in my living room." He glances over at his wall of fame. The chief in photos with two governors, a senator, a congresswoman, a dozen business leaders. "I'll make it simple. I have a brain tumor. It's not malignant, and it is operable. I could hang on, of course. I could have the surgery and hope the potential for neurological deficits . . ." He pauses long enough to laugh. "Neurological deficits? Well, at least my vocabulary's improving."

"Finally." This from Gloria Meacham.

"Always a vote of confidence from Gloria." Black's tone makes their past conflicts obvious, but that's not where the chief's going. "I've had enough, Delia. Last week, my daughter, Veronica, gave birth to a baby girl. Leila's my third grandchild—there are two boys as well—and my only goal now is to spend time with them while they're still young."

Black lapses into silence, and I find myself filling the void. I still don't know why I'm being told any of this.

"So you're resigning? You're retiring?"

"All of the above. And we want you to replace me."

I have a big mouth, and I'm not afraid to use it. But now I'm struck dumb.

Gloria Meacham speaks first. "A new beginning, Delia, for the whole town. But it's only a beginning. There's work to be done, including our drug problem and the resulting crime. To be frank, we need an insider who can put a strategy together, then systematically implement that strategy, somebody we know isn't corrupt. You'll have help, too. The start-up money includes funding for our police department, enough to put on twenty-five new officers. Each of them, by the way, subject to your approval. There's also money to expand Baxter's treatment programs, which gives you another way to go."

"What about the cops already on the payroll?" My voice returns as an image of Gloria's brother, the Dink, rolls into my consciousness. "I'm not gonna name names at this point, but there are cops on the force I wouldn't hire to weed my garden."

"Including my brother?"

"Especially your brother."

I'm again caught by surprise when Gloria reaches across the desk to place her hand on mine.

"We're looking to you because we want a professional department. You'll have compete autonomy. Your only constraint will be the law itself. Don't start shooting suspects. Other than that, I can promise the city council's backing. You have my word." She gives my hand a little squeeze. "I don't intend to blow this opportunity because my little brother's an asshole. Do what you need to do."

I'm not stupid enough to make any further comment, and the chief takes up the slack.

"We want to introduce you at the press conference. I'll say a few words, then call you to the podium. You'll outline the investigation you headed and take a few questions. Three murders solved. The perpetrator behind bars. On Monday, we'll hold another press conference, at which time I'll officially resign. The mayor will then announce your appointment as acting police chief, pending confirmation by the city council."

"Which," Gloria Meacham is quick to add, "I guarantee. Absolutely."

I'm almost dizzy as I leave the chief's office. Of course I'm taking the job. It comes with a twelve-thousand-dollar raise, better health insurance, and a guaranteed pension if I hang on for another fifteen years. And I can't wait to tell Danny, which I'll do tomorrow morning, Saturday, when my little inmate's allowed to have visitors.

His momma the chief of police? He'll be thrilled.

Vern looks up as I enter the squad room. He gives me a thumbs-up, and right away I know he'll be in charge of the antidrug task force I intend to put together. Vern knows the people in Baxter, including the lowlifes. He grew up with them.

Three hours later, when I'm finally satisfied that every detail has been tended to, including Carl Schmidt's dinner, we lock it up. I'm retrieving my purse when Vern stops me.

"We did good work, Delia. Police work. We wrapped it up."

I don't dispute the claim, but I can't fully accept it, either. That's because there's one more task ahead of me. A ride out to Henrietta's Hattery.

# CHAPTER THIRTY-NINE

## GIT

Zack doesn't comment when I come through the door an hour late. He's huddled with two men and a woman in the living room. They're sitting on the edges of their chairs, leaning forward, heads close together. Only the woman looks in my direction. Her gaze is distinctly hostile.

"That's my nurse," Zack explains.

The woman nods once and gives me a little wave. If Zack says I'm okay, I'm okay. I nod in return, then head for the kitchen and a cup of coffee. When it comes to Zack's visitors, it's strictly don't know and don't want to know.

Thirty minutes later, all three are out the door and I join Zack in the living room. I'm assuming he'll leave his company and whatever they spoke about unmentioned. What with Carl Schmidt's arrest, there's plenty to talk about. But this time, Zack surprises me.

"Big happenings," he announces. "This city's gonna explode when the news goes public."

"What news?"

"A factory's coming to Baxter. A car company? Amazon? Apple? I haven't got all the pieces yet, but I know where they're goin'."

"The Yards."

The response is meant as a joke, but it turns out the joke's on me. "Exactly right, Git," Zack tells me. "Once Baxter Packing closes, the Yards will be fully open to redevelopment. Yeah, there are still a couple of thousand residents, but they're gonna be relocated to the eastern edge of the industrial zone. Like it or not."

"And they're gonna live in what? Tents?"

"Nope. They're gonna live in new housing built with money supplied by the feds and the state. Them and another couple thousand new workers. And guess who's gonna be part of the consortium that builds that housing?"

"Consortium?"

Zack laughs until he chokes, which doesn't take all that long. "Yeah, consortium. If I said that word in a bar fifteen years ago, I woulda got beat up. But it's happening, Git. There's a new day comin' for the Yards. Night when I close my eyes, I see a giant factory runnin' three shifts. Small businesses lined up along new-paved streets. Traffic jams in and out, morning and night. The future's on the way."

———

Maybe Zack's future is bright, a sunrise on a cloudless morning, but it doesn't help me any. I came home from his place an hour ago, at seven A.M., to find Connor Schmidt parked across the street. I couldn't miss the car, a Lexus sedan, one of the few (and the only red one) in a town that prefers battered pickups. Connor was slumped behind the steering wheel, his head barely visible. He didn't move when I pulled into our tiny driveway, got out, and walked into the house.

Now it's an hour later, and I'm feeding my daughter. Scrambled eggs with small cubes of ham, apple juice, and two slices of whole-wheat toast. Charlie's excited. Charlie's scheduled to leave for a three-day overnight camp in less than an hour. The camp's not free, but I signed her up because a number of her classmates will also be there. I didn't want her to lose touch over the summer.

Stupid? Especially because I'll be leaving the city in a couple of weeks. But Charlie has yet to understand the consequences of our move, and I'm in no hurry to make them plain. We won't be coming back, simple as that, and she'll never see these kids again. She'll have to make new friends in a town where just about everyone's richer than her mother. A lot richer.

Going back a day, that was my greatest fear. That we'd never belong, that Charlie would become a perpetual outsider. Now I've got Connor sitting across the street, and I'm thinking maybe he'll solve my Charlie problem. Permanently.

"Mommy, will Samantha be there?"

Samantha is Charlie's current best friend, her fourth this year.

"Her mom says yes. I called yesterday."

"Can I have some more juice?"

"Take your glass into the kitchen and pour it yourself. Carefully. Then get dressed. We have to be out of here in forty-five minutes, and you haven't decided what you want to wear."

Charlie jumps off the couch, probably assuming the sooner she gets dressed, the sooner we'll leave. The girl's not big on clocks.

"Connor's gone," Mom tells me once Charlie's out of the room. "He drove off a couple of minutes ago."

"He never should have been here in the first place."

"There was no other way."

"Way to do what?"

"To leave this town without having to look over your shoulder for the rest of your life. Or do you think New Jersey's so far away that Connor won't be able to find it?"

"Nobody recognized me, even after the cops showed my photo."

"Except Henrietta. You know, the woman who made the hat? The woman you bought it from, using a credit card in your own name? And even if she doesn't rat you out to Connor, that cop, Mariola, is sure to find her. If she hasn't already."

She's right. And Henrietta's not the only one who's seen me in the hat. A month ago, I wore the hat to a wedding. Have any of the guests phoned the cops? Has Henrietta? I don't know, and I can't ask. But I do know that if the cops identify the woman in the hat, they won't keep it a secret. They can't. Not after the press conference.

The waiting has me on edge as I flash back to a day long ago. I'm nine years old, just a bit past Charlie's age. Mom's passed out on the couch, wearing a bra and panties. Her latest boyfriend's drunk, too, but awake. His name is Harmon, and he's sitting in a chair next to the couch, staring at Mom with a look in his eyes I already know well. I'm watching television in our minuscule living room. Watching television and definitely in the way. Harmon, he's not the sort of guy who resists his impulses, probably why he's been to state prison twice.

"Get the fuck out of here, kid."

"It's my house."

A casual kick to my shoulder sends me spinning. It also sets me straight. I've seen Harmon beat the crap out of my mother—who was giving almost as good as she got—and I want no part of the damage. I run out of the trailer and onto the tiny plot of cleared land around it.

Now what? We're more than a mile from the nearest house, and it's midsummer. Aside from a small woodlot behind the trailer, the surrounding land is cultivated. Long rows of head-high cornstalks extend from all sides, narrowing in the distance to what seems like a solid wall. The most prominent distraction is a fallen oak, a giant torn up by a passing thunderstorm a few months earlier. The branches have yet to wither. They hold the trunk off the ground, creating a dark tunnel beneath. My cave.

The property holds another attraction for me at age nine. A large pile of discarded junk. Not garbage, but ordinary household articles. Chipped dishes, cups with broken handles, a three-legged table, a wooden chair with no legs at all, a pair of cracked lamps, a collection of bent and battered pots.

The best of these items have already been salvaged. I've arranged them in my cave to form what I think of as my other home. A home for me. A home for my imaginary friends.

My cave home is especially enticing on this particular afternoon. The deep shadows beneath provide a refuge from the heat and from the sounds pouring through the trailer's open windows.

Thump, thump, thump, thump, thump.

The saddest part is that I know what those sounds mean. At nine years old.

An opening among the tightly packed branches serves as my front door. There's a rug on the ground, one end burned off, and a stained tablecloth on top of the rug. Cups and saucers, dinner plates, a teapot with no spout, bent knives and forks and spoons adorn the tablecloth. I've created a dining room that's as close to the dining rooms I've seen on television as I can get it. A family's dining room, peopled with the television-inspired community that fuels my imagination.

My eyes close in the middle of an imaginary party, and I drift off. When I open them again, it's well past sunset. Rising winds, a harbinger of thunderstorms I can hear in the distance, stir the drying leaves of the fallen oak. Farther away, the branches on a mix of birch, oaks, and aspens rattle like colliding bones, now loud, now fading. The moon as it dances along the edge of a fast-moving cloud throws vague and grotesque shadows across the patch of dirt behind the trailer. I'm hungry and scared, and young enough to believe in demons and devils, not to mention the flesh-eating zombies who populate Harmon's favorite DVDs.

Unable to move, I watch the corn sway back and forth, driven almost to the ground by gusts of wind that whip the branches on the trees into a frenzy. Hoping that Mom will come to get me, I look toward the trailer. I'm not comforted, though. Nor is my courage boosted by the appearance of an animal, a raccoon, at the edge of the yard. The coon rises on its hind legs, its nose extended, holding the pose for a few seconds before dropping to all fours. A moment later it vanishes into the forest of corn that surrounds us.

At nine, I still think raccoons are cute. But there are other things out there as well, including coyotes and bad-gers that might want to eat a nine-year-old girl. I have to get inside.

It's about then that I notice that Harmon's car is gone. Its absence boosts my courage. I no longer have to choose between Harmon's temper and becoming a meal for a pack of hungry coyotes. Now all I have to do is cross fifty feet of hard-packed dirt and circle around to the front of the trailer. Where anything might be waiting.

The wind picks up, and the first drops of rain speckle the dirt. That's enough. I crawl between the branches, skyrocket around the trailer, and explode into the house. I find Mom in the bedroom, snoring away, but no sign of Harmon. There's a third reward in the refrigerator. Two slices of American cheese and a plum, withered but still fresh enough to eat.

A half hour later, I strap Charlie into the car seat. No sign of Connor as I pull away, heading uptown on Baxter Boulevard. Beside me, Charlie's mouth doesn't stop moving. What games, she wants to know, will they play? What will they eat? Who will be there? What if it rains? When does she have to come home? I alternate between working the mirrors and the vague answers distracted parents always give their children.

I want Connor to be tailing me, and I don't want Connor to be tailing me. I want to pretend that he'll go away, but there's no use pretending. I'm a woman with no man to protect me. A woman with a sick mom willing to rat her out and a young child who needs protecting of her own.

Easy meat.

# CHAPTER FORTY

## CONNOR

'm thinking I made a mistake. Rushing in. It's too close to my father going down, too close to Mariola's threats. Mariola wants me in prison—it's like a crusade—and judging from her press conference, she's gonna have the authority to pursue her ambitions. Chief Black and the mayor practically kissed her bull-dyke ass. So maybe what I should've done after talkin' to Celia Graham was step back and let things cool down before I went after the money. Because the money's mine, no issue, no question about it. Maybe the broad—Gidget or whatever her name is—stole it from Bradley, but the money was never his. It was always mine.

So I gotta do something, right? But I don't gotta do it right now. Except I have to do it right now because I parked in front of her house, like the asshole I am, and the bitch saw me out there. She didn't look like much, a mouse really, like her mom claimed. And the way her head jerked back, that fear look in her eyes? Bein' in the loan-shark business, I'm real familiar with that look. I've seen it on the faces of a hundred trapped deadbeats. It turns me on, actually, and what I'm thinkin' now is I can get my money back, no problem, if I catch her alone.

The phone rings while I'm workin' my way through a bowl of cereal instead of Mom's waffles. It's Augie. He's got a line on a manager at Baxter Packing who wants a loan. This foreman claims he can provide exclusive access to Baxter workers if we ease up on his vig. And me, the first thought to work its way into my little brain? I'm bein' set up. That's how bad Mariola's gotten to me.

"How'd you meet this guy, Augie?"

"At the Dew Drop. Frankie introduced him."

That would be Frankie Thomas, who takes out a new loan the second he's paid off the old one. Frankie's been late a few times, but he's not a deadbeat.

"Check it out, Augie. Like careful, all right? We're hot just now, in case you haven't noticed."

"Gotcha, boss."

Maybe I'm paranoid, but my biggest fear right now is that Gidget'll run to the cops. Fear can do that to ya. I know because it's happened before with deadbeats. It's not right, because they knew the deal when they came to me, but there's no suin' deadbeats, no garnishing anyone's pay or freezing their bank accounts. I know it, and they know it. So if you welsh, you should live with the obvious fact that I have only one way to collect.

Two men went to the cops, two I know about. Lucky our guy in the department gave me a heads-up and I backed away. And I think that's what I'm gonna do here. I'm gonna convince Gidget to return my eighteen large. I'm gonna tell her, no harm, no foul. Then I'm gonna back away until everything cools down. Until Mariola buries herself in someone else's crimes. Until Gidget believes that I've forgotten all about her. Until it's Augie time, and I have an unbreakable alibi.

One thing's sure, you don't steal from Connor Schmidt.

Mom caught an early flight to Denver, where her sister lives, and I'm alone in the house. I wanted her far away in case my old man has resources I don't know about. She didn't take much convincing, but it still feels completely weird. The house is ridiculously big for one person, and I don't know how she's gonna live here by herself. I could always move in, of course, but that doesn't seem right, either. So, what to do? Sell the house, find a smaller place for Mom? Meanwhile, I don't even know whose name is on the deed. Or the bank accounts, or any other legal document. That's why I asked Lorimer Taub—Dad's former lawyer, now Marjorie Carver's—to pay a visit.

I didn't have to ask twice. Lori's a coke addict, and addicts dance to their supplier's tune. And I'm not surprised, either, when he rings my bell at eight thirty. Right on time.

Lorimer's not lookin' all that great. He's always been skinny, like he's waitin' for the big, bad wolf to blow him over, and the owl-eyes glasses only make it worse. Today, though, I'm thinkin the coke's getting' the best of him. Rich druggies can hold it together for a long time, but not forever. Lorimer's got maybe six months before a stint in rehab. His third.

I seat him at the kitchen table, pour him a cup of coffee, and settle into a chair on the other side of the table. "Marjorie holding up?" I ask.

"Solid as a rock. You worried?"

"Not really." I lean forward. "I asked you here for a different reason. With my old man in prison, I need to get a handle on my mother's finances."

"That's quite a coincidence, Connor, because I've been meaning to have a conversation about finances with you." He waits for me to wave him on before speaking again. "Nissan's coming to Baxter."

"What?"

"Nissan's gonna build a plant right here in Baxter. In the Yards, after the packing plant closes down. This is comin' straight from the governor's office. Believe me, it's happening. It's happening, and it presents a major opportunity for anyone smart enough to take advantage. That means early, Connor, before everybody and their grandmother figures it out. We've already got the big chains—Gap, Nike, Starbucks, Nordstrom—scouting locations. That's because there's gonna be a lot of white-collar money on the table."

"Like who?"

"Like the plant management, like the engineers and machinists who'll keep the robots running. And the workers, too, earning the kind of wages this town hasn't seen in decades. And the owners of all those new businesses sure to spring up." Lorimer takes a handkerchief from an inside pocket of his tan suit and coughs gently into it. "Any event, there's a bunch of us taking a hard look at the property around City Hall Park. The money to rehab the park's already been allocated, and the city's looking for the right landscaper. The idea is to surround the new park with restaurants and shops, with antiques and boutiques, to create a destination zone. Add new apartments with the right appliances and the right view, and there's real money to be made. Legit money, Connor. Money you don't have to hide."

I glance at the clock on the wall. It's nine o'clock, and I need to get moving. "You inviting me to join this—"

"Corporation."

"And what's that gonna cost me?"

"Minimum, fifty thousand."

"And the maximum?"

"There isn't one. But if you can put a quarter mil together, you'll own enough voting shares to have real clout."

I nod and tell him I'll think about it, but I'm not stupid enough to get in bed with a coke junkie. Especially when the payoff's at least five years down the line. Still, Lorimer's got me thinking. If he's not full of shit, Baxter's gonna be flooded with out-of-town construction workers a few months from now. They're sure to have the kind of needs that only a man in my business can satisfy. Plus, if I wanna go legit, there's an offer already on the table.

Jimmy Santini's lookin' to sell a piece of the Dew Drop, which is where I mostly hang out anyway. And I trust Jimmy.

"So what about my mom? She gonna have to file for bankruptcy?"

Lorimer shakes his head. "There are bank accounts, savings and checking, in both their names. Maybe thirty-five total. The big money, the working capital, is stashed."

"And you know where?"

"Yeah." He doesn't have the balls to ask what's in it for him. But I know I can't scare him into talking. Lori's practice covers three counties, and he's represented some of the most violent criminals out there. The man's been threatened many times.

"An ounce, Lori, to show my appreciation." I hesitate before adding. "Of the best."

"Excellent. Okay, your old man wanted me to know in case he got busted and needed to make bail. There's a major pile hidden beneath the floorboards in Marjorie's bedroom."

"He trusted her? Marjorie Carver?"

Lorimer finally smiles. "He told her if a single dollar vanished, he'd kill her kids while she watched. And from what I could tell, he meant it. One thing about your old man, he was tight with a buck."

I get rid of the lawyer a few minutes later. I'm anxious to put Gidget and the stolen money in the past. Between dealin' with my old man and the rest of the bullshit, I've been stuck in neutral. No more. I'm startin' to think ahead.

That's because Lori's right. I need to be ready when the money pours in, ready to collect my piece.

I lock the door behind me when I leave the empty house and walk over to the Lexus. I've got a gun stashed under the driver's seat. Not because I'm worried about Gidget. I'm packin' the gun for the same reason I sent Mom to Denver. I don't think my old man's got anyone he can ask for help, but you never know.

I transfer the gun to my blue Toyota, slide behind the wheel, and start the car. But I don't put it in gear, not right away. Instead, I lean back in the seat and close my eyes for a minute. I'm remembering the video from Randy's, the girl in the hat and the green dress. Remembering the red light flashing in those sequins, remembering how the hem of her dress rose halfway to her crotch, remembering the red mouth and the green eye shadow. And now I'm thinkin' it'd be appropriate if Gidget paid a little interest on her debt. Or even a lot of interest.

# CHAPTER FORTY-ONE

## GIT

The red Lexus is nowhere to be found, despite a nervousness that has my eyes moving from the windshield to the rearview mirror to the side mirrors. My mistake, as it turns out. That mistake is remedied when I turn onto Poplar Street, a road that leads to Baxter Park, and a blue Toyota sedan follows. There are no cars between me and the Toyota, but when I deliberately slow, the Toyota slows as well.

An urge to slam the gas pedal to the floor seizes my body and my brain. But it's too early to panic. The last thing I need is a confrontation while Charlie is in the car. It doesn't come. I pull to the curb behind a long line of cars at the camp area and get out. Charlie unbuckles her seat belt and joins me at the curb. She takes my hand, which she tends to do when she's excited, and we stroll over to join the line at the registration table. I chat with the other mothers, those I know. Our conversations alternate between Carl Schmidt's arrest and the departure of Baxter Packing. The talk isn't pleasant either way, but I'm barely paying attention. It's taking all my self-discipline not to check on Connor.

Charlie gives me a final hug after I attach a name tag to the front of her T-shirt. Then she's off to join Samantha, who's waving to her.

"Goodbye, Mom."

"Have a good time, honey. I'll pick you up on Sunday evening. Maybe we'll have a pizza."

And maybe you'll be motherless.

An illegal U-turn takes me right past Connor's parked Toyota, but I don't turn my head. I work my way to Baxter Boulevard, then south to a strip mall anchored by a Walgreens. I'm too pissed off to be afraid, but still not stupid enough to park at the edge of the lot. I find a space almost in front of the entrance and head inside. When I'm certain that Connor's not going to follow me, I take out my phone and call Mom.

"He's on my tail," I tell her. "Only he's driving a blue Toyota instead of the Lexus."

"If he doesn't want to be noticed, he's gotta be serious."

This I already know. "You ready?"

"Yeah. But take care, Git. You have a little girl to get home to."

Mom's referring to our shared belief that Connor's armed. His father's threats are common knowledge. But

Baxter's not an open-carry city. You need a special permit to go about armed. How likely is it that Connor's obtained the permit? Or that he'd carry a gun on his person if he hasn't? Close by is one thing, but not on his person.

Still, there's always the chance.

Outside, I walk to my car, press the button that unlocks the doors, then look around as I pull the door open. When my eyes land on Connor, still sitting behind the wheel of the Toyota, I flinch. Not too obviously, but enough for him to draw a simple conclusion—that I know he's there and I'm scared.

The car's been sitting in the sun for the past fifteen minutes, and my air-conditioning isn't functioning. No big deal over the winter, but now I'll have to find the money to fix it. Not today, though. I let the windows down, all of them, start the car, and head off.

I head north on Baxter Boulevard, my speed gradually increasing, then finally turn onto Route 74, a state road. The speed limit here is 55 mph, and I blow past the limit almost immediately. Connor follows, not hesitating even when I weave in and out, passing cars on either side. I imagine him enjoying the chase. I imagine him imagining a terror I don't remotely feel. No, what I'm feeling at the moment is rage.

Would-be gangsters like Connor haunted my teenage years, mine and every other fatherless girl longing to be loved. They used us and abused us and threw us away. I should know. I ran with a dozen of them and actually married one. Well, Connor's attitude, if I'm right about it, is all to the good. He's thinking that I'm still one of those hapless fools. He's thinking that he found me on his own. He's thinking that I'm defenseless.

Or so I hope.

I make a quick (but not too quick) move to the right, onto an off-ramp. Connor follows. We're almost in corn country now, on a two-lane road, speeding past a series of ranches. Buffalo, not beef cattle. I can see a small herd grazing in a long meadow. The grass they rip from the ground is bright green and rises to their knees. For a moment, I'm envious. Their world seems utterly peaceful. But then I see them led along a chute to the killing floor, hear them bellowing as their nostrils fill with the scent of blood. Not me, not me.

With Connor on my tail, I take four sharp turns, to the right, then the left, a small animal desperate to escape. Only when we're far from any main road do I make a quick left onto a hard-packed dirt road. Long abandoned, the single-lane road is studded with small rocks making their way to the surface. It runs straight between cornfields for thirty yards, then curves sharply to the left, the fields now screening me from view. A final curve to the right feeds into a small clearing, with no way out except the way I came in. The trailer's long gone, the place where it rested overgrown with grass and weeds. My tree cave, its branches now in pieces, has fallen to the ground and begun to rot. Even the cornfields seem closer, and there's just enough open space in the clearing to accommodate Connor's little sedan.

I'm out of my car, half stumbling toward the edge of the nearest cornfield, shoulders slumped, eyes downcast. An utter waste of time as the dust settles behind me to reveal an empty road. My heart drops. Connor hasn't followed. My gamble has failed. I touch the Czech .32 jammed behind my belt. If Connor had trailed me in, he would not have driven back out.

A few seconds later, Mom barrels up the road in a borrowed pickup. We'd planned to box Connor in, to allow him no room to escape, even if he stayed in his car. Now we're left staring at each other. Mom doesn't speak, but I know what she's thinking. That's because I'm thinking the same thing. We took a big risk going to Connor. Sure, he would almost surely have discovered the identity of the girl on that video from Randy's. Eventually.

But eventually is eventually, and now is now.

# CHAPTER FORTY-TWO

## DELIA

The woman who answers my knock doesn't seem very surprised by my appearance. More dismissive. Her name is Celia Graham, and she's the mother of Bridget O'Rourke. I know this because I conferred with Vern after my visit to Henrietta's Hattery. He remembered Celia because he once arrested her for an assault that came to nothing when the victim OD'd a few days later. But though he'd probably come across Bridget in high school, he couldn't place her. But he knew her by reputation. A straight shooter, she'd never been arrested, never accumulated so much as a parking ticket.

"Detective Mariola, ma'am." I display my shield, to no apparent effect. "I'm looking for Bridget O'Rourke."

"I know who you are." Celia Graham's smile reveals tobacco-stained teeth and a tongue the color of pea soup.

Sick doesn't describe her condition. More like walking dead. "Whatta ya want?"

The single-story house is surrounded by a small yard. The grass, though far from lush, is neatly trimmed and the narrow flower beds of alyssum are well tended. Except for the windows, the house mirrors the homes of many hundreds of respectable Baxterites. The difference here, despite the heat, is that every window is closed and the shades have been drawn behind them.

"I already told you, Celia. I need to speak to your daughter." I stop for a moment to stare into her eyes. My knowing her name hasn't fazed her. "I need to speak with your daughter, and you're annoying the fuck out of me."

But Celia's not giving up, or maybe a bad attitude is the only attitude she has. "You got a search warrant?"

"For what? You have something you need to hide?"

"What's that supposed to mean?"

"Last chance, Celia. Is your daughter home?"

"Last chance? Wha'cha gonna do, hit me?"

"Exactly right. I'm going to punch you in the face, then charge you with assaulting a police officer."

Bridget herself rides to the rescue, appearing behind her mother before I have to make good on my stupid threat. "Can I help you?"

Bridget's no longer the party girl who displayed herself on that bar stool in Randy's. A trim woman about my height, I'd describe her as housewife-next-door—she's wearing a pair of jeans and a violet T-shirt with the sleeves rolled up—yet her eyes are as cold as her mother's.

"You should've paid cash for the hat," I tell her.

"You don't have to talk to the cops." This from her mom. "You have rights."

"True," I admit, my eyes focused on Bridget, not her mother. "You're a material witness, not a suspect. That means I can take you to headquarters and ask you for a statement, making sure every cop in the house, not to mention every civilian employee, gets a good look at you. But it won't matter, right? Because Connor Schmidt's already found you. That's why the shades are drawn."

"Mom, catch a smoke outside." Bridget waits until her mother disappears around a corner of the house, then steps back to let me pass. I walk into a small, cozy, and very hot living room. Well-worn but obviously comfortable, a pair of couches and two upholstered chairs almost fill the small space. I'm tired and would like nothing better than to settle my butt onto one of the seats. No go. Bridget leads me to a dining room table with two straight-backed chairs on either side. She points to the closest one.

"You want some iced tea?"

"Yeah, sure."

Bridget turns without a word and walks into the kitchen, her gait assertive. I'm left to look around, and I take advantage, being nosy by nature. A pair of travel posters, one of Yosemite and one of Grand Teton National Park, grace the windowless wall before me. Both are of snowcapped mountains, and I read a kind of flatlander yearning into them. Beyond the pair, my eyes are drawn to a pile of toys in a corner of the living room, which instantly raises the stakes. A frame house like this will allow a 9mm round to penetrate every wall before exiting. It'll penetrate flesh as well, the flesh of a child as easily as the flesh of an adult.

"You have children, Bridget?"

"One," she calls from the kitchen. "She's at camp."

"Is that a matter of convenience? Her being away?"

"Call it whatever you want." Bridget walks out of the kitchen bearing two glasses on a tray. She hands one to me, then says, "I didn't kill Bradley."

"I know that."

"And I didn't steal his money."

"I know that, too."

"Do you know who did?"

"Yes, and it wasn't Connor Schmidt." Now I'm smiling. "But that leaves you with a bit of a problem. Because the way Connor sees it, if he didn't steal the money, you must have. So where does that leave you? Without any money to return."

When I leave it there, Bridget has the good sense not to pursue the issue. She stares down at the table for a moment while she sips at her tea, then suddenly raises her eyes.

"I don't have time to spar with you. Ask the question."

"Did Bradley Grieg tell you that he was expecting someone after you left?"

"Is that what you want me to say? That he was expecting someone?"

"No, Bridget—"

"Git."

"Sorry?"

"My name's Git. No one calls me Bridget."

"All right, Git, but what I want you to say doesn't really matter. I need to know the truth."

"But you won't know, not really. Bradley's dead, and there isn't anyone to confirm or deny whatever I say. I can make it up as I go along."

"I want the truth anyway. And I think you need to be straight with me. You have a child, remember?"

I'm hoping to shock her into cooperation, but Git only laughs, and I know I'm dealing with someone who's seen the worst. An innocent witness who suddenly finds herself the target of the good and the bad guys. So the joke's on me. I'd come to reassure Bridget O'Rourke, the woman in the hat, but this is one woman who doesn't need reassurance. She's not backing off, not an inch.

"You want Connor Schmidt, I'll give you his head on a platter," she tells me. "Gift wrapped and tied up with a bow. All you have to do is ask."

# CHAPTER FORTY-THREE

## CONNOR

T he Dew Drop's my bar of choice after a busy day, and I'm sitting here now, trying to relax. It's only seven o'clock, but I feel like I been at it for a week. Startin' with the broad, Gidget. It was fun chasin' her around the county, somethin' different, and I would've most likely caught her. Or she maybe would've given up and faced the music. But a call came through as she turned onto this dirt road, a call from Augie. Last night, one of the kids in Little Ricky's crew, an asshole named Harlan Brown, piled his car into a traffic light on Baxter Boulevard. Stoned out of his mind, if you can believe that, and carryin' half an ounce of cocaine. The coke was layin' on the seat next to him.

It took most of the afternoon to get him bailed out, and now the prick, escorted by Augie, is on his way to the Dew Drop. For a little talk.

The Dew Drop's slow this early on a Saturday night, but the place'll fill by nine. Meantime, the owner, Jimmy Santini, has nothin' to do. In his late sixties, Jimmy's approached me about becoming a partner, and I'm takin' the offer seriously. The Dew Drop's not much to look at—there's about a thousand names carved into the bar top—but it's the first bar you pass on Baxter Boulevard when you leave the Yards. If the Yards are developed, that would mean thousands of workers drivin' by every day. And not the kind of deadbeats who'll nurse a draft beer all night. I'm seein' men and women, some of them far from home, with paychecks to spend.

I'm still bullshittin' with Jimmy when Augie walks in, pushin' Harlan Brown ahead of him. Brown, who can't be more than nineteen, looks beat to shit, what with spendin' the night in jail and coming down off whatever he's been using. What I heard, there was more coke on his fingers than in the bag.

I motion Augie and the kid over to a corner table. Once they're sittin' down, I get straight to the point. "Harlan, I'm thinkin' you're too stupid to live. I should put you down, like right now, and I would, except Little Ricky spoke up for you. But here's what I'm sayin'. You're outta fuckin' business. No more dealin', no more crimes. You so much as pinch a Snickers bar from CVS, I'll make you dig your own grave. Think I'm kiddin'?"

The kid doesn't ask me to repeat myself. "No, and I'm sorry, Connor. Really. I know I fucked up."

Before I fire off a last volley, I watch him rub at one of a line of pimples that trace his right cheekbone. "Here's what's in it for you, Harlan. First, the best lawyer in the county is gonna represent you. That would be Lorimer Taub. Second, Ricky's gonna toss you a few bucks every week to keep you goin'. Third, Lorimer told me there might be a problem with the search, so where there's life, there's hope. But if things go wrong and you gotta do some time, then you gotta do that time. I have people in with the cops. If you turn rat, I'm gonna find out. Now go home and sober up. And also grow up while you're at it. Life ain't a game for kids."

Brown dismissed, I order a pizza from Sal's, the only Italian pizza joint in Baxter. The Dew Drop's menu is limited to potato chips or pretzels in plastic bags. Somethin' else that needs fixin'.

"So what about the broad?" Augie asks. "You wanna lay that off on me?"

Actually, what I don't wanna do is admit how much money I'm out. And I'm also concerned that Augie's methods could draw attention that I can't afford right now. That means I'm gonna have to handle the situation myself. Do I walk right up to her door and say, "Hand it over?" Do I wait for her to show herself? Or do I maybe kill the bitch and forget about the money? Do I put the bullshit behind me? One thing sure, I don't need any more distractions.

I lean back in my chair, about to answer Augie's question, when the door opens and Gidget walks into the bar, resolving my problems. She's wearing a dark red, silky blouse, two buttons undone, a triple chain of black beads, and dark blue earrings that look like buttons. Her white jeans fit her ass like they were spray-painted by a graffiti writer.

I'm instantly suspicious, but I don't think she's wired up. The pants and blouse are too tight, and she's not carryin' a purse. She's brazen, though, as she walks over to our table and stares down at Augie. I'm lookin' at the expression on his face and thinkin' he's about to jump out of his chair and pound her in the face. And I'd probably let him if we were alone.

"Give us some room, Augie." Ignoring his disappointed look, I wait for Augie to walk away. He'll get his chance. Gidget waits, too, then sits without being asked.

"You want somethin' to drink?"

"I'm not gonna be here that long." She lays her hand on the table and leans forward, giving me a second to enjoy the view. "I've got something you want," she tells me.

"No. You got something that belongs to me."

"That's what I heard. But I took it from *Bradley*, not you. And the way he treated me, what he did? Let me put it this way. I think I was poorly compensated for what I went through."

"If you wanted to get even, you should've cut his balls off when he passed out. What you took was never his."

"Now we're goin' around in circles."

I've had enough. "Why don't you just say whatever it is you came to say."

"Before he fell asleep, Bradley told me I had to leave because he was expecting someone. That would be you, Connor. That would be you."

"You're lyin'."

"Does that matter?"

Jesus, the balls on her. I'm thinkin' she takes lessons from the other one, her mother, because when I look into her eyes, I'm not readin' fear.

"Don't be a jerk. The cops don't wanna hear that. They got a locked-up case against my old man. They'll laugh you outta the station."

"I grew up in the Yards, Connor. I don't talk to cops. No, I'm thinking I should talk to your father's lawyer."

That stops me for a minute. The evidence against my father falls apart if Bradley was expecting me to come calling. The gun was in the old man's closet, true, but it's not like I didn't have access. Or like he isn't gonna claim the gun was planted anyway.

"You do that, you won't live long enough to testify."

"I don't expect to testify, and I don't expect to keep your money. I'm just tellin' you where it stands."

"Then what do you want?"

She leans forward a little, and I can't help myself, I stare down at her tits. I think she's gotta be wearin' a bra, but I can't see it.

"I work seventy-two hours a week, Connor, and I'm getting exactly nowhere in life. Every month I'm juggling the bills. Paying this one, putting that one off until next week, or next month if I can get away with it. I have a daughter, too, real smart according to her teachers. I'd like to see her go to college, which I never got a chance to do, but college tuition goes up every fucking day. If you don't have rich parents, you're so deep in debt by the time you graduate that you'll never get out from under." She leans back, finally, and crosses her legs. "I'm sick of the way I'm livin', sick of it. You shouldn't have to work as hard as I do and still be a paycheck away from sleepin' in your car. But the bad's on me, Connor. I thought I could stay straight and still lift myself up. What a joke, huh? For people like me, the American dream is exactly that. A fucking dream."

A nice speech, which has exactly no effect on me. That's because feeling other people's pain is not my strong point. "Forget the sob story. Tell me what you want, or take a hike. Like before my pizza's delivered."

"I have a proposition for you . . ."

Right away my antenna starts to vibrate. "Legal?"

"Yeah. I want you to buy Microsoft and let me run it." Her laugh, when it comes, is cool and light, almost mocking, but not exactly. "No, not legal. Not even close."

Rushing into deals ain't my style, simple as that, and I take a minute to look around. Three men stand around a battered pool table on the other side of the room. A drunk, here all afternoon and soon to leave, sits hunched over a beer. Two kids, early twenties, in jeans and T-shirts, occupy a table in the center of the room. I've never seen them before, and they're just old enough to be cops.

Gidget isn't surprised when I stand up. Like she knows how these things work. I tell her, "Outside," then walk across the room and out the front door. Which way to go? Six vehicles—two cars, three SUVs, and a pickup—are scattered across the parking lot. None are occupied, front or back. There's a gas station across the street and a drugstore next to the bar. The store is closed, and the gas station's been out of business as long as I can remember. Every window's broken.

Still, I'm not satisfied. I lead her to an SUV parked fifty feet away. The SUV's parked at a sharp angle. Standing behind it, we can't be seen from the road.

"Trust? It's not my thing, Gidget," I tell her. "I gotta pat you down."

"You want to make sure I'm not wired? Well, knock yourself out." She moves her arms away from her side, still smiling that same smile. There's no fear in it. No humor, either. "That's your only motive, right? Being sure I'm not wearing a wire?"

It's not my only motive, no, but it's one of them. I gotta be sure. I run my hands under her arms and around her tits. She doesn't flinch. Not even when I place my hands on either side of her right ankle and work my way up to her crotch, or when I cover the same territory on her left leg.

I can't help it. The balls on her, on her and her halfway-to-the-grave mother, turn me on. Maybe I been payin' for it too long, but I'm seein' her next to me in the clubs where I do business. My woman.

I step back, and she returns her arms to her side. "Okay, Gidget. Say what you gotta say."

"My name's Git."

"What?"

"My name is Git, not Gidget." She pauses, but I got nothin' to say. "Okay, it's like this. My cousin, Wyatt, who lives in Jackson Lake, moves top-shelf cocaine. All he can get, which is never enough, especially during the tourist season. Me, I want to supply him, simple as that."

"That's noble, and I appreciate family values. Just ask my daddy. But what does your cousin in Jackson Lake have to do with my money?"

"Two ounces, that's the trade. I give you back your money, which from my point of view I think I earned, and you front me two ounces of first-cut blow. Front me, right? As in I'll pay for it in a couple of weeks."

I can't help myself, I burst out laughing. This is not a conversation I expected to have when me and Augie ordered that pizza.

Cool and calm, Git waits for me to finish. She's not kidding, and I'm already getting ideas. Doing regular business means regular visits. Lots of contact.

"Don't get me wrong, Connor. I came up in the Yards and I know how things work. You take care of me and I'll take care of you. The money will always be good and always be right. I just need this front to get started. After that, it's cash on the barrelhead." A smile, long in coming, lights her face. "I think we'll get along, Connor. Really. In fact, I think you could become a coconspirator with privileges if you play your cards right. Would you like that? Privileges?"

# CHAPTER FORTY-FOUR

## CONNOR

So, yeah, I would, and I proved it by takin' one of Dew Drop's regulars, a skank named Sarah, home for the night. It seemed like a good idea at the time, only I can't put the woman, Git-not-Gidget, out of my mind. But I can put Sarah out of my little cottage, which I do as soon as she finishes her shower. I'm not cruel about it. Humiliation was Bradley's game. I tell her I've got business I need to get started on, so please . . .

I'm dreaming of the girl in the hat before the door closes behind Sarah. First the look in her eyes when she put that coconspirators-with-privileges deal on the table. Then the video of her on that stool in Randy's, of the dress with all those sequins, of her long, smooth legs when she crossed them. This is a woman who knows what she wants. This is a woman who grew up hard enough to do whatever it takes. No delusions.

My phone rings twice before I finish my breakfast. The first is from Mom. She's getting along with her sister, and Denver agrees with her. The mountains are spectacular. The second is from Lenny Krone. He needs to "refuel," which amounts to a key of coke, not necessarily first grade. I don't bother with yes or no. For all his big mouth, Lenny's always been reliable. Yeah, he'll whine about the price or the place of delivery or the fucking weather. But the money's always there. I never have to chase him.

I get on the burner right away. A hard unit of regular and two soft units of the best. A key and two ounces. I'm thinking of the ounces as an investment. Roughly four grand in exchange for eighteen grand. What happens next depends on Git. Just now, I'm hoping we'll get along, because I've been lookin' for an out-of-town distributor. But the deal can go bad, and I tuck a Colt .38 auto inside my belt as I head out the door.

The cool weather catches me off guard. It's been sweltering for the last few days, but now it seems more like early May, when the last of the winter snow has finally melted. The weather out here is the worst. Freezing winters followed by blazing hot summers. A winter wind that doesn't quit. Motionless air in summer that weighs on you like a wet overcoat.

But not today. I ride north with the Camry's windows open, a steady breeze whipping through the interior, an AC/DC classic blasting away. My destination lies sixty miles west, in a shopping center off I-80. Unlike the mostly abandoned strip malls in Baxter, this one's anchored by a Lowe's, a CVS, and a Kroger supermarket. It's closing on eleven when I arrive, and the mall is busy. I have to cruise around for several minutes before I spot the gray van parked in a corner close to the I-80 on-ramp. The swap goes quickly from there, a package from me, a package from a dark-skinned man I've never seen before, and on my way.

No more AC/DC, no more high volume. Now it's country and western, some wannabe cowboy moaning about his lost love. Swear to God, it could've been written twenty years ago. Or fifty. But it's safe, which is how I like to play it when I'm transporting product. Not that I'm worried. Our guy . . . No, it's my guy now, John Meacham. He called me this morning. Mariola and her partner, Vern Taney, have been summoned by our district attorney to work on my father's prosecution. On a weekend, no less. They'll be out of action until late afternoon.

Forty minutes out of town, I stop for coffee and a doughnut. I'm in the car, sipping at the coffee, when I call Git on my personal cell phone. The burner's reserved for business with my suppliers.

"Git, you know who this is?"

"Yeah, I do."

Her confident tone cheers me. I'm thinking more and more long-term. "Is it a go?"

"It is on my end. And you?"

"I'm on the way."

"And you have . . . what you promised?"

"Thirty minutes, Git, and you're not runnin' the show."

"I wouldn't dream of it."

I pride myself on discipline, the waiting game. Just ask my old man. But it takes everything I have not to ram the gas pedal into the floorboards. I can't afford to be stopped, maybe subjected to a random search, even if it wouldn't stand up in court. Cool, cool, cool. Just another hunk of metal rolling down the street. Not worth more than a glance. Meanwhile, I can already feel the silky smoothness of Git's inner thigh beneath my fingertips. I have a slow hand, like in that song, call it the long game . . .

I come into town on the northern end of Baxter Boulevard, headed directly for Git's house on the other side of town. For once, the lights work in my favor and I coast all the way to city hall before a police cruiser, lights flashing, pulls into the intersection ahead of me. I turn the wheel instinctively, trying to go around, when a second cruiser pulls in from the opposite direction. Now the intersection is totally blocked, and I don't have to look into the rearview mirror to know there are cruisers behind me.

An adrenaline surge threatens to overwhelm me. I've been sold out, and I don't have to guess who did the selling. She's dead, of course, because I'll never stop coming after her. No. I warned the bitch. I told her, You'll never testify. And she won't. The only issue is whether I settle for her or whether I kill her kid, too. And there's John Meacham, standing outside of his cruiser, gun in hand. He looks like he's about to cry, and I know he's been suckered. Him and me both.

"You know the drill, Connor." It's Mariola, over the cruiser's public address system. "Get out of the car and lie on the ground."

And that's it. Just the one command, like the bitch is hopin' I won't obey. But I'm not stupid. The dope's locked in the trunk, along with the Colt, and I'm enough of an optimist by nature to hope the cops don't have a warrant. I open the door slowly, get out slowly, lower myself to the ground, slowly. The cops swarm me a few seconds later, searching me for weapons I don't have. I'm expecting the handcuffs next, but I'm pulled to my feet instead. Mariola's right there, standing a few feet away, the expression on her face unreadable.

"Mind if we search your car?"

"You have a warrant?"

"Nope, just a tip that you're transporting drugs."

"A tip? From who, Detective?"

"It's Lieutenant Mariola, and please answer the question. Do we have your permission? Yes or no?"

Four cops, including Vern Taney, stand close enough to hear my response. "No warrant, no search. You don't have my permission."

Mariola looks over at Taney. Both are smiling now. "Get the dog," she says.

The dog's an ugly mutt that reminds me of the dogs you see in a cage on ASPCA commercials. Pitiful, right? Only the animal's all business, yanking on the leash as she circles the car, stopping on a dime when she reaches the trunk, barking madly as she drops into a sitting position.

In court, they call it probable cause. In court, the dog justifies the search.

I look directly into Mariola's eyes while Taney opens the Camry's front door and tugs on the trunk release. I'm trying for defiance, or at least rage, but my heart drops as the trunk's lid rises. Everything I worked for, every dream, gone now. Several cops peer inside as the dog's pulled away, but it's Taney who reaches in to retrieve the zipped backpack. I watch him open it, listen to him shout, "Bingo," watch him lift the kilo into the air.

"Field-test it," Mariola orders. Then, to me, "How much am I lookin' at, Connor? A pound? A kilo?"

"I'm not talkin' to ya. I want a lawyer."

"Good idea, Connor, because that much cocaine? We're talkin' a Class A felony. You'll go to prison for the next thirty years. But look at the bright side. Maybe you and daddy can share a cell, enjoy a bit of family time. Or maybe you can put out hits on each other."

Mariola reaches out to spin me around. I want to kill her, to kill every fucking one of them, to grab the bitch who set me up and burn her alive, but I offer no more resistance than a five-year-old. And I don't resist, either, when she pulls my right hand behind my back and locks the cuff around my wrist, or when she does the same with my left. It's her words that stop me, and the triumphant tone. She said she'd get me, and now she has.

"You have the right to remain silent, you have the right to a lawyer, anything you say can be used against you."

# CHAPTER FORTY-FIVE

## GIT

D elia stays until Connor's call, then heads out to lead the arrest team. Vern Taney's already on the street. We're hoping, all of us, including Mom, that Augie Barboza's traveling with Connor, two birds with one stone. I want the pair of them off the street until I pick up Charlie. Then we're out of here.

Clothes, personal possessions, important documents, and that's it. We're leaving the furniture behind, and I'm going to sell my car for cash after we settle in New Jersey. Delia thinks Connor's organization will crumble, what with father and son behind bars, but there are no guarantees. And it's not Delia or her boy under threat. It's me and Charlie and Mom.

Mom's moving about the house, restless, her nerves on edge. I know she wants a drink. Alcohol has always been her refuge. That's not happening, but I can taste her gratitude when Delia calls an hour later. And the news she conveys is good, for her at least. In addition to the ounces meant for me, Connor was transporting a larger amount of cocaine, probably a kilo. The cocaine part is definite, confirmed by a field test.

"He'll be arraigned tomorrow before Hang-em-High Dunn. Bail will be close to half a million dollars, cash. Connor won't be able to raise that much right away, if he can raise it at all."

Am I supposed to be cheered, relieved, even grateful? Augie Barboza wasn't in the car when Delia closed the trap on Connor. Connor was alone, hardly surprising since he was en route to the home of a woman he expected to screw. Meanwhile, I'm more scared of Augie than of Connor.

Zack described Augie and Connor as joined at the hip. Worse, according to Zack, Augie's mainly a loan shark and willing to do whatever's necessary if borrowers don't pay. Dealing out pain is an everyday occurrence. Again, in Zack's telling, Augie was in high school, Connor a few years past, when he and Connor met. Out of control at that point, Augie was in fights every day, usually over an imagined slight. Connor took a chance on him, a chance that paid off and earned him Augie's unconditional loyalty. That made Connor one for two. He'd taken a chance on Bradley Grieg as well.

Mrs. Finder at Charlie's camp isn't pleased when I tell her that I'll be coming for Charlie tomorrow morning.

"You know," she tells me, her tone sweetly conde-scending, "the children find sudden changes traumatic. It's only one more day."

"I'll be there by ten o'clock. I'd appreciate you having her ready. But one way or the other, she's leaving."

"Well, you're the parent . . ."

Yes, I am, and I prove it by hanging up. Now I have a choice, and Mom knows it, too. The look on her face is expectant. She's waiting for me to decide. I'm due tonight at Resurrection, where I'll be reasonably safe, but that can't happen. I won't leave Mom alone to deal with Augie.

"Maybe he won't think it's you," she says out of nowhere.

Mom has a habit of leaving important information out of her conversations, like I'm somehow following the thoughts traveling through her brain. But this time I get it. I went into the Dew Drop wearing jeans that haven't fit me in a couple of years and a blouse tight enough to hug my belly and back. No purse. We'd assumed that Connor would be suspicious, and we wanted to put him off his guard. In fact, one of the black earrings I wore, the size of a sweater button, contained a tiny transmitter. A block away, Delia picked up every word, probable cause to search Connor's vehicle. The dog was insurance, and an added factor to confuse Connor. Hopefully.

"You're talking about the second package?"

"Yeah, Git. Connor had your ounces, plus another kilo. So who set him up? You or whoever was buyin' the kilo? Or maybe no one, maybe Connor was bein' harassed and the cops got lucky."

"He'll figure it out fast enough when I disappear. And if there's a trial, I'll have to show up."

"True, but with Connor and his old man lookin' at decades in prison, what's left of the crew's gonna have enough on its hands without worryin' about you."

"What about Augie?"

"I been knowin' Augie since he was in high school. He ain't got the leadership skills of a virus. It'll take a miracle for him to run his own operation. He won't be lookin' to run someone else's."

The idea is so enticing, it takes me a while to come up with the flaw. "What about the money? The eighteen thousand everybody thinks I stole? And Augie knows. He was in the Dew Drop when I arrived. The look in his eye, Mom. He wanted to beat the crap out of me, then and there. No, I gotta think he's gonna make a move. I think he's gonna make a move, and he's not the type to wait around."

I call Zack Butler. Reluctantly. I don't want to admit that I set Connor up, not to Zack, whose relationship with the legit world is shaky at best. But that's why I need his advice, if not his protection. With him, it's been there, done that.

"Hey, Git, you won't believe this, but I'm in Chicago. Workin' on my consortium."

"Well, the shit's hit the fan back here. Connor's been arrested." I take a few seconds before I work up the courage to reveal the important part. "I set him up, Zack. After he found me, right?"

"You say he found you?"

"He was outside the house when I got home yesterday. And he followed my car later on."

"Tell me the story, Git. All of it."

And I do, leaving nothing out, including my attempt to lure Connor into that clearing and my trip to the Dew Drop.

"Connor's off the street, which is all to the good. And Connor had a kilo that was meant for someone else. Maybe he'll blame whoever it was meant for instead of me."

"Git, you can testify against him. That's motivation enough, even if you didn't set him up. And another thing you might consider. If you should die an unnatural death tonight, Connor has a perfect alibi." He clears his throat. "Best move on the board? Don't be where Augie can find you. And what about Charlie?"

"Charlie's at a mini-camp. And I'm taking your advice. I'm gonna pick Charlie up tomorrow and head for New Jersey. But I don't know how much that helps. Like you said, I'll be needed if there's a trial. That means I'll have to let Mariola know where I'm living. Can she keep my address secret? If it's in a file somewhere? Or will I spend the next five years looking over my shoulder, suspecting every strange face? Or worse, be caught off guard?"

"Look, the Schmidts' operation ain't the Gambino crime family. Get out now, let the future take care of itself."

Chad Gotosky smiles at Mom as we march through the front door of Rapid-Fire Arms, the larger of the two gun shops in Baxter. Mom and Chad are roughly the same age. They were in high school together and at least marginally involved. That's what she told me on the way over, but Chad's grin speaks to something deeper. Contemporaries or not, they're a study in opposites. Chad's in great shape, with cannonball biceps and forearms thick enough to roast. His neck is wider than his head.

"Hey there, Celia. Haven't see you in . . . let's see, maybe five years."

"Guess you lost my number."

"C'mon now, girl. I been inside this store six days a week for the past fifteen years. I ain't hard to find. So what can I do ya for?"

"I'm not here to buy tomatoes, Chad. I need a gun."

Handguns dominate a display case that runs the length of the shop, the exception being a three-foot section at one end exhibiting knives of every size and shape. The walls, too, are crowded, though here most of the weapons are rifles and shotguns. Just behind us, accessories crowd a freestanding display case, everything from a purse with a built-in holster to thick body armor. While I'm not afraid of guns, my technical knowledge of how they work is strictly limited. I doubt if Mom is any more experienced.

"It's for home protection," I tell Chad, which is technically true.

"Uh-huh. And who's gonna do the protectin', you or Celia?"

Mom cuts me off. "I am, Chad"

"What's your skill level?"

"Pull the trigger, try not to flinch."

Chad's personality suits his occupation. His smile is quick and genuine. "Well, Celia," he says, "that approach is fine when you're plinkin' away at a shooting-range target. But if there's a man in your home, an intruder prepared to do you harm, pullin' the trigger and hopin' for the best won't cut it. When you do fire your weapon, you wanna be damn sure that you put whoever's in front of you on an express train to hell." Another smile, this one accompanied by a wink and a nod. "Now, most gun dealers, at this point, would recommend one of these shotguns." He gestures at several displayed on the wall behind him. "Only there's a problem usin' a long gun of any kind in a home. Too many obstacles to avoid. You poke it around a corner and it maybe gets knocked out of your hand. No, I got somethin' that does the same job without the drawbacks." Not missing a beat, he removes a black box from the display case in front of him and opens it. "Now, full disclosure, this Remington Tac-14, which fires 12-gauge shotgun shells, ain't a shotgun. Not by the feds' definition. That because it don't have a stock. It's manufactured with a pistol grip. That's not an alteration, folks. What you're seein' came out of the factory just like that."

The weapon, with its short barrel, appears to be less than two feet. That's my guess, and I'm off by only a couple of inches.

"Twenty-six-point-three inches," Chad declares. "And the way you hold it, down near your hip, it's ready to fire. Now—"

Mom stops him. "That gun's about as long as my forearm. And you're tellin' me it's legal?"

"Yes, it is, Celia. See, according to the feds, a shotgun has a stock you press into your shoulder. This weapon has a pistol grip, so it fits into the category of general firearms. It's a hundred percent legal." Another smile before Chad presses the grip against his thigh. "You don't aim this gun. You fire from the hip, with your hand pressed tight against your body to handle recoil."

"And it's accurate?"

"Put it this way. You won't be firin' at a duck flyin' two hundred feet in the air. No, ma'am. You'll be shootin' at somebody on the other side of a room. You won't miss."

We make a stop on the way home, at Jackson Movers. Weekends are prime time for people moving, and I'm not surprised to find it open. But I haven't come to arrange a move. I'd have to give my new address to the movers. I'm leaving all the furniture behind, even the dishes.

I buy a dozen small boxes, carry them back to the house, and begin to pack. Clothes, a few books, Charlie's toys, of which there are many, important papers, of which there are few. A closet shelf bears all there is of the family's past. A few photos of my grandparents, of Charlie as a baby, of my wedding (which I'd as soon forget),

292

Charlie's report cards, a birthday card Charlie made for me at school. The birthday card is bright red and shaped like a heart.

The look on Charlie's face when she handed it to me rises up, as clear as a photograph. So proud, so proud.

Suddenly I'm sitting on the edge of the bed, crying. I'm remembering my own expectations, the hope that's every child's birthright. Smashed, torn apart, beaten down. And what of Charlie's future? Without me, she'll be thrown into the same cauldron that shaped my own life. I'm what stands between her and . . . I don't want to think about it. Foster care? Try Hell on Earth.

"C'mon, Git. Suck it up. If the scumbag shows his face tonight, we're gonna find ourselves free and clear by morning."

Mom looks so frail, like a spring breeze would knock her on her ass. She has no right to her optimism, but she seems eternally hopeful.

"Don't worry," I say. "I won't make any mistakes. But it seems so unfair."

The phone interrupts a conversation that was going nowhere. Delia calling.

"What's the news, Lieutenant?"

"Connor's in a cell, and he'll stay there at least until tomorrow. But we had to give him his phone call."

"Lemme guess . . . he didn't call his lawyer. He called Augie Barboza."

"That's right, Git. Are you home?"

"Yeah."

"Then you need to get out. I'm going to have a patrol car cruise past your place tonight, but I can't station a unit in front of the house."

At six o'clock Mom goes to the refrigerator in search of dinner. I'm thinking that a last meal ought to be elegant, but we settle for hamburgers. I'm not up to making spaghetti sauce. I haven't the patience, yet I know this is all about waiting. I throw a quick coleslaw together while Mom panfries the burgers, the two of us working in silence.

Fifteen minutes later we carry our dinners to lawn chairs set in the shade of the trees at the western edge of the property. Before I take my first bite, I stare into a woodlot that covers an acre of ground. I mark the narrow trails created by the feet of Charlie and the kids next door—and probably children running back through the generations. When Charlie was younger, two or three, I'd hold her hand and watch her head swivel, her eyes afraid and awed as I guided her along the shadowed trails. I think she was five before she first ventured into those shadows alone. I watched her from the yard, watched her take a step, then a few more, then run back and throw her arms around my legs.

At dusk, I go back into the house and Mom drives away, the shotgun on the seat beside her. She's not going far. Only around the block, to a driveway forty yards from where I stand. The home on the property is vacant and for rent. Mom's there to keep watch. I've set my phone to vibrate and have it in the front pocket of the loose-fitting jeans I'm wearing. If Augie shows up, Mom will call and I'll be waiting.

Settled in, I unlock the window next to my bed as the evening slides from dusk to dark. One benefit of a single-story house is convenient access to the outside in case of fire. No jumping from a second-story window. Our plan, if you can call it that, is simple. If Mom calls, I'll exit through the window and circle the house. Mom will approach from the neighbor's driveway, bearing the shotgun. Between the two of us, we should have enough firepower to handle whatever's coming our way. Add the element of surprise and . . .

Seconds like minutes, minutes like hours, the night gradually passes, until I'm fighting sleep at four in the morning. Until enough time has slipped by to leave me hopeful. Maybe Connor's smart enough to hold off, not compound his problems. Maybe Augie's already been here. Here and gone when he found no car in my driveway. My nerves aren't just on edge, they're inflamed. I need to pee. I need to get up and pace. I need resolution, the waiting unbearable. I force myself to stay where I am, on a chair beside my bed. My phone has already gone off twice, robocalls from 800 numbers. But it took minutes before my heart quieted down. I'll have to deal with that if Augie shows, the adrenaline surge. I can't afford to hesitate, to rush in or freeze in fear.

My eyes find the digital clock on the dresser, almost willing the numbers to flip as daybreak approaches. I'm thinking of the rented trailer I'll need to haul the packed boxes to New Jersey, where I'll find it, how long it will take me to load up, when to collect Charlie, how long to put Baxter behind us. Then I hear it.

No warning, no vibrating cell phone, just a crunch from the living room that I recognize instantly. Someone's using a pry bar on the front door. The hair on my head literally rises, and my heart kicks into overdrive. Did Mom fall asleep? Did they spot her in that driveway? And where's my gun? For a second, I forget where I put it, although it's lying in my lap. Then I happen to glance at the dresser, and my eyes settle on a framed photo of Charlie sitting at table with a baby's bib, pink, tied around her neck.

Move, move, move. I'm on my feet, easing the shade up and the window open, sliding over the sill. My thoughts have slowed, and I pick up the plan worked out earlier. I close the window behind me and step to my left so that I can't be seen from inside the bedroom. The little Czech .32 is in my hand, my finger already through the trigger guard as I quickly review the basic strategy: circle to the front, come up behind the intruder, pull the trigger.

I raise the pistol, extend the barrel forward, and turn the corner of the house to find myself facing a man twenty feet away. He's walking toward me, but we both stop in mid-stride. Then we stare at each other for several seconds while a rage boils up inside me. Here's another one, another Bradley Grieg, another Connor Schmidt, another childhood demon come to life. His hand moves toward his belt as I pull the trigger once, then again, then again, then again.

The moon is still high enough to reveal a little color when the bullets rip into his chest. I watch him look down at the blood, his eyes wide, before I pull the trigger one more time. The shot crashes into his forehead, and he drops backward, his head slamming into the grass.

The man on the ground's not moving. He's not moving and he's not Augie and he's not the intruder ripping at my front door. Instinctively, like a small nocturnal animal caught in a sudden light, I dash for the safety of the woods, for the deep shadows. Fear drives my feet, but they're not fast enough. The gunshots—two quick explosions, then a third—buzz past my right ear like enraged hornets. They emit a distinct snap as they tear by, the sound vaguely regretful. I'm not about to give them an opportunity to redeem themselves. I enter the woodlot on a path that Charlie and I have walked many times, then veer into the deepest shadows.

Bullets follow me, but my luck holds. The ground is a tangle of roots and vines that snatch at my ankles, tripping me before I cover ten feet. I fall on my face and taste blood from a cut lip, but I hold on to the gun, my hand locked on the grip. I can't see the man I assume to be Augie Barboza, but I place him on the lawn when he fires three more shots. They cut through leaves and brush ten or fifteen feet to my right, then slam into a trunk. The solid thuds motivate me, and I begin to crawl deeper into the woods, ignoring the low branches that claw at my body, the rocks digging into my knees.

Augie stops shooting, and I assume he can't see me. I don't know if he'll follow me into the woods, but I'm sure he won't turn tail and desert his injured partner. My strategy is obvious either way. All I need do is remain hidden for another five minutes, ten at most, until the cops arrive. We have neighbors to the east. Surely they've already dialed 911.

Unlike Augie, I know where I'm going, and I continue to crawl until I reach one of the footpaths running through the woodlot. By this time I can see well enough to mark a pair of half-rotted stumps. They're all that remain of timber harvested generations ago, but they lock me in. The path runs a short distance toward the back of the lot before intersecting with a path that extends in a half circle to the edge of a blackberry patch. Here the bushes stand higher than my head. Here the darkness is near absolute.

Long tendrils reach for me as I start down an impossibly narrow path. I keep my hands before my face to ward off thorns that dig into my arms. Nevertheless, I'm calm, mostly because Augie has no idea where I am. He proves this by firing off a pair of shots that fail to connect with anything close to me.

I finally reach the end of the path. My backyard's in front of me, but I don't intend to expose myself or confront Augie. I'm assuming that time is still on my side, and I expect to hear approaching sirens any second. The upstairs windows of the house next door are lit. But it's not to be.

Augie stands on the lawn, close to the back of the house. He's not facing me or the woods. He's looking over his shoulder at my mother. Mom's standing thirty feet away. She's holding the shotgun, pointing it in Augie's direction.

Augie manages a grimace probably meant to approximate a smile as he slowly raises his hands without dropping his gun. He's not fooling me, and I can't imagine him fooling Mom. Yet she simply stands there, frozen, and I know Augie's working up his courage. He's not going to surrender, no way. He's going to make the first move, and I know he'll take her out even if she manages to pull the trigger.

Suddenly I'm aware of the gun in my hand, my little .32, and I'm wishing I'd taken it to a gun range, that I'd practiced for hours on end. Augie's forty or fifty feet away. I need to hit him in the head to stop him. The odds against pulling that off are massive.

"Evenin', Celia."

"Put down the gun."

"Gotta admit, girl, you did a hell of a job, you and your daughter. Had me completely fooled. Connor, too."

"Put down the gun."

"But you were always hell on wheels. Never knew you to take a backward step."

"Put the gun down, Augie. Else I'm gonna pull this trigger."

"Now, Celia . . ."

I can't let it go any further. I have to do something, have to act, even if the best I can offer is a distraction. I pull the trigger four times, fast. Augie's face registers the shock even as the barrel of his gun turns in my direction.

Again, I fire, the only effect a broken window far to the right of where Augie stands. Then Mom finally pulls the Remington's trigger, the roar of the shotgun drowning out time itself. I can't see the buckshot as it rips across the space between Augie and Mom, but the loose shirt Augie's wearing jumps as though hit by a sudden gust of wind. Then the blood, black in the moonlight, begins to run from the side of Augie's face and neck. His blue shirt darkens, and he puts his hand to his side before raising his eyes to meet mine. He seems confused. This isn't how it's supposed to end, two women refusing to submit, two women standing firm. His mouth opens for a moment before he falls forward, his weapon dropping from his hand. Only then do I hear the onrushing sirens.

My attention finally turns to Mom. She likely forgot to brace the shotgun against her hip. It's lying ten feet away, and she's sitting on the grass, a lopsided grin dominating her face.

"Time to assume the position, daughter," she tells me.

When she drops to the ground, face-first, stretching her arms before her, fingers splayed, I get it. The cops are responding to a report of shots fired, and they'll be jumpy. I step onto the lawn, drop my .32, and take a few more steps before I join Mom on the lawn. Submissive at last.

# CHAPTER FORTY-SIX

# ONE WEEK LATER

## GIT

Charlie's sitting in Delia's lap at the kitchen table. Calling her Aunt Delia. I don't know where Charlie picked up the aunt part, and I'm not in a hurry to inquire. Charlie's wearing Delia's gold badge—proudly, of course—while I'm reduced to standing by the stove, tending the scrambled eggs, watching the toaster, cutting an orange into quarters. I don't mind, not at all. I'm still . . . adjusting? Beyond that, Delia seems genuinely fond of Charlie, and maybe fond of me as well. Delia's pretty much openly gay, so maybe that's part of it. But there's something genuine about the woman that I find attractive. She seems to love her life, and to be living it easily.

Augie and his gangster pal (Little Ricky, according to Delia) are both dead. They deserved what they got, no question. And what they got was justified. No question, either. Not from Mariola or the state police unit that processed the scene or the coroner at an inquest that took place yesterday.

So that part of it, the legal part, is over and done with, a closed book. But not the other part, the notoriety. Notoriety as in notorious. I'm the girl in the hat who followed Bradley Grieg into Cabin 909. At best a slut tearing off a piece of ass. And at worst? At worst, I lured Bradley there to be murdered by Carl Schmidt. I'm not surprised by the speculation, because so many of the facts are unavailable to the virtuous citizens of Baxter. They don't know that Bradley was by himself when he checked into the Skyview, or that Bradley and I hadn't even met prior to that night, or that I didn't know Carl Schmidt's name before Bradley was killed. Connor's, either.

"When folks don't have the facts at hand, they make facts up to fill the gaps." That's what Zack told me as we made our goodbyes last night. "As long as the stories they tell are half-assed logical, they believe 'em. The only arguments are over the details."

"Like, is Bridget O'Rourke a slut, or did she get paid? Is she a pig or a full-blown whore?"

"Yeah, just like that."

Zack spoke gently, and I could sense his regret. He'd offered me a job earlier, as his "second-in-command." Two weeks ago I would have jumped at the chance. But I can't have Charlie grow up as the daughter of a notorious woman. When I refused, Zack passed me an envelope—a "bonus." I didn't count the money until I got home. Eight thousand dollars. Enough now, with Mom's three thousand, to complete nursing school if I keep working. A bachelor of science next? Every credential includes a financial bonus. As an RN with a college degree, I'd start at eighty thousand a year. Without overtime.

"We're gonna go up a mountain," Charlie tells Delia.

"Is that right?"

"Uh-huh. A real one. Not like Mount Jackson. Mom says Mount Jackson is only a hill."

"How high is this mountain? Is it the biggest mountain in the world? Can you see China from the top?"

Wrong question. Charlie lives part-time in an alternate universe called Map World. She can locate the capital of Cambodia on her tablet in under a minute.

"No, silly," Charlie declares. "China is on the other side of the Earth."

"Oh, yeah, I forgot." Delia gives my little girl a hug. "But you're still gonna go to the top of a mountain, right?"

"Uh-huh." Charlie looks at me. "Right, Mommy?"

"Right."

After I wrap things up with Delia, Mom, Charlie, and I are taking off for New Jersey. Our itinerary includes a stop at a small resort, Vista View House, in the Appalachian Mountains near the Ohio-Pennsylvania border. We're not talking about the Alps here. The elevation's only a bit over two thousand feet. But Charlie's lived all her life on the midwestern flatlands. The prospect of a real mountain has captured her imagination and hopefully taken her mind off the craziness. When she asked me to explain the violence, I told her that bad men came to hurt me and Grandma. I expected an endless series of whys, but she left it at that. At least for now.

The news about the Nissan factory helped as well. It broke two days after the shootings, and I'm pretty sure Delia leaked it. I know she's on my side, like I know she'll always put her job ahead of her emotions. But even if she wasn't the leaker, the news has electrified Baxter. The *Baxter Bugle* published a banner headline: NISSAN TO CONSTRUCT NEW PLANT IN BAXTER. It ran from one side of the first page to the other. Speculation followed, about the number of workers the plant's construction would employ, about the number of workers who would have permanent jobs once the plant begins operations, about new housing needed to accommodate all those workers, about new businesses attracted by workers with money in their pockets.

Of course, the slut-nurse wasn't totally forgotten in the excitement, but at least the reporters stopped hanging around my house.

"Eat up, honey, we've got a long trip ahead of us."

Charlie picks up her fork. "Thank you, Mommy."

"You're welcome."

Already impatient, I lead Delia into the backyard. "Whatever you have to say, Lieutenant, say it quick. I don't have time for games."

Delia's not impressed, though I sense respect in her attitude. I fought back, and that counts for something in her world.

"Okay. You're off the hook as far as the homicides go. Self-defense is self-defense, and I don't see evidence arising to challenge that classification. And maybe you'll get lucky again. Maybe the Schmidts will cut a deal and plead guilty. But even if they do, Connor will probably test the system by challenging the evidence. Was it legally seized? Did we have probable cause? Was it entrapment? If that should happen, Git, you'll have to testify. Now, I could keep you here, even hold you as a material witness, but that's not happening. You go in peace. God knows you've earned it. But I'm asking you to settle down where I can find you. One phone call, okay? No games."

"Understood, Lieutenant."

"I'm glad to hear that, because I know you'll be placed under oath and asked questions you'd rather not answer. Like, did you steal money—which we both know you didn't—from Bradley Grieg? Like, why did you say you did when you didn't? Remember, you made some damaging admissions to Connor, and I have them on tape. And then there's the part about you claiming that Bradley told you to leave the motel room because he expected Connor to show up. Talk about a wild card."

Now I'm smiling. "Are you giving me reasons to run, Lieutenant?"

"Nope. I'm giving you time to prepare." She returns my smile and extends her hand. "You've been lucky so far, and maybe you'll be lucky again. Our district attorney's under pressure to deal with the Schmidts as soon as possible. The city fathers don't want a show trial drawing attention to our drug problems. They'll cut deals if there are deals to cut."

"And what about you, Delia? Now that it's over, now that the pressure's off, what's in it for you?"

Delia's chocolate-brown eyes narrow as her mouth opens into a broad smile. "Well, after I leave you this morning, I'm heading off to watch my son play baseball."

"Your son?"

"Danny. I sent him to baseball camp for a couple of weeks, and he must've impressed the coaches. They invited him to play in a summer league. He'll be traveling all over the state."

Her pride in her son is obvious, and I know she's feeling the way I feel when Charlie sounds her way through some difficult paragraph in *Watership Down*.

"Long-term," she continues, "this city has a drug problem that needs to be addressed. Before Nissan begins to hire."

"You really think you can stop drug use in Baxter? It's anywhere and everywhere. And anything your heart desires."

"Can't argue the point, but according to our dear mayor, Nissan drug tests new hires. And they'll bring in outside workers if they have to. That'll leave the folk living here with the same nothing they have now. I'm not a magician, Git, but I don't plan to just sit around and hope for the best. You know, it's funny . . . You've lived here all your life and you can't wait to get away. I'm only here for a couple of years and I've become a booster. Anyway, good luck to you and your family. I wish you well."

For a moment, an eyeblink really, I think we're about to hug. But then Delia thrusts her hand out and we shake instead.

"You don't mind," she says, "I'll say goodbye to Charlie."

"Good idea, and don't forget to collect your badge on the way out."

Two hours later we're cruising east on I-80. Charlie's strapped into her car seat and sound asleep. Mom's beside me. We haven't really spoken about what happened, most likely because Mom had fallen asleep in the car and almost got me killed. I can still hear the bullets passing my head, the angry buzz, the little snap. But I'm not expecting an apology—that's not my mother's way—and when she finally begins to speak, I don't get one.

"This here is about somethin' I witnessed a long time ago. When I was about Charlie's age, I had a best friend named Sandy who lived just down the road. She—" Mom stops as suddenly as she'd started, her eyes darting to a cornfield alongside the highway. "Funny, how things stick with ya. You'd think I'd be over it, but I ain't and never will be. Anyway, I was at Sandy's one afternoon, playin' with her new puppy, when her mom and dad got into a fight. They was both drunk, screaming at each other and throwin' punches. This was nothin' new to me and Sandy, and we was tryin' to ignore the show." She pauses again, this time for almost a minute while she stares out the window. "All right, I'm gonna make this short because it don't bear talkin' about. Or even thinkin' about. So, it got to the point where Sandy's momma couldn't take it no more. She ran into the house and come out with a rifle, a .30-30, and started firin' away at her husband. Didn't hit him, though. Nope, hit her daughter instead. I was standin' a few feet away, and I seen the blood when the bullet come out through Sandy's back. A pink haze that followed her to the ground like it was chasin' her."

"Look, Mom—"

"No, let me finish, daughter." She continues when I nod. "Sandy's mom and dad started screamin', the both of them, standin' over their daughter, lookin' down like they was scared to touch her. I think she was dead right then, but she surely was by the time an ambulance showed up. And me, I stayed still as a statue, Git, like my feet was nailed to the ground. Didn't say nothin' and probably didn't think nothin', not until later when your granny come to bring me home. Then I started shakin' so bad that Mom thought I was havin' a fit. And it continued that way, on and off, for months. And even now it comes back time to time, like I can't bury it deep enough."

"And that's the way it'll happen to me? Little Ricky and Augie popping up out of nowhere?"

"That's right, Git. You have to go on, ain't a choice in the matter, but some things in life don't disappear. You just have to live with 'em."